Reverie

Lauren E. Rico

New York 2017

Reverie by Lauren E. Rico

Published by Harmony House Productions

Reverie by Lauren E. Rico

For permissions contact: Lauren@LaurenRico.com

ISBN-13: 978-0-9974303-2-5

Visit the author's website www.LaurenRico.com

Also Written by Lauren Rico...

From Harmony House Productions:

Rhapsody
ISBN: 978-0-9974303-0-1
Kindle ASIN: B01KR8OGG8

Requiem
ISBN: 978-0-9974303-4-9
Kindle ASIN: B01MDP56PH

From Entangled Publishing:

Solo
ISBN: 978-1545256800
Kindle ASIN: B06ZYQYTXW

Blame it on the Bet
ISBN: 978-1975633202
Kindle ASIN: B074ZLDGZR

Don't miss a new release! Sign-up for my newsletter at www.LaurenRico.com

The Music of Reverie

The musical selections mentioned, both in passing and in detail throughout this book were carefully selected to complement the mood of each character and to reflect the tone of the of the story at that point in time. If you have the opportunity to listen to some of the selections as you read, I think you'll find the music adds an entirely new emotional depth and dimension. Happy reading and happy listening! -Lauren

JS Bach: Suite No.1 for Unaccompanied Cello

Sergei Rachmaninoff: Cello Sonata

Dukas: Villanelle for Horn and Piano

Tchaikovsky: Symphony No.4

Mozart: Horn Concerto No.3

Richard Strauss: Horn Concerto No.1

Luigi Boccherini: Cello Concerto

Edward Elgar: Violin Concerto in B minor, Op.61

Antonin Dvorak: Piano Concerto in G minor, Op.33

Camille Saint-Saens: The Swan

Franz Schubert: String Quartet Death and the Maiden

For Vanessa, who told me I could.
For Tom, who told me I should.
For Janet, who told me I would.

Part One: Julia

1

If it's true you don't get a second chance to make a good first impression, then I'm in serious trouble here. I'm late, I'm out of breath, and I look like a wild, sweaty mess as I sprint the final length of the hallway to the concert hall—the concert hall where my audition should have started nearly ten minutes ago. All around me, clusters of musicians are loitering in my path.

"Excuse me!" I gasp as I dart in and around them, skirt hiked-up and long strands of red hair plastered to my damp face. All the while, there is what looks like a small coffin strapped to my back.

"James? Julia James?" I hear my name being called from somewhere in the distance.

"Here!" I yell, not bothering to excuse myself as I become entangled in a gaggle of pianists.

"Last call for Julia James, cellist, McInnes Conservatory!"

I'm closer to the voice now.

"Here! Wait, I'm here!" I bellow with as much volume as I can muster.

I spot the girl with the clipboard twenty feet in front of me, but she steps inside the auditorium doors before I can get her attention.

No. No way I'm going to get this close and blow it now. I dig deep and summon the extra burst of energy I need to propel myself through the heavy doors before they can bang closed in my face.

"I'm here!" I yell, too loudly, I realize, as three sets of eyes swivel in my direction from the judges' table. But that doesn't stop me. Clipboard Girl has to duck into a row of plush red seats just to avoid being mowed down as I head straight for them.

An older man peers at me curiously over his horn-rimmed glasses.

"Miss James?" he asks a little skeptically.

I nod, too breathless to speak for the moment.

"You're late Miss James," says the woman next to him. She puckers her mouth in distaste while she scowls at me.

"Yes, ma'am," I begin, still wheezing. "I apologize. You see, I couldn't get a cab and I had to run here…"

Sourpuss leans forward across her table of judgment. "Miss James, if I were you, I wouldn't waste what's left of my audition slot making excuses."

Seriously? If this woman had any idea what kind of a morning I've had… But, of course, she doesn't know. And I'm quite sure she doesn't care.

"Yes, of course," I say, swallowing my irritation.

I drop the casket-esque case where I stand, and pop it open to reveal my cello and bow. I grab both more roughly than I should, and scramble up the stage steps. The enormous platform, which usually holds over a hundred musicians at a time, is empty, save for a single folding chair and a music stand. They are dead center, and my shoes clop noisily as I make my way across the floorboards to sit down. I can feel the spotlights hot and bright above me, no doubt accentuating my disheveled appearance. But that, I realize, is the least of my problems. In my haste to get up on stage, I have left my music folder down with my case. Damn! If I try to go back and get it, they'll probably end the audition altogether.

What am I going to do now?

I take a deep breath and try to suppress the wave of panic that is rising within me. I'm just going to have to play something from memory.

It's okay. I'm okay. I can do this.

With that thought, I close my eyes and give the slightest nod of my head as I set my fingers free to dance across the fingerboard. In my right hand, the bow is an extension of my arm. I swing it effortlessly over each string, digging in—grabbing hold, pivoting and leaping like a gymnast on the uneven bars. I coax and tease and pull the notes from my instrument, fingers rocking back and forth from string to string.

The Prelude from Bach's Cello Suite No. 1 feels as if it is pouring out of me and spilling into the theatre. It is only when the very last note has died away that I'm able to open my eyes again and, when I do, they are all staring at me. And I mean staring. Like in disbelief over what they've just heard. I'm not quite sure what to do next, so I just stare back at them silently, waiting. Finally, Glasses Guy clears his throat and speaks.

"Thank you, Julia. Thank you very much. I hope the rest of your day is a little less hectic."

I stand up and speak in a voice that sounds tiny in the vast, empty space of the concert hall. "Thank you all for your time. I apologize again for being late."

I pick up the cello, which is almost as tall as I am, and take it back off the stage to return to its case. As I do, I can still feel their eyes on me, and it's freaking me out. I can't get back up the aisle and through the double doors fast enough. I breathe more easily once I'm back out in the corridor, but I really need a minute to decompress, so I turn in the opposite direction from where I came in. When I find an empty bit of hallway, I set the cello case down and stand with my back against the wall. Slowly, I let myself slip down into a sitting position on the floor, closing my eyes and trying to steady my frantic pulse.

"That bad?" asks a winded voice.

I open my eyes and he's standing there, bent over, palms on knees as he tries to catch his breath. My best friend, Matthew Ayers, is looking at me expectantly. "What are you doing here?" I ask, momentarily forgetting my own problems. "You're supposed to be in rehearsal! You didn't blow it off to come hear my audition, did you? Matthew, you just got that job…"

"Just hold on a second, will you?" he says, straightening and holding up a hand to stop me.

It's funny how all of our lives, people have been surprised to find out Matthew is a viola player. It's like they think that classical musicians are supposed to be pasty, geeky and dull. Well, that's certainly not the case with this particular classical musician. Someone who didn't know him would probably believe he's one of the best tennis players in the world before they'd believe he's one of the best violists. He's tall and muscular with thick, light brown hair that seems to be perpetually disheveled. Matthew is forever raking his hands through it in a losing battle for control. There's nothing fancy, or pretty, or overworked about Matthew Ayers. He's handsome in that easy, casual way.

Right now, he seems to just fold in on himself as he slips down to join me on the floor. When we are eye-to-eye, his amber to my emerald, I'm flooded with a sense of relief. I don't know why he's here, I'm just glad he is.

"I didn't skip rehearsal," he reassures me. "I just asked if we could skip the coffee break and wrap it up early instead. They were fine with that, so as soon as we were done, I hauled-ass down here to try and catch your audition. I actually snuck up into the balcony, but you were already gone. One of the pages said you went this way. She also said you nearly mowed her down," he adds with a slight smile to his lips.

"Yeah, well, I was late and she was in my way," I grumble.

"How late is late?" he asks with a hint of concern.

"I barely made it in there. That page was starting to cross my name off the list as a 'No Show,' but I ignored her and went straight to the judges' table."

"Did they let you play?"

"Yeah. But I only got five minutes."

His brows shoot up in disbelief. "God, that's barely enough time to get tuned!"

"Who tuned?" I cry. "Matthew, that five minutes included apologizing, unpacking and getting my butt on the stage. And, to make matters worse, I didn't bring my music up with me. The only piece I could think of to play was the Bach Prelude."

He considers this for a few seconds. "Okay, well, that's not such a bad thing is it? I mean, you kill that piece every time you play it."

I shrug and roll my eyes. "I don't know. I played it well enough, I guess, but it was only like three minutes. Is that enough time to compete for a spot in the Kreisler International Music Competition? I mean, everyone else got here on time, and was able to play whole movements for the committee. I don't know that they're even willing to judge me based on what I did," I say dejectedly.

He drapes his arm across my shoulders and I sink into his broad chest. This is a safe place for me. "I had a feeling something was wrong when you didn't pick up your cell this morning, so I called the lobby. Marcus told me he wasn't able to get you a cab in the rain and that you were going to try and run the twelve blocks here."

"Still, you shouldn't have come," I protest.

He shrugs. "I was worried about you. I just wanted to make sure you got here okay."

I shake my head, not sure if I should be touched or furious. In the end, I give him a kiss on the cheek and am rewarded with the sweet smile that makes those amber eyes crinkle. We grew up together in some pretty tough circumstances, and there is no one on this earth that I trust, admire, and love more than Matthew.

For him, it would have been an easy move out of the friend zone and into 'lovers' territory. Not so much for me, though. I lost too much, too early on. If our relationship becomes romantic and things don't work out, we could lose everything. And I'm simply not willing to jeopardize the only stable, loving relationship I have ever known. It's been a constant source of conflict between us for years.

"Come on. Let's go get something to eat. If I know you, you were probably too nervous to have your breakfast, and now you're starving," he says.

I smile sheepishly. I'm always starving.

He gets to his feet and offers me a hand up before grabbing my cello case and swinging it easily over his shoulders. As we walk back down the hallway that I sprinted through not a half-an-hour ago, I have the luxury of taking in a lot of what I missed the first time. Musicians are everywhere, chattering excitedly, pacing nervously. There are a lot of us, and not just cellists. This year, the Kreisler categories include piano, violin and French horn, too. We've all worked so hard to get to this point, and it's just the beginning. Even if I'm lucky enough to make this cut, there are semi-final and final rounds still to come.

"Look," I say, pointing inside one of the warm-up rooms as we pass. "There are Jeremy and Cal from the horn section. I should have known they'd be auditioning too."

I catch Cal's eye and give a quick wave. He's playing, but manages to convey a hello with a lift of the eyebrows and tilt of the chin. I know that Jeremy sees us too, but he doesn't give me a second glance.

Matthew doesn't even bother to look. "Good for them," he mumbles, gently pulling me along out of the building and into the crisp fall air.

2

The McInnes Conservatory of Music is my home away from home. It's not quite three blocks from the illustrious Juilliard School, but the two couldn't be more different. McInnes doesn't offer its students high-rise dorms looking out over the Hudson, or a fitness center. There are no high-tech, climate controlled practice rooms equipped with Steinway grand pianos.

Most people walk right past the unremarkable building which houses McInnes, thinking it's just another New York City public school. That's probably because it was exactly that before the conservatory took over the grim space with its cinderblock walls and yellowed linoleum floors. But the thing about McInnes is that you don't come here for the amenities, you come here because it's intimate. There's no getting lost in the crowd here. Although, today is one day when I'd welcome the opportunity to do exactly that.

It's been a few days now since the first round of Kreisler tryouts, and with dozens of McInnes students in the running, the entire building is buzzing. Pianists are comparing notes, violinists are gossiping, and my cello colleagues are passing judgment on one another's performances. It's a musician-eat-musician world over here in Lincoln Center. Personally, I'm trying to keep a low profile because I don't want to hear the insincere good luck wishes. I don't want to see their glances, or notice their giggles and whispers. I'm talented enough, and lucky enough, to sit first cello in a world-class conservatory, but that doesn't give me an advantage around here. Quite the opposite actually. All it does is put a target on my back. There are more than a dozen other cellists walking around the building at this very moment who would happily push me under a bus to move up a chair or two in the McInnes Conservatory hierarchy.

It doesn't help matters that I'm a little shy and embarrass easily. I have a hard time being the center of attention—not a great trait to have when you're in my line of work. So, I avoid orchestra politics, I don't sleep around with my professors and I don't pay attention to the petty gossip and rumors that always seem to be whirling around me. You'd think staying above the fray would make people respect me. Not so much. Instead, they call me 'The Mouse' behind my back.

For now, I just pretend to be invisible and make my way quickly and quietly through the halls, up the stairs, and into one of the oldest, dingiest practice rooms in the city. Since they constructed new ones downstairs, very few people bother to come up here anymore. I'm alone as I slip into my usual spot at the far end of the hall, and unpack my cello. I don't bother with the music stand, because I won't need it for this little exercise. Once I'm settled, bow in hand and instrument between my knees, I reach over to the light switch on the wall behind me and turn off the buzzing fluorescent lights above. I'm sitting in complete darkness.

If I can't see the music to read it, then I have to recall it from somewhere deep inside of me. I have to play it by feel, rather than sight. With a breath and a nod, my fingers begin their journey up and down the fingerboard. Bach makes me stretch, and reach and work for every note. But it's not just about hitting the right place on the right string at the right time. It's also about how you land on that string. The passages can be quick, which means I have to be decisive. My fingers are committed, moving deftly across the four strings in a blur—then there are the melodies that linger on each string. The bow in my right hand draws them out, but it's the left hand that does the heavy lifting, each finger rocking in place or, almost imperceptibly, from side to side, giving that long bowed note the most delicate vibrato.

Here, in the darkness, it's almost as if the cello and I are a single entity. I supplement the instrument's delicate panels of wood, and tough lengths of gut string with my own flesh, blood, and breath. I inhale every phrase, and my entire body moves in a circular pattern, cello lovingly embraced between my knees. It takes me to places I don't usually allow myself to go, places buried deep in the back of my mind.

My mother lives here, in this place where the music brings me. She's a young woman, not much older than I am now. I can see her pretty, fair face. She has freckles like me, and a head full of coppery curls. I imagine her leaning over me and tucking me in. She brushes the hair from my forehead and tells me to have sweet dreams. But they are not sweet at all. As my bow slices across the strings, I hear her and my father yelling through the night. I dig into the Bach harder, recalling the crash of objects hurled and the smack of a hand on someone's face. Whose? I don't know.

My fingers move frantically now, recklessly. The music could break apart and shatter in an instant. But it doesn't. It slows and begins the lament. The crying. Her tears. There it is. *He* slapped *her* this time. The cello is a wordless voice, heaving and sighing with the weight of her sorrow. The bow carries my fear with it as it swings to each string in turn. My parents are so volatile. They cannot hold our fragile life together. It just spirals out of control, picking up speed again, until it reaches a fever pitch.

Without warning, my hand slips across the D string, lurching forward and sending my bow flying across the room. It hits the floor with a sickening 'thwack,' returning me instantly to the tiny, pitch-black room in which I have lost myself once again.

I mutter obscenities under my breath as I carefully lay the cello on its side and drop to my hands and knees to find the bow. I'd turn on the lights, but I'm afraid I'll step on the damn thing and turn it into a three-thousand-dollar pile of toothpicks before I can get to it. I fumble blindly until I find it under the piano bench. I'm done. It's a dangerous thing, to open yourself to this kind of emotion, and it's possible to go too far if you're not careful. I'm very careful.

I pack up and start back out the way I came in, noticing the light on in another practice room. Now that's weird. I can count on one hand the times I've run across someone else up here ever, let alone at this hour of the night. I walk carefully, so my shoes won't clack on the floor and disturb the person playing…what is that? A trombone? As I move closer, the tone is better defined. No, that's a horn. When I'm standing in front of the room, I take a quick glance through the small window on the door and see the back of a chestnut head of hair.

Oh, now this really is a surprise! Jeremy Corrigan is practicing, just like the rest of us mere mortals. Since our freshman year, there have been rumors that he doesn't practice. He doesn't want to, he doesn't need to. He's just that good. And yet, here he is, in the middle of the night working on what? Weber? No, Strauss. Yes, definitely one of the Strauss Horn Concertos. I'm mesmerized as I hover in the shadows, listening as he tears through the intricate passages without breaking a sweat. This guy is amazingly good.

My thoughts are interrupted when he stops playing suddenly and turns his head to the side, as if sensing he's being watched. I scurry away as quickly and quietly as I can, but something tells me he might just have gotten a glimpse of me. I use the rickety old back stairs and duck out of a side exit and onto the sidewalk, shiny from a late night shower. It's just wet enough that the cars create mini-tsunamis as they whiz through puddles. There are a lot of people out and about tonight as I turn in the direction of home. They are a reminder that there are other people in this world, that I'm not the only one fighting the ghosts of the past on a Tuesday night at two o'clock in the morning. I find that strangely comforting.

It only takes ten minutes for me and the coffin case to get home to the Strathmore Building where—in apartment 16D—it's obvious that Matthew has been waiting up for me. Or, at least, he was before he fell asleep on the couch in front of the television. Well, there's no sense waking him now. If I do, it'll just be another lecture about staying out this late at night, getting my rest, and more sage, sound, practical advice than I can stomach at this hour. It's been a long, stressful day and all I want is to crawl into bed.

I set the cello down in the foyer and slip my shoes off so I can tiptoe through the room without disturbing him. I make my way to where he's passed out, arm splayed over the side of the couch, glasses hanging from his nose. Gently, I take them from his face and put them on the coffee table. The remote has fallen out of his hanging hand and I pick it up from the floor, using it to turn the TV off. I grab the throw blanket I keep in a basket near the couch, and drape it across his still, silent body. Finally, I turn out the light and slip down the hall.

Inside my room, I breathe another sigh of relief. As happy as I was to get out, into the night air and away from my demons, I'm equally grateful for the respite of my very own space. I've shared this apartment with Matthew since the day I turned eighteen. Growing up in a foster care facility, I never had anything to myself. Now, at twenty-three, I still get a thrill out of having a room all to myself.

I pull a nightgown over my head and set my phone on the nightstand to charge. I should have checked my texts earlier in the evening. No wonder poor Matthew stayed up for me, he sent me six messages while I was busy indulging in my little bit of music therapy. I know he's just worried about me, but I don't have the energy for it, or anything else at the moment. It's so much easier to just slip under the covers and allow the darkness to overtake me. Unfortunately, sleep is no guarantee of escape. Sometimes, the demons follow me there, too.

In my dream, it is always the same. I hear the smack of the aluminum storm door, as it slams closed. I look out the window and see my mother walking across the front lawn, carrying a small suitcase. The sun catches her bright auburn hair, making it look as if she has a fiery halo. My father is close behind her.

"Get your ass back inside!" he yells.

She ignores him, getting into the beat-up old Chevy.

Something feels terribly wrong and I go running out the front door barefoot, in my pink princess nighty.

"Mommy?" I call out.

She starts the car.

"Mommy? Where are you going?"

I walk towards the car just as she starts to pull out of the driveway. And then I am running but she keeps driving, the car kicking up a cloud of dust around me.

I'm screaming for her now. I know she can hear me.

She doesn't slow down. She doesn't even glance back in her rearview mirror.

I'm five years old.

This is usually the point where I wake myself up sobbing, drenched in sweat, and today is no different. It takes me a few minutes to get my heart rate back to normal.

"Julia?" comes Matthew's voice from the hallway outside of my room.

Pause.

"Julia, are you awake?"

A rap on the door.

"Go away!" I mumble from under the covers and pull the pillow over my head to block out the sound.

"Hey, are you okay? Was that another bad dream?"

He's in my room now, standing by the bed.

"Julia, come on," he coaxes. "I brought you a cup of coffee…"

Hmmm. Bribery. I lower my overstuffed shield slowly and allow my eyes to get used to the light.

"What time is it?" I croak squinting up at him.

"It's almost nine," Matthew says. "You really need to get moving. You don't want to be late for rehearsal or Maestro Hagen might throw his toupee at you."

I smile sleepily, and sit up in bed, propping myself against the pillows. He's not kidding either. Our crazy conductor actually pulled off his ill-fitting hairpiece and flung it at the trombones after they missed a cue during rehearsal. Now they duck whenever he even glances their way.

Matthew hands me a steaming mug of coffee. I take it in one hand and pat the side of the bed with the other, inviting him to join me. He climbs in and we sit, side by side, against the headboard. "What time did you get home?" he asks. "I didn't even hear you come in!"

"Mmm…just after two, I guess."

"You're insane!" he says, shaking his head at me. "No, I take that back. You're obsessed. God, you must be practicing five hours a day!"

More like seven, but I'm smart enough to keep my mouth shut on that point. So I do what women have done for centuries. I deflect. "Matthew, I'm trying to make it into the next round of the Kreisler's. If that means I have to live on catnaps and coffee for a while, I'm going to do it."

He looks as if he's about to start lecturing me, but I hold up a finger before he can reply.

"Besides, Mr. Pot-calling-kettle-black, who do you think you're fooling? You spend just as much time practicing as I do."

I conveniently neglect to mention the fact that he's not in school anymore. But he doesn't. "Not the same, and you know it. Besides, I'm not a grad student, am I?"

"You were," I point out.

"Yes, I was. And maybe I was running on too little sleep when I was finishing up at McInnes and getting ready to audition for the Walton, but now that I've got the job, I'm taking better care of myself."

"See? Exactly!" I say victoriously, slapping the mattress and making my coffee slosh dangerously close to the rim of the mug.

"What?" he asks, perplexed.

"You put in the hours. You did what you had to do and look at you now! You finished your degree and won a spot in the most elite string quartet in the world. Tell me it wasn't worth it," I challenge him.

He can't. Instead, he just rolls his eyes at me. "You're impossible, Julia James."

I smile at him with a frothy milk mustache and he laughs. "But I'm cute, right?"

"Yes. Very cute," he concedes begrudgingly.

"Seriously. Are you okay? That nightmare sounded pretty bad, even from out in the hallway."

I nod. "It's just the stress of the last couple of weeks, that's all. Things should calm down after they announce the audition results."

"How do you figure?" I don't answer and he nudges me hard. "Unless, of course, you're not expecting to make it to the second round. Is that what you think?"

I should have just kept my mouth shut. Why didn't I just keep my mouth shut?

"I don't know what to think, Matthew. There was some pretty stiff competition. I just don't want to get my hopes up too high."

"You've got this. I know you're going to win it," he says without the slightest hint of doubt.

I smile and, not for the first time, wish I had as much confidence in myself as he does. "What? Win it? God, we don't even know if I made the first cut. Let's not hang that medal around my neck yet, okay?" I laugh.

"I know it, even if you don't," he says, snatching the now-empty mug from my hand and untangling from me. "I'm headed out to rehearsal, I'll see you tonight." He raises the mug as if to toast me.

Once he's gone, I haul myself out of bed and rummage around in my dresser for some clean clothes. I'm about to close the drawer when the pair of framed photos on the dresser catches my eye. The smaller of the two is terribly faded. Even through the glass that now protects it, there are visible folds and creases from years of keeping it under my pillow. The man and woman look happy. He's strong and tall with sandy blonde hair. His arm is draped easily over the shoulder of the woman by his side, a petite redhead whose emerald green eyes are still striking, even after the picture has had so many years of abuse.

She's holding a toddler with a crop of strawberry blonde hair and those same eyes. Me. What I wouldn't give to be able to call to mind memories of the happier days of my young life.

I carefully return the plain, black frame to its spot and pick up its partner. There's a little less mileage on this one. It is a candid of Matthew and me under the big apple tree out front of our home. The North Fork Children's Home where we were foster kids together. Neither of us could have been more than eleven or twelve-years-old in it. Even now, he claims that this was the moment he fell in love with me. I put this one back too, close the dresser drawer and start my shower running in the bathroom.

Matthew has never once hidden the fact that he wants something different from our relationship than I do and, over the years, he has held fast to his belief that we are destined to be together. The truth is that there is nobody I love or trust more on the face of this earth than Matthew. That's the problem. I'd be lost without him in my life, without our relationship. If we give in and sleep together, if we try to live as a couple rather than best friends, there is no guarantee that we won't screw it all up. We have too much to lose if things don't work out for us and for me, that's an unacceptable risk.

I'm really not interested in romance at this point. I'm barely twenty-three. There'll be time for love later on. Besides, I've had more than enough chaos and drama to last me a lifetime. No, what I want right now, is to play my cello and finish my Master's degree. And, I suppose if I'm really honest with myself, I want a slot in the Kreisler Competition. But, that's such a long shot that I don't dare consider it. Not seriously, anyway.

3

I'm sitting on stage in the concert hall, rubbing rosin on my bow and waiting for the orchestra rehearsal to start. I use the term 'concert hall' loosely. It's actually a cafeteria retrofitted with seats and stage.

"He talked to me the other day, you know," says my stand partner, Mila Strassman.

I look up to see who it is she's talking about, and I'm not at all surprised to find that it's Jeremy Corrigan. Of course that's who she's talking about. He's the guy most of the girls in the orchestra talk about.

His entrance is the same every time. He unpacks his horn, tucks it under his arm like a football and lopes—actually lopes—up the steps onto the stage. Long, lean legs stride easily past the first violins, then the harp and finally the percussion to take his place at the head of the French horn section.

If even once Jeremy would go around the other way, if he would just turn right at the conductor's podium instead of left, he'd walk right past the cello section. That would certainly make Mila and several other female musicians very happy. But he never makes that turn. Personally, I think it has something to do with the violin section, which looks like something out of the talent portion of the Miss World Competition. I've never seen so many beautiful women playing in the same string section.

"Julia, you should have seen him at the auditions last week," Mila is saying.

"I did, actually," I correct her, but she doesn't seem to notice.

"God, he is so hot! I asked him if he was nervous," she informs me. "Do you know what he said?" I consider answering, but she continues before I can. "He told me he just takes whatever he wants." Now she turns to look at me. "I mean, how sexy is that?" I nod politely without comment. "I wouldn't mind if he took me," she mumbles under her breath.

The thing with Mila Strassman is that she's a talker. Chatter, chatter, chatter about anything and anyone—to me, to herself, to no one in particular. And I have to say she's not the most stimulating of conversationalists either.

"So the Kreisler list is out this week, right?" she asks.

"That's what I hear," I reply as she flips through our music folder and pulls out the Tchaikovsky Symphony No.4.

"Aren't you just dying to know?" she presses. "I know I am! I mean there were, like, hundreds of cellists going for it. Pretty much everyone here is hoping to be invited to play for the committee. And then there are, like, cellists from all over the country. What will they take, like ten or something? And that's from all over right? So who knows how many cellists are trying out for it that we don't even know!"

All of that without taking a single breath. I've taken to clocking Mila's ramblings just for the fun of it. She once yammered on for nearly a minute and half without so much as a tiny gasp for air. When I don't respond to her latest monologue, she just keeps going.

"Well, like I said, I know pretty much every one of the cellists here auditioned, probably the violins, too. But I'm not sure anyone here is really good enough..." She stops and turns toward me. In a rare moment of clarity, Mila realizes she may have just offended me. "Oh, gosh, I didn't mean you aren't good enough… It's just…well, you know. All those people from around the country…"

"The world, Mila. That's why they call it the Kreisler *International* Music Competition," I say a little too sharply and immediately regret it. She looks stricken.

"I'm sorry," I say, quickly. "I'm just tired. I was practicing late last night."

Her face instantly becomes sunny again, and she picks up her prattling where she left off.

"Well, the horn players, I think at least one of them has a good chance, don't you? I mean Cal is so solid. Never misses a note that one. And Jeremy...well, you know. He's so...you know…" She smiles as she leaves that sentence hanging.

I do know. Jeremy is one of those guys who is just enough of everything. Lips that curl into just enough smirk, stubble that gives him just enough ruggedness and hair just tousled enough to look neat, but not too neat. His brows appear to be set in a perpetual arch, framing brown eyes. I've never been close enough to get a good look. In fact, I've never even spoken to him, but you can clearly see he's just one of those guys. You know, the funny, charismatic ones to whom people are just naturally drawn. It wouldn't surprise me if he had the same effect on the Kreisler Competition judges, especially the female ones.

Mila looks about ready to launch into another conversation with herself when, to my immense relief, the concertmaster stands up and faces the orchestra, violin under his chin, bow poised. Once we have all quieted, he nods to the principal oboist who plays an A for the group to tune to. Across the orchestra strings, winds, brass all align themselves into perfect unison. The concertmaster nods and takes his seat again and we wait.

It's only a few seconds before the stage curtains part and Maestro Gunther Hagen takes his spot on the podium. He's a small, older man with the aforementioned floppy patch of wild hair that, since the unfortunate trombone incident, we can now confirm is not real. Sometimes, when he's conducting a particularly energetic piece, the faux hair will shift and he'll actually swipe at it with his baton.

Like many Maestros, ours is prone to the dramatic and right now, he's standing on the podium, eyeballing us, when he should be telling us what we're going to start with. There are a few soft coughs and shuffling feet until, finally, he smiles with twinkling blue eyes and wishes us a good morning in his soft German accent.

"I'm sure most of you are familiar with the Kreisler Competition. And if you're not, you should get out of the practice rooms once in a while," he chuckles.

Polite laughter from around the orchestra.

"As you know, this competition only takes place once every four years, and it is divided into three rounds over the course of three months. The gold medal winner of The Kreisler Competition will not only receive a substantial cash prize and a recording contract, but will also embark upon a concert tour that takes him or her around the globe. To say that this could launch a young musician's career is an understatement."

Hagan pauses to look down at his podium for a long moment before he picks up a single sheet of paper, and holds it above his head for all of us to see.

"It just so happens that I have a friend on the committee and he slipped me the preliminary round results a little early."

Suddenly, he has our undivided attention.

"We usually have one McInnes Conservatory student make it into the competition." Another dramatic pause that leaves us all hanging on the edge of our seats. "This year, we do not have one."

An audible stir of disappointment crosses the entire orchestra like a wave. The Maestro waits until he once again has the full attention of the one hundred musicians before him, then he gives us a sly smile. "I'm so proud to report that we don't have *one* student in the running, we have three!"

He shouts the number with an excited little hop that makes his hair shift slightly to the left. "Please stand up so we can recognize you…Calvin Burridge, French horn! Stand up, Cal!"

All heads swivel to the back of the orchestra and the horn section. Always calm and composed, Cal stands up, still holding his horn and gives a brief wave to his cheering colleagues. Everybody loves Cal. He's working on his doctoral degree and he's not just talented, he's a decent guy. I'm really happy for him.

When the applause has died down, the Maestro continues.

"Congratulations to *another* horn player, Jeremy Corrigan!"

If Jeremy is surprised, he doesn't show it. He simply stands and nods smugly as if to confirm what he has known all along. Now we all face front again to hear who the Maestro will call next. It's so quiet that I can hear Mila's stomach rumble next to me.

"And then there was one!" Hagen teases with an impish smile on his face. He looks around the orchestra, from one section to the next until he cannot contain his excitement anymore.

"And finally, please join me in congratulating….our principal cellist, Miss Julia James!"

Wait. Did he just say my name? Everyone has turned to look at me, so I must have heard him right. I can feel the warmth rising from below my collar up to my forehead. I'm sure I must be turning a lovely shade of scarlet as the people around me applaud and whistle. I'm shocked, thrilled, and terrified. Mila has to give me a push to get me to stand up.

Don't look down at your feet, Julia, don't look down at your feet...

But there is no controlling the blushing. I notice one of the girls in the violin section pointing and whispering to her stand partner. I pretend not to notice them giggling at me.

I hear someone call out "Mouse!" I hate that nickname.

"All right! Congratulations to the three of you! I expect you will represent us well, and I hope you will all make it through to the next round!"

Finally, our cue to sit down once more.

"You made it!" squeals Mila.

"Yes, I did," I mumble under my breath as I open up the Tchaikovsky.

4

French toast. It's all I can think about in my last hour of practicing. I realize why when I glance at my watch—I've worked through lunch and dinner. Now that I've cleared the first hurdle, I have less than a month to put together a program to play as I compete against two-dozen other cellists. Time, as they say, is of the essence.

It's after midnight, and I'm absolutely starving. But this is nothing new. The waitresses at the diner across from Lincoln Center know me by name now. They give me the booth in the back where there's extra space for my cello.

"Hi, Leslie," I say with a wave to the gray-haired woman who's been serving me midnight breakfast since I was a freshman.

"Hey there, sweetie. Have you been over there at the school practicing again?"

"Always," I groan. "And I'm starving. Any chance you've got a fresh pot of coffee on?"

"As a matter of fact, I do."

"Don't worry, I'll get myself seated," I say, starting to head for the back.

Leslie leans over the counter toward me and speaks in a stage whisper. "Julia, I'm sorry but there's someone in your usual spot. If I'd known for sure you were coming…"

I wave a hand at her dismissively. “Don’t worry about it. I’ll park this beast somewhere else,” I say, patting the case on my back.

As I turn the corner to look for an alternative booth I stop in my tracks. Sitting there is none other than the dashing Jeremy Corrigan. He’s writing something in a notebook when he looks up suddenly and spots me. Damn. No stealthy retreat possible. It’ll look rude if I turn around now. Won’t it?

I give him a small smile of recognition and a nod to acknowledge that I know him.

Okay, that was fine.

He cocks his head as if trying to place me and I see the sudden light of recognition cross his face. I’m about to slide into a booth a few down from his when he decides to speak to me. “You’re out late,” he observes.

“Oh, it’s still early for this one!” Leslie pipes in as she arrives with a pot of coffee and a fresh cup. “Where did you decide to sit, honey?”

“Uh—I think over here…” I gesture to the spot I’ve picked but he interjects.

“Please, join me.”

I must be looking at him funny because he says: “Unless, of course, you’d rather be alone…”

Now he and Leslie are both waiting for me to say something. Well, I might not ever get an opportunity like this again. “Sure, thanks. The company would be nice.”

And then he bestows upon me a beautiful, gleaming, crinkly-eyed smile. I think it’s maybe the nicest smile I’ve ever seen. It’s warm and welcoming, friendly and familiar. With this one expression he makes me feel as if he’s been here, counting the minutes till my arrival. I like this smile very much.

I set the cello down in a corner and slide in across the table from him.

"The usual?" Leslie asks as she pours my coffee.

"Yes, please."

When she's gone, I have no choice, I have to look at him.

"Julia, right?"

"Uh, yes"

"You don't sound so sure about that." The corners of his mouth twitch up and his smile turns teasing.

"I am. Yes. Julia. Sorry…"

"I'm Jeremy," he says, as if I don't know.

"Yeah…"

This is getting worse by the second. He must think I'm a total idiot.

"Congratulations on making the Kreisler list," he says, by way of an icebreaker.

"Um, thanks. You, too."

"Are you just leaving the practice rooms now?" He glances down at the watch on his wrist.

"Yes. How come you're out so late?"

"I was covering for a friend in one of the Off-Broadway pit orchestras," he explains "Just got out a little while ago and I'm starving. I love breakfast for dinner." He leans forward and says this last part softly, as if he's letting me in on his deepest, darkest secret. It makes me smile.

"Me, too. I'm a regular here," I confess with a giggle.

"I could tell when she asked if you want your usual. What is your usual, by the way?"

"French toast. But on the thin bread, not the challah, with warm syrup and crispy bacon."

"Now I'm sorry I ordered the eggs and home fries." Again he leans forward conspiratorially. "And you know, I'm a big fan of warm, sticky syrup."

Now he looks a little…what? Impish? Naughty? Sexy as hell is what he really looks like, and I'm fairly certain he isn't talking about breakfast food anymore.

Don't blush. Don't blush. Don't blush.

"You don't say much, do you?" he asks when I ignore the comment and sip my coffee.

"Oh, sorry! I don't mean to be rude. I'm just wiped out from practicing all day."

And I'm totally tongue-tied by your rugged good looks. Did I mention my knees are knocking, too? Being this close to him has made me a nervous wreck.

"So, do you know what you'll play for the next round?" he asks, steering my thoughts back into safe territory.

"Bach for sure, I'm still consulting with my teacher on the rest. What about you?"

"I don't know yet. I'm thinking one of the Mozart Concertos. Oh, and there's the Villanelle for piano and horn. That's an option, too."

"Oh, I love that Villanelle. I heard you play it at your senior recital last year. It was amazing!"

My sudden enthusiasm seems to take him aback. His dark eyebrows knit together as if he's trying to remember something. "You were there? At my recital?"

I nod and take another sip. The coffee cup has become a life raft that I'm clinging to in an attempt to keep from drowning. I take a quick look around. Where is Leslie? I'm going to be fake-sipping soon if she doesn't get me a refill quick.

"How could I have missed that?"

"Missed what?" I ask, turning back to him.

"You."

Oh.

"I'm easy to miss," I say in my usual breezy, self-deprecating manner.

But he doesn't smile back at me. In fact, every bit of humor has left his face. Oh, hell. What have I said now? This isn't going well at all.

"Is that what you think?"

"What?"

He sighs with exasperation. "You think you're easy to miss?"

I look down at the table in front of me, hoping he won't notice the redness I can feel in my cheeks. "Apparently," I mumble.

"Meaning what?" he demands, suddenly sounding a little defensive.

I look up. I can tell I'm irritating this pretty boy, but there are some things that even quiet little Julia can't let go by. "Jeremy, we've been playing in the same orchestra and sitting in the same classes for five years. Five! And you weren't even sure of my name until just now."

He doesn't move, doesn't respond for what feels like the longest time, and just keeps his eyes squarely on mine. Hazel. They aren't brown after all—they're definitely hazel.

Dammit! Focus, Julia! I have to will myself not to look away. Not this time.

Finally, to my utter shock, Jeremy is the one to look down. "You're absolutely right, Julia. And I apologize, I won't make that mistake again."

I'm spared from having to respond by Leslie, who brings our plates out and sets them down in front of us. She catches my eye, gives a little gesture toward Jeremy with her eyebrows and winks at me.

We prepare our food in awkward silence. He slaps the bottom of the ketchup bottle. I pick up the syrup, look at it and put it back down again.

"What?" he asks. I giggle a little. *"What?"*

"You've made my syrup seem…dirty," I admit with a smile.

He looks perplexed for a moment, and then a sly grin crosses his face. "Then I've done my duty for the night."

I roll my eyes and smile, the tension suddenly broken. Mila is never going to believe this. "So how are things back in the horn section?" I ask, moving on to a more neutral topic. "Is it weird with you and Cal Burridge both in the running for the horn slot at the Kreisler's?"

He shakes his head as he chews a piece of rye toast. "Nah. No more than usual. I'm not worried about it anyway."

"Oh? Are you that certain you can beat him out?"

He shrugs. "Is he a good horn player? Absolutely. One of the best in the country for sure. Is he better than me? I don't think so. But, I guess we'll just have to wait and see what the judges think."

"Huh."

The single syllable comes out sounding a little more snarky than I had intended.

"You disagree?" he asks, picking up on my disapproval.

"Disagree? No… Well, I guess a little. It's just so different from the way I look at things."

"Okay, so what's your thought process then? You're the top cellist at one of the most exclusive conservatories in the country. What did it take, mentally, for you to get here?"

"It wasn't a mental process for me."

One of those arch-y eyebrows shoots up skeptically. Really? He wants to debate philosophy of success over eggs?

Fine. I may be reserved when it comes to a lot of topics, but music isn't one of them.

"It was…it *is* a physical process for me. I practice until I have calluses on my fingers. Most days I'm running on five hours of sleep so I can spend the rest of the time prepping for rehearsals and lessons. I have a cello teacher, an accompanist and an audition coach. In other words, I work my butt off. That's my process."

"Okay, so hard work is how you got there. Fair enough. But let's take the music out of the equation…"

"What?"

He holds up his palm. "Please, just indulge me for a second. You beat out a lot of fine musicians to become principal cello at McInnes. There must be a dozen of them who would love to see you lose. You're not naive, you know that they're gunning for you." He pauses and looks at me quizzically. "You do know that, don't you?"

I shrug.

"What's that supposed to mean?" he presses, looking at me with an intensity I didn't know he possessed.

""I'm not naive. Nor am I an idiot. Of course I know that, Jeremy. Hell, Mila Strassman would skewer me with her bow to move up a chair if she thought she could get away with it."

"She'd never get away with it," he interjects. "That girl can't keep her mouth shut. She'd be telling everyone what she'd done in under thirty seconds."

I give in to a tiny chuckle because he's right, but I want to finish my thought. "As I was saying, I am aware. I just choose to ignore it."

"Ignore what? You don't think they all talk about you, behind your back? Don't forget, I sit behind you, Julia, and I've got a great view of your section. I see the other cellists snickering when you're singled out to demonstrate how something should be played. I was in Maestro Hagen's office when Tom Carson came in to complain about you last semester. I think you were out sick or something, and that idiot was petitioning to take your spot!"

He has become louder and more animated. In the mirror on the wall next to me I can see Leslie look up from where she's clearing another booth. I purposely drop my volume a little lower, hoping he'll get the hint.

"What do you have to be so indignant about?" I ask with a half-smile. "The cello crazies are my problem. And the truth is, Jeremy, that if the Maestro doesn't think I deserve my spot, he'll demote me. If any of them is a better cellist than me, they deserve to sit first chair. That's the way it is."

He starts to jump in, but I'm on a roll.

"And you know, for a guy who didn't recognize me when I walked in the door, you seem to pay very close attention to what people are saying about me."

"I pay very close attention to what people are saying about everybody," he says coolly.

"Life can be unfair," I begin slowly, "even tragic at times. There are things far worse than people talking about you behind your back."

Now I'm done. And I'm immediately sorry to have been sucked into this debate with a guy I barely know.

"Such as?" he asks, his voice trailing off.

"Such as what?"

"What 'far worse' things have you encountered?"

Nope. Not going there.

"You know, Jeremy, maybe you should leave the cello section drama to me and focus on the other four players in the horn section. They hate you. Seriously hate you."

I'm not totally surprised when a wide, brilliant smile passes across his face. "That, Julia, is exactly the effect I'm going for."

I sigh in exasperation and flag down Leslie for the check. I think it's about time to wrap-up this bizarre late-night rendezvous. Besides, my French toast is gone and I'm feeling a sugar coma coming on.

He opens his wallet and drops a few bills on the table as a tip. "I've got this," I say, as Leslie approaches.

"Absolutely not," he says, plucking the black folio out of her hand before I can even reach for it.

"No, really, thanks, but you don't have to…" I protest but he shakes his head at me resolutely.

"Not gonna happen," he says as he pulls more cash out and tucks it in with the bill.

I sigh in exasperation. I guess this is one of those "pick your battles" moments.

"Well, thanks," I say getting out of the booth. "That was very nice of you. I'll see you at rehearsal tomorrow…" I can't even get the sentence out before he's on his feet, grabbing the cello case and swinging it over his shoulder. "Oh, no, thanks, Jeremy, I can…"

"Are you nuts? You're all of five-feet-tall. You think I'm going to let you walk home alone in the middle of the night with an expensive instrument hanging off your shoulder? My mother raised me better than that, Julia." He flashes me that crinkly smile.

How do I argue with that? I nod reluctantly, and follow him as he leaves the diner with my instrument in tow. I practically have to run to keep up with his long stride.

"Someone waiting up for you?"

"Nah. My roommate is asleep by now."

"That's Matthew Ayers, right? He knows my brother. Good violist."

"He is," I agree.

We're about to dash across the busy street when he seems to realize he doesn't know which direction to go in. "Which line are you on?"

"Excuse me?"

"The subway. I want to get you to the subway station, at the very least."

"Oh, no. I live just around the corner, right off of West 62nd."

He gives a long, low whistle. "Pretty steep rent over there."

"I just rent a room. It's Matthew's apartment."

We're on the move again and I fall in beside him quietly until my building comes into view. "I can take it from here."

Jeremy stops, looks around, and then up. "What, here? You and Matthew live in the Strathmore Building?"

"Thanks again for seeing me home, Jeremy," I say, holding out my hand to take the cello from him. But he's still looking up.

"Jeremy?"

"Oh, yeah. Sure. Here." He pulls the strap from his shoulder.

"Goodnight," I say with a small wave.

"Hey, you don't really think that no one notices you, do you?" he asks.

I sigh. It's not what I think—it's what I know from years of experience. "Goodnight, Jeremy," I repeat, ignoring his question and turning my back on him.

Carl the doorman has come out to usher me and the coffin/case in.

"Goodnight, Julia," I hear him call out from behind me.

I hold up a hand without turning.

"Carl?" I ask when I'm safely in the lobby and out of earshot.

"Yes, Miss James?"

"Is that guy still out front?"

He gives a quick, stealthy glance over my shoulder, trying not to look too obvious.

"Yes, Miss. He's watching to see you're safely inside. Seems like a gentleman," he says approvingly.

"Yes, he does," I mutter to myself as the elevator doors slide closed and I push the button for the sixteenth floor.

5

When I push open the doors to the performance hall, I'm almost knocked over by the cacophony. It sounds as if every musician in the orchestra is playing something different, all at the same time. The noise doesn't usually bother me, but I'm running on not much sleep, and I'm more than a little anxious about seeing Jeremy again after our impromptu meeting last night.

I'm breathing hard as I slip into my seat on the hardwood stage and get my cello situated between my knees. Bow, bow, bow. Pluck, pluck, pluck. That'll have to do for a warm-up today. From next to me, I feel a jab in the ribs.

"Hey, look!" Mila says, thrusting her chin toward the front of the orchestra.

And there he is. Jeremy Corrigan, horn under his arm, strides up the steps to the conductor's podium…and makes a turn to the right. Wow. He's actually going to pass by the cello section. I hunch down a little, grab a pencil and pretend to be absorbed in writing notes on the music in front of me.

"Hi."

He's stopped beside my chair.

"Hi," I reply, putting down my sham pencil and sitting up straight.

"Nice talking to you last night," he says just loud enough so that I can hear him. "I'm sorry if I was a little…pushy with my opinions."

"No need to be sorry." I smile. "It was an interesting night. And hey, thanks again for walking me home."

"The pleasure was all mine. This time, anyway."

Can this guy say anything without it sounding like a sexual innuendo? Before I can reply he's gone, moving on to take his seat with the horns.

"What the hell was that?" Mila asks in a hushed squeal. "He walked you home? From where?" she demands.

Oh, this might get a little bit ugly.

"It was nothing. I stopped by the diner after practicing last night and he was there. He asked me to sit with him, and he made sure I got home safely. He was just being polite."

"Since when are you even interested in him?" she demands, shaking her head at me in disbelief.

"Mila," I begin, trying to diffuse the situation, "It was nothing. Really. I went to the diner, where I often go, and he just happened to be there. I didn't go there looking for him, he didn't go there looking for me. It was a total coincidence."

She cocks an eyebrow skeptically and I'm reminded of my conversation the night before. This girl isn't my friend. Not really.

"You expect me to believe that?"

I sigh and turn back to the music in front of us. "I really don't care what you believe."

I can tell the comment has surprised her. She's not used to me having an attitude with her, and now I can feel her staring at me in disbelief. I have to say, I kind of like it. So this is what it feels like to actually say what you're thinking!

By the time rehearsal ends, Mila has given me no fewer than ten loud sighs, twelve sidelong glances and one 'humph!' I don't give her even a moment's notice. Aside from the counting, that is. She's quick to flee the cello section when we're finished, and I decide to give her a few minutes to clear out. We'll sort it out later when she's had a chance to calm down.

"Nice job today, *Julia*."

The unmistakable voice—his voice—is coming from behind me. I turn around and see him coming toward me on his way off the stage. Mr. Smarty Pants wants to let me know he hasn't forgotten my name.

"Well, thank you, *Jeremy*," I reply, with equal emphasis. "Twice in one day!"

"What?" he stops and asks.

"You. You never come past the cello section…but here you are."

A wicked little smirk crosses his face.

"Why Julia, I had no idea you kept track of my movements so closely."

Ugh! I walked right into that one. He starts to leave, but then stops and turns back.

"You know, next time you come across me in the practice rooms, you should stop in, instead of just lurking out in the hallway," he says, then resumes his trip off the stage without waiting for comment.

I can't help but notice the fact that Jeremy Corrigan looks just as attractive going as he does coming.

6

"You're sure you'll be okay?" Matthew asks as he zips his tux in the garment bag and hangs it from a hook on the back of his bedroom door.

I roll my eyes at him.

"Yes, I think I can manage without you for a few nights."

"It's not a few nights, Julia, it's a few weeks. And you don't have to be so damned independent, you know. A guy likes to feel he's needed," he says with faux indignation.

I walk up from behind and give him a bear hug.

"I do need you. We need each other. But we're both going to be just fine. Matthew, this is your first tour as a full-fledged member of The Walton String Quartet! You've worked your whole life for this. Why are you worrying instead of being excited?"

He pats my hands around his chest. "I'm excited. It's just a long time to be away from…home."

"Well, you go ahead and be homesick, but I'll be busy here. I have a competition to prepare for," I say, letting go of him so he can finish packing his overnight bag.

"Yes, you do," he replies as he grabs socks and underwear from his dresser drawer. "But I hope you're going to do more than just live in the practice rooms while I'm gone."

Despite my protests, Matthew has the smaller of the two bedrooms in our apartment. That's not to say he's living in a hovel or anything. Our two-bedroom apartment is large and sunny with windows that run from floor to ceiling. At night, the city view is spectacular. There's a gas fireplace in the living room, and the kitchen is like a little oasis of stainless steel and granite. My favorite amenity is the small balcony overlooking Lincoln Center.

I can't tell you how many nights we spent as kids, lying out on the lawn of the North Fork Children's Home, looking up at the stars and planning what our lives would be like when we "grew-up" which, in the case of un-adoptable foster kids is eighteen. Up until that time, we had no control over where or how or with whom we lived. We swore it wouldn't be like that forever. And it hasn't been.

Unlike most kids coming out of that living situation, Matthew has money. Lots of money. When he came of age, he was finally able to take control of the estate his parents left him when they were killed in a boating accident. He doesn't like to take rent from me, but that's non-negotiable, as far as I'm concerned. I may not be rich, but I do well enough teaching lessons on the side.

"So what are your plans for the weekend?" he asks now as I perch on the edge of his bed and watch him collect his toiletries.

"Oh, you know, the usual. Dinner, dancing, a show. Maybe a carriage ride around Central Park."

"Well, you've always been a hopeless romantic."

I giggle. "Nah. I think I'm probably going to plant myself in a practice room for the next couple of days, depending on how my lesson goes this afternoon. Dr. Sam has made it very clear that if I don't get my act together on the Rachmaninoff Cello Sonata, I can't use it for my audition."

"I thought you had that one down already. You've been working on it for months," he says, tossing some T-shirts into the suitcase.

"Yeah, I thought so too," I sigh, watching as he adds jeans and a wad of socks to the heap.

"So, what's the problem then?"

I start pulling the clothes back out and folding them. "Oh, you know Dr. Sam. He's big into the meaning behind the piece. The composer's intention, blah, blah, blah..."

"And he doesn't think you know the meaning behind the piece?"

"You'd think, right? Nope, he wants me to spend some time with the third movement in particular to see if I can find an emotional connection to it," I say, with rolled eyes.

"Could he have been a little more vague, do you think?" he asks with a sarcastic smile.

"Tell me about it!" I return the newly folded items to his suitcase. He looks down at them appreciatively, and then joins me on the edge of his bed.

"Does it have to be this piece? I mean there are hundreds of other sonatas and concertos you could do instead."

I sigh and look hard into his golden brown eyes, the color of amber. They are clouded with concern. I hate to worry him about this stuff, but it's impossible to get anything past him. He knows me too well.

"Matthew, this is the one," I say finally. "With the Rachmaninoff and the Bach, I think I can win the cello category."

"Okay, well, there it is, Julia," he nods firmly. "If you feel that strongly about it, then the answer is somewhere in here," he says, tapping his chest over his heart. "Not," now he taps his head, "in here. Get out of your head and trust your heart."

"I know you're right," I whine, "but that's easier said than done."

"Of course I'm right!" he quips as he gets to his feet again. "And no one ever said it was going to be easy, Julia. Now, if you'll excuse me, my driver will be here soon and I've still got things to do."

"Ah, yes. I'm sure your adoring public will be waiting for you at the airport," I tease. "Are you going to wear sunglasses so you won't be hounded by the paparazzi?"

I duck with a squeal of laughter as he throws his deodorant at me.

7

The stove and I are not friends. Right now, it seems to be mocking me as I stand in front of it, thinking about how much I'd love a grilled cheese sandwich. It's just a frying pan, two pieces of bread, some cheese and butter. How much damage could I do? I turn back to the fridge with a sigh and pull out some turkey. Cold sandwich it is. I'm just a terrible cook, so it's Matthew who ensures there's a meal on the table once in a while. But now that he's away for the next two weeks, I can see a lot of diner meals in my immediate future.

He's only been gone a couple of hours, and the apartment already has a strange, empty vibe. How is it possible for me to live in a building with hundreds of other people, in a city with millions of other people and still feel alone? Well, I won't be here for long anyway. I'm going to have my lunch and head over to McInnes. I don't have any time to waste with that Rachmaninoff if I plan to have it ready to go on Monday.

DING!

I jump at the sound. My phone, sitting on the breakfast bar, is suddenly bright with a text message.

Coffee on the counter. Microwave dinners in the freezer. Don't use the stove!

I laugh as I send back a smiley face emoji. Maybe this won't be so bad, after all. He's even set out my favorite mug for me next to the carafe. I add sugar and cream to the cup and start to pour in the coffee, but the lid isn't quite tight enough and the scalding hot liquid wicks underneath the carafe and down my hand.

"*Ouch!*" I yelp loudly, putting the coffee down hard on the counter and rushing to the sink.

As I hold my hand under a stream of cool water from the faucet, I'm almost knocked over by a sense of déjà vu. I've been here before, in almost this exact position. The smell of the coffee, the spilled drops on the counter, the sting of the burn, they all take me back nearly two decades to our ramshackle little house in one of Long Island's seedier neighborhoods. My mother was gone by then, leaving me scrambling to keep my father happy. Even at the age of six, I knew that keeping my father happy was crucial to my wellbeing.

The early morning hours were the best. I'd wake up with the sun streaming into my tiny bedroom. The sheets were warm, my pillow was soft and I enjoyed several groggy minutes in that state between asleep and awake. Minutes that didn't involve pain or hunger or cold, minutes that ticked by without threats of violence or humiliation. They were the best minutes of my day. And, they were swiftly followed by the worst minutes. My father banging around the kitchen, demanding I get out of bed and make him a cup of coffee.

I remember having to pull a chair up to the counter to stand on, just so I could reach. The image is frighteningly clear in my mind. Me, teetering on the chair, pouring the water and measuring each spoonful of coffee.

"Please, God, let Daddy like the coffee today. Please God. Please," I prayed.

And, if God didn't happen to be listening on that particular day, I would find myself just as I am now, watching the angry red welts rise on my stark white hand. Only, back then, it could've just as easily been my arm, or my face. Rex James had no patience for the daughter his wife had saddled him with when she ran off.

In those days, it wasn't hard for a quiet little girl to fall through the cracks and, the truth is that by the time I was six, I had become an expert at hiding in plain sight. I knew just how to fade silently into the background, a survival skill that served me well at home. On the days that I actually managed to get to school, things weren't much different. I was silent. Unremarkable and unnoticed until, one Tuesday afternoon in December, someone finally saw me.

Miss Evans blew through my elementary school like a breath of fresh air, taking over after the crotchety old Miss Smith broke her hip. The young teacher watched me. And the more she watched, the more I willed myself to disappear. It didn't work, though. Jen Evans wasn't like the other teachers who saw only what they wanted to see. She noticed as I stood by the heater on the far end of the room every chance I got, teeth chattering and shoes soaked trough from the slushy snow.

The day I came in walking slowly, wincing with nearly every movement, was the day she stopped watching and did something.

"Sweetie, is your back hurting you?" she asked softly, squatting down next to my desk so the other children wouldn't hear.

I nodded.

"Did you hurt it?"

I nodded again.

"Can I see?"

A sickening wave of panic seized me. I knew my father would be furious if I told.

I shook my head. No.

"Please, Julia, just let me take a peek."

When I finally nodded my consent, she ushered me to the small bathroom in the back of the classroom. After a brief look she pulled it down gently and smiled reassuringly.

"Don't you worry about a thing! Everything is going to be okay," she promised.

I was not convinced. And for good reason. Even at the age of seven I had the definite feeling that everything was about to change.

What Jen saw when she lifted my clothing was a huge bruise, already turning a rainbow of purples, yellows and blues. It took up most of my back and was in the perfectly outlined print of a size ten work boot.

While we waited for Child Protective Services to arrive, Jen took me to the nurse's office and brought me a tray from the cafeteria. After I gobbled up my lunch she passed me hers so I could eat that one as well.

"Sweetie, what was the last thing you had to eat?" she asked, trying to sound casual.

I shrugged.

The rest of that day felt as if it was stuck on fast forward. A blur of doctors and police and social workers peppered me with questions about my home life and my parents. Terrified of the beating I'd get from my father, I never uttered a word. But I needn't have worried about my father because I was never going to go home again.

That night I was brought to an emergency foster home and a kind woman called Miss Mavis.

"Why, you're just as quiet as a little mouse," she said, as she gently washed the grime from my body and combed the tangles from my hair.

In the bedroom where two older girls were already sound asleep, she tucked me in tight under the covers and picked out a teddy bear for me to cuddle from a shelf on the wall. A pink princess nightlight glowed in the corner. Miss Mavis brushed the unruly hair back from my forehead and kissed it tenderly.

"Everything is going to be alright, sweet little mouse. You hear me? You are going to be alright."

Somehow, when she said it, I believed it, and for the first time in my short life I felt warm and full and safe.

"These are good minutes," I thought as I drifted off to sleep that night.

Now, so many years later, sitting in a safe home of my own, I put a hand to my cheek. I'm surprised when it comes away damp, covered in salty tears.

I do understand why my mother left my father—I just don't understand how she could have left me behind.

8

I have to get out of the apartment. With Matthew gone, I'm better off just jumping into my practicing than sitting around, watching television and letting my mind go to places that I have locked away in the deepest recesses. When I get to the McInnes lobby, the night watchman barely looks up as I come through the front lobby door.

"Hi, Gordon," I say with a wave as I pass his desk.

"You've got company tonight," he informs me without looking up from his crossword puzzle.

I pause, and turn back to him. "Excuse me?"

"You're not alone. There's a French horn player up there right now."

He gestures absently toward the back staircase.

"Which one?"

Now, why did I ask that? Does it really matter? There are five horn players altogether—three women plus Cal and Jeremy. It could be any one of them. Gordon finally looks up at me through his thick-framed glasses.

"The guy. The tall guy," he says.

I smile and nod. There's a little bit more spring in my step than there was thirty seconds ago, as the cello and I take the steps two at a time. When my feet hit the third floor landing, I'm greeted by the muted strains of Mozart. I pause for a second to slow my breathing and smooth my hair. When I'm confident that I don't look too eager, I stroll slowly toward the source of the sound, the first practice room on the left. I can see the back of a dark head of hair through the small rectangular window in the door. Just before my knuckles make contact with it, the horn player turns to the side and turns out not to be Jeremy Corrigan at all, but rather Cal Burridge. I can't help feeling a little disappointed as I head a few doors down and take my usual spot at the end of the hall.

Inside the tiny, dimly lit practice room, I set my case on the floor and rest my back against the closed door. What the hell was that? First excited, then disappointed? Is it possible I'm a little more attracted to him than I'd like to admit? I have to get real here. Jeremy Corrigan is a player and I'm not the kind of girl that players look for.

"Ugh…" I groan out loud and roll my eyes.

Time to stop acting like a lovesick teenager and put on the big girl pants. I have plenty of things that require my attention at the moment, and Jeremy isn't one of them.

With that self-lecture out of the way, I get myself set up, and dive into the Rachmaninoff Cello Sonata. The faster movements go by in a blur that will surely impress the judges. The slow movement, though, that's where the problem lies. I've got to find a way to wrap my head around it, so I start out with a little deconstruction. I take the melody apart, one measure at a time. When I've got that, I string several measures together. Nope. No good.

It sounds disjointed. Okay, maybe getting my eyes off the music will help me to loosen up. I close my eyes and try playing from memory. No go. I miss more notes than I hit. I'm about to try playing it while standing on my head when I hear a gentle rap on the practice room door. When I turn around, Cal's smile fills the tiny window. He raises his eyebrows to ask if he can enter. I smile back and nod.

"Hey, Julia! I thought I might run across you here," he says, seeming to be genuinely happy to see me.

"Yeah, Rachmaninoff and I are having a knock-down, drag-out fight right now," I explain with exasperation.

"Well, don't feel too badly, I've just gone ten rounds with Mozart and I think he's the winner."

I laugh. Cal is such a pleasant change from the other devious little sharks that swim around in the McInnes waters. What you see is what you get. And what you see in Cal Burridge is an easy-going, affable guy who just wants to make music.

"So, I'm just about done here," he says, "and I was thinking I'd head over to the diner for something to eat. I've never been, but I know you're there all the time, and I thought I might give it a try. Feel like joining me?"

My first instinct is to say no and keep pounding my head against the wall with Rachmaninoff, but my stomach puts a stop to that thought immediately. Apparently, skipping that turkey sandwich was a mistake that I'm about to pay for. Well, it's not like I'm making any progress here anyway.

"That sounds really great, Cal," I agree, and watch his face light up.

"Let me just pack up and drop my cello down in the locker room. Meet you out front in five minutes?"

"Great!" he says with a little too much enthusiasm. "Uh, great," he repeats, sounding cooler the second time.

I'm not blind. I know that Cal has had a little crush on me since he was accepted into the graduate program last year. Thankfully, he's never acted on it, so I haven't had to endure the awkwardness of turning him down. He's a great guy, a handsome guy, and a talented guy. But he's definitely not my guy. That would just be too easy, wouldn't it? No, instead, I have to obsess over my last late-night breakfast companion, the bad boy of the brass section himself. And right now, I'm about to return to the scene of the crime.

This time, when Leslie sets my breakfast plate down on the table, she shoots me an interested *'hey, what gives?'* glance. I've been coming here either on my own or with Matthew for five years and now she's seen me here with two different guys in less than a week. I give her a *'for me to know and you to find out!'* brow raise in return and she scuffles away, shaking her head and smiling.

I pick up the bottle of syrup and turn it over in my hand.

"Something wrong?" Cal asks, noticing.

"Oh, nothing. Just remembering something someone said to me recently."

Something naughty.

Cal lets it go with a shrug of his broad shoulders. He's a big guy. Not heavy, just big. So big, that as he sits across from me in the booth, he looks like a grown man sitting on tiny furniture at a child's tea party. Now, he runs his large hands through his sandy blonde hair.

"You've got to have one of these pancakes, Cal," I say, slathering them with the sexy syrup. "They're amazing, but I'll never finish them. Cranberry and walnuts. Here..." I offer, starting to offload a pancake from my plate but he waves his hand.

"No, thanks, Julia. I wish I could, but I'm allergic to nuts."

"Oh, Right! Sorry, I knew that! Is it a problem if I have them?" I ask with concern.

He shakes his head. "No, not at all. So long as I don't come into contact with them, I'm okay. I just have to be really careful."

"So," I say, between bites, "how did you know I like to come here?"

"You're in *My Orbit*," he says simply, as if I should know what he's talking about.

"I'm sorry, did you say I'm in your orbit?"

His mouth is full of chicken salad but he nods and raises a finger, indicating I should hang on a second until he's swallowed his sandwich.

"Yeah, the app. *My Orbit*."

Why does it seem like he's speaking a foreign language all of a sudden. App? What app? I haven't bothered to put anything on my phone but music. I wouldn't even text if Matthew didn't insist.

"I don't even know what that means…"

He gives me a teasing smile. "Not as savvy with the phone as we are with the cello, then?"

"Not so much," I mumble.

"Let me see your phone."

He holds out his hand and I put the requested item in his hand. Then, I watch with some interest as he scrolls, punches, pinches and types his way to an "Aha!"

"Aha?"

"Yup, aha," he repeats, coming around the table to sit next to me in the booth. He points to a small icon in the top right corner of my screen. "See that tiny little icon?"

I nod. "Yeah, it looks like Saturn."

How come I never noticed that there before? Maybe because I rarely look at the damn thing.

"Exactly. That means the app is active in the background."

"Cal, you keep talking about this app like I put it there or something. If it didn't come with the phone, then I don't know how it got there. I mean, what does it do, anyway?" I can hear the frustration creeping into my tone.

"Okay, look…" He taps a few more times and suddenly, I'm looking at a street map of this block. There's a dot on the diner. "That red dot is you. Now, if you had it set to notify you, the app would send you an alert every time someone in your contacts is nearby, or 'in your orbit.' You get it?"

"Not really..."

"So, the way it works most of the time," he continues, trying to dumb it down even more for me, "is that the app pulls all of your contacts' information and is able to track their movements within a certain radius of your location. Any time one of them enters that radius, you should, theoretically, get an alert."

"What kind of alert?"

"It would look like a text and it says something like *'Cal Burridge is in Your Orbit!'* Then, if you're interested in seeing where I am, you can tap on the message, and it'll take you to this map. My location will be marked with a pin."

"But I don't see you on this map. And I don't ever get messages like that. I think I'd have noticed..."

"Well, let's see," he mumbles, poking and swiping and clicking in a blur of gestures across my screen. "Okay, here it is... You're set to transmit your location to all of your contacts at all times, but you've turned off the setting that tracks *your* contacts."

"Wait, wait, wait," I say, trying to process. I know there's something really important about what he's just said, I'm just not sure I'm understanding it clearly. "So...anyone who has this Orbit app *and* has me as one of their contacts *and* is set-up to receive notifications, will know whenever I'm somewhere close by?"

"Exactly!" he smiles, pleased that I'm finally grasping this...but not grasping that I'm growing more concerned.

"And, if I wanted to, I could track my contacts, too."

"That's it! You've got it. See, I knew you could wrap your head around tech concepts. You don't give yourself enough credit, Julia!" he says, giving me a friendly nudge.

"Cal?"

"Hmmm?"

"So…if *I* didn't put that app there, and it's not configured to let me *know* it's there…is it possible that someone *else* installed it with the sole purpose of tracking *me*?"

I see the smile slip from his face as he digests what I'm suggesting. Now he's seeing what I'm seeing…that this could be something else, entirely.

He clears his throat. "Uh, well, yeah, I guess. If the thing isn't set to let you know when people are around you, then you wouldn't even know that it's there in the background, broadcasting your whereabouts."

Holy. Crap.

My phone's been acting as a double agent, alleging to keep me safe and in contact, while alerting anyone with an internet connection that I'm hobbling around town with several thousand dollars' worth of cello strapped to my back…*and* delivering a map to my whereabouts while it's at it!

Cal slips back around to his side of the booth and gestures the waitress for more coffee. "Hey! Don't look so worried," he says, after she's topped us up. "I'm sure it's an innocent mistake. It's easy enough to uninstall. Besides, it's not as if everyone doesn't already know that if you're not home, or in the practice rooms, you're here."

My newly warmed coffee is almost to my lips when I stop and put it back down on the table.

"Am I really that predictable?" I ask, astonished by this revelation.

"Nothing wrong with a routine," he shrugs.

"Yeah, well. I guess I'd better mix it up a little so I don't get boring."

"Oh, I think you're just fine the way you are," he murmurs, trying to hide his smile in a sip of coffee.

Time to get him onto another topic. And fast. "So, how's it going with you and Jeremy?"

Now it's his turn to set the coffee cup down on the table. His smile is gone. "What do you mean?"

The abrupt chill in his tone catches me a little off guard.

"I—I don't know..." I stumble, feeling as if I've hit a nerve that I didn't intend to. "With the competition, I guess. Is there any friction between the two of you over it?"

Cal's brows knit together and he looks down as if contemplating the sandwich in front of him. "There's always friction where Jeremy is concerned," he informs me coolly.

"What do you mean?" I press, suddenly all ears.

"I mean he and I don't exactly get along. Actually, Julia, very few people get along with him."

"I don't know," I shrug. "I get along with him just fine."

My words come out sounding contrary, and he looks up to meet my gaze. Suddenly the happy-go-lucky Cal has vanished.

"Julia, Jeremy's a complicated guy. He's really talented, and I know he can be very charming. I'm just not sure he's the kind of guy you should be friendly with."

Is that what I'm doing? Being friendly with Jeremy?

"What kind of guy is that, Cal?" I ask.

He takes a long second to choose his words.

"In my experience, he can be...well, let's just say I've seen him when he's not at his best. He can be *difficult*. Especially if he doesn't get his way."

Oh. Maybe this is a *'guy thing.'* Or even a *'horn player thing.'* I give him a gentle smile.

"You know, I don't doubt that the two of you have had your run-ins. I mean, Mila and I, we're always butting heads. It just goes with the territory around here. All the pressure to perform, all the competition. And that's just the everyday stuff at McInnes. Now, you throw in the Kreisler Competition…"

He's shaking his head before I've even finished speaking. "It's not about that. Not about competition. There's always an angle with Jeremy," he explains. "I'm telling you Julia, you're better off keeping clear of him."

Poor Cal. I don't know why he's so jealous—it's not as if I have a snowball's chance in hell of having a relationship with Jeremy. Honestly, I'm surprised Cal hasn't had issues with Matthew. Maybe he's smart enough not to go down that road.

I look down at my pancakes, half eaten and cold. I'm not so hungry anymore.

9

"No, No, No!"

I jump a little and stop bowing mid-note when Dr. Sam yells at me. He never yells at me. But today I'm testing his patience and, apparently, his nerves. I watch him silently as he takes off his glasses and pinches the bridge of his nose. Oh, this is not a good sign.

Sam Michaels was a Kreisler Gold Medal winner at the age of twenty, and principal cello of the Chicago Symphony Orchestra less than a year later. Now, in his sixties, he's one of the most sought-after teachers in the country. And I'm one of a handful of students he's willing to teach.

Finally, he puts the frames back on his face and considers me for a long moment.

"Julia," he begins, voice lowered and hands steepled, "I don't know what else I can say to you. You're just not grasping this movement…and without this movement, there *is* no sonata."

He's telling me I can't use this piece in the first round of the Kreislers. But, as far as I'm concerned, there is no other piece. He can see this in my eyes.

"It's not the notes. You just fly through the tricky passages in the other movements but this one…it's like you're phoning it in."

We've been having this discussion for the last three weeks—ever since we found out I made the first cut. But I've always wanted to perform the Rachmaninoff Cello Sonata and now, finally, I have the opportunity. I don't know what to say to convince him. I drop my eyes to the floor and he keeps talking.

"Maybe we should take a look at some other possibilities. I mean, we only have a couple of weeks left here, Julia. We can't afford to waste time on something that you can't…that you won't…" His voice trails off.

"I can do this," I say to the floor, my voice sounding smaller than I'd like.

He doesn't respond.

"I can do this," I say more firmly this time, looking up again.

"Julia, you are a phenomenal cellist."

Uh-oh. I feel a 'but' coming.

"And we both know that even more than professionally, I care about you personally. I have been teaching you since you were a little girl, and there is no student that I'm more proud of than you."

Here it comes.

"But I care about you and your future too much to let you play a piece you're not ready to play in front of thousands of people."

"Give me a few more days," I plead.

He holds his palms up and shakes his head. "Julia, we do not have the luxury of waiting…"

"I *will* get it," I insist.

If he says no, that's it. I'm done. You don't disobey Sam Michaels if you want to remain his student. That rule applies even to me.

"There's a lot on the line here."

"I know."

"Honestly, in your heart of hearts, do you think a few more days will make any difference?"

I respect this man enough to give him my most honest answer.

"I don't know. But I won't be able to move on to another piece unless I give this one more try. I swear, if it's not where it needs to be by my next lesson, I'll let it go and I'll commit myself to whatever you think I should do."

He takes a deep breath, and I wait for the 'no' that I'm sure is coming. "Alright then," he agrees, to my shock. "But not one day longer."

I beam at him and wish—not for the first time—that I could just throw my arms around him and give him a hug, the way I did when I was a little girl. I know he wouldn't mind, but I also know that no one is safe from the McInnes rumor mill. On impulse, I set the cello on the floor, open the door of his studio and take a look down the hallway. It's deserted. I close the door, scoot back in, and give him the quickest of kisses on the cheek. "Thank you, Dr. Sam," I whisper.

"You're welcome, kiddo. Now get out of here before I change my mind."

I do, because he just might.

By the time I get to my Chamber Music Lit class, there are already three violins and a tuba propped up against the wall. My cello joins them and I manage to slide into a seat on the aisle with a minute to spare as the professor gets her sound system setup. I feel a light tap on my shoulder and turn to find myself looking into the eyes of Jeremy Corrigan, which are more green than brown today.

"Hi," I say with a shy smile.

"Julia, I missed last class. Is the test today?" he whispers.

I hope not. I think hard for a second to be sure.

"No," I shake my head. "Not till Wednesday. She wants to cover the Schubert Quartet today and Monday."

He sits back in his chair, clearly relieved. "Thanks!"

I nod and face forward, but not before I catch a glimpse of Tom Carson, a cellist from my section, in the seat next to Jeremy. The little creep sits just under Mila and, as Jeremy reminded me recently, he tried to stage a hostile takeover of the cello section while I was sick last semester.

"Hey, *Mouse*," he says, twitching his nose as if he has whiskers.

Before Mila came along, Tom was my very jealous second chair and stand partner. One day, he noticed a birthday card sticking out of my music folder and snatched it up, reading it aloud against my protests.

"My dear, sweet little Mouse," he recited in a mock old-lady voice. "It has been such a long time now since you first came to me, so shy, so afraid…"

This went on and on, my face beet red, tears stinging my eyes as until Matthew managed to rip it from his hands. But, by then, the damage had been done. From that day on, I was known as 'The Mouse' throughout McInnes. And not in the kind, affectionate way Miss Mavis had intended.

Normally, I'd just ignore him and let it go. But I'm having a really crappy day, and I don't need his nonsense on top of it.

"Oh, hi there, Tom!" I say brightly.

His eyes narrow with suspicion.

"Say, I noticed in rehearsal today that you were out of tune in that soft section of the Strauss. Again. Just keep in mind, I'll have to ask Maestro Hagen to move you back a row if you can't get that worked out."

I watch the snide look slide right off his face. He's too stunned to even give me a smartass answer and I hear Jeremy chuckling as I turn back around, taking out my notebook and pen.

10

"Dammit!" I yell out in frustration and kick the music stand in front of me. It goes flying across the tiny practice room, nearly missing the piano and sending my music flying to all corners.

I've been sitting in what feels like a claustrophobic, dimly lit jail cell working on the same five measures for hours, and I'm no closer to getting the sound right than I was when I started. Now, I'm exhausted and frustrated and, without Matthew around, I feel totally and utterly alone. Overwhelmed, I drop my head into my hands and start to cry. And not the pretty kind of crying either. The kind where you snort and hiccup and have to wipe your nose on the sleeve of your shirt.

My little pity party is interrupted by a knock so soft, that I'm not sure I've heard it at all. I lift my head to see a face peering in at me from the small square window in the door, but I can't quite make out who it is.

"Hello?" I sniff.

The door opens slowly and a head full of chestnut brown hair pokes inside.

Oh, no. Oh, God! No, no, no! This. Is. Not. Happening!

But it is…and I'm certain that my blotchy, tear-stained face fully communicates the horror I feel at this very moment.

"Hi," Jeremy says, his own face full of concern. "You okay in here?"

I quickly swipe at the tears and run my hand through what I'm sure is a tangle of hair on my head. "Uh, yes, thanks,"

I mutter, wishing the floor would suddenly collapse and send me plummeting to my death.

The rest of his body moves languidly around the corner of the doorway and joins me in the room, letting the door close heavily behind him.

"I couldn't help but overhear—even through the soundproofing in here."

"What? My temper tantrum or the nervous breakdown that followed?"

"No," he laughs. "Well, both, actually, but before that the Rachmaninoff."

"You know it?"

"A little." He folds his arms across his chest and considers me. "What's the problem?"

"The third movement. Dr. Sam is really unhappy with the way I'm playing it. He says I'm missing something."

I stop talking and imagine how he must see me, unkempt, teary, and babbling. "I'm sorry, you don't need to hear my sob story."

He puts up a hand and waves away my apology. "Missing how?"

I clear my throat. I hate having to explain this to him.

"Emotionally, I guess. I've got all the notes down but he thinks it sounds…flat."

"And you don't hear what he's talking about?"

I sigh and try to rub the stress from my temples. "I do…and I don't. I'm usually really good with this kind of thing. So I get that he wants something deeper but there's just something about this piece. I'm having trouble connecting with it. You know what I mean?"

Of course he doesn't. He's not just stunningly handsome and charismatic, he's a brilliant musician, too. I'd bet no one has ever told Jeremy Corrigan he's lacking in anything.

"I think so. You want to play it for me?"

What? Now?

"Not really," I mutter.

"Oh, come on. Don't be embarrassed," he cajoles me, righting the music stand from where it's lying on the floor and gathering the pages I scattered a few minutes earlier.

When he has the piece setup in front of me again, he moves around to the back of my chair so he can watch over my shoulder as I play.

Oh, what the hell, it can't get much worse than this.

I pick up the bow and it's all I can do to keep my hands from shaking as I play. I only get through the first few notes before I stop in frustration.

"Still not right," I mutter, dejectedly.

And then, there is his breath, warm and sweet against my cheek. He's so close that our faces are almost touching. "Sex," he whispers in my ear.

"Excuse me?" I croak.

"This piece is all about sex. When you play, think of the piano as trying to seduce the cello."

"I don't…I'm not sure how to convey that…"

Out of nowhere I feel his large hand resting on my shoulder. "No, wait. I'm sorry to cut you off Julia, but what I just said isn't quite right. It's not sex. It's more than just the physicality of it. It's making love."

Oh. My. God.

"Look, I'll show you…"

He reaches around me to pluck the accompanying piano part off the music stand. Before I can ask him what he's going to do with it, he has left my side and is pulling the bench out from under the piano.

But he doesn't play piano. Does he?

"Third movement!" he directs, getting himself situated quickly. "In three…two…"

"Wait…!"

"One!" Jeremy starts to play the solo piano opening.

I'll be damned! He does play the piano. And well, too!

Under his fingers, the opening is a nostalgic reverie. I'm hearing things that I missed before. Romance with just a hint of something darker. Not sinister so much as...broken. No, fragile. Bereft? That's it. Bereft. The mood he creates is so hypnotic that I nearly miss my entrance.

"You're coming up here..." he calls out over his shoulder.

There's no time to think, so I just play. This time, as I pull the bow across the strings and allow my fingers to stretch across the fingerboard, I imagine the sound of the cello as a voice, professing its love—a sentiment echoed lovingly by the piano. It goes back and forth, this romantic dialogue. They are separate. They are together. And suddenly the two voices are so intertwined that it's hard to tell where one starts and the other ends.

In an instant, it's clear to me what I've been missing all this time. Jeremy is absolutely right. This is the sound of lovers, clinging to one another. I'm so drawn-in that I can feel my own pulse quicken as the intensity mounts. It crests and slowly dissolves into the quietest, most intimate of utterances. When the last note is played I can only sit there, staring at the music, bow hanging from my hand. He has turned around and I can feel his eyes fixed on me, gauging my reaction to what has just happened.

"Wow," I say when I can finally bring myself to meet his gaze. It comes out as barely a whisper. "That was...*amazing*."

He smiles at me and, in an instant, he's on his feet. I watch in stunned silence as he takes the cello from me and lays it gently on its side. He squats down so that we are at eye level, and presses his lips to mine. It is delicate and firm, confident and tentative all at once. After a long moment, he extricates himself from me and walks over to the door.

"Now do you understand?" he asks softly.

I can only nod dumbly.

Jeremy smiles, nods, and slips back out into the hallway, letting the soundproof door shut tight between us.

11

Spending time in the stacks at Childress Music is like wading into an archaeological dig. It's hard work, and you get dirty, but the historical discoveries that you can make are absolutely worth the effort. Broad wooden filing cabinets take up nearly every square inch of floor space, most of them topped by solid oak bookshelves that touch the ceiling. They're all stuffed to capacity with sheet music, scores and etude books. This is where the most rare of editions can be found lurking among reams of mass-produced Mozart, Beethoven and Bach.

Surprisingly few musicians that I know bother with this place. Why come all the way downtown to crawl, climb and root around the narrow, dusty aisles for something they can just as easily find online in a fresh clean copy? Not me. I don't even come here with a specific piece in mind. I relish the hunt—the thrill of standing on a shelf, knocking over a pile of concertos and having a rare sonata fall on my head. It's happened! And I love it.

Right now, I'm sitting on the floor of the cello aisle, examining a musty-smelling edition Dvorak score. When I hear footsteps approaching, I lean forward without looking up, ensuring that whoever it is doesn't have to step over me to get past. But the shoes don't pass. They stop right next to me. I glance over and find myself inches from a pair of white Chuck Taylor's.

Really? Tell me there isn't another cellist who wants to be right where I'm siting right at this instant. Chuck Taylor coughs and I look up, following long, jean-clad legs up to a t-shirt and button down-shirted torso and, finally, the finely chiseled face. I'm stunned to find that Chuck is none other than Jeremy Corrigan. I've been working hard to avoid him since that day in the practice room. The day that he kissed me. I suppose there's no avoiding him now.

"Well, look who else is digging for buried treasure." He's smiling down on me.

"Uh, Jeremy, hi," I mumble up at him.

I'm going to break my neck if I have to keep this up, so I tuck the Dvorak under my arm and start to pull myself back onto my feet. And then his hand is there, on my arm, helping me up.

"What'd you find?" he inquires, nodding toward the music I'm holding.

I use my hands to slap the dust off of my backside and thighs. "Oh, it's a really old edition of the *Dvorak Cello Concerto*. I've never seen it before."

"Now that's what I love about this place," he proclaims with a wide sweeping gesture around the store. "You have to get a little dirty, but you never know what's going to turn up. I mean, look what I found hidden in the bottom drawer over there, under a heap of Mozart horn concertos!"

He's brandishing a yellowed, fragile looking piece of music. "It's this really rare Schubert song for soprano, horn and piano. I had no idea the damn thing even existed! All I can think about is how great it's going to sound on my graduate recital." He's grinning like a little kid with a new bicycle. "Look," he beckons me closer, opening the score to show me.

The pages themselves are a work of art with a cover printed with intricate scrollwork and calligraphy. Inside, the notes themselves almost appear to have been hand written.

"Oh, Jeremy, this is so beautiful," I marvel, gently running my index finger along the imprint of the melody line.

"Hey, are you done here? I was going to grab a slice down the street before I head back to Brooklyn. Why don't you join me?"

Hmmm.... Dust mites and Mozart or pizza with Jeremy? Tough call.

"Yeah, sure," I agree, and we pay for our purchases at the front counter. While we're there, I hand the cashier the little pink claim ticket for the bag I checked when I came in. The man hands me a large shopping bag in return.

"What've you got in there?" Jeremy asks, eying the bulky box inside the bag as we leave the store.

"Boots."

"Boots? What, like snow boots?"

"No, silly! Fall boots. The tall leather kind with a long zipper on the side."

"Oh! *That* kind of boots. I like those boots."

"You do?" I ask, scrunching my face in surprise as we walk toward the pizza parlor. "Why's that?"

He glances at me sideways and I catch sight of a very naughty looking smile.

"Because it seems like they usually go with short skirts."

I laugh and shake my head.

"What? What's so funny?"

"Nothing, it's just that you're right. I wouldn't have expected a guy to notice that kind of thing, but I guess when you put it in the 'short skirt' context...well...that makes sense."

"So...are you planning to wear *yours* with a short skirt?" he asks, with one eyebrow cocked.

"I don't own a short skirt," I pout dramatically.

"Well you know, I'd be happy to go with you if you want to buy one...I could help you pick it out," he suggests, a little too helpfully.

"Yeah, I'll keep that in mind..." I grin.

We take our cheese slices and sit on stools at a high countertop, looking out onto the busy city street.

"So," he begins between bites, "isn't boot shopping one of those things you girls do in a pack?"

"A pack?" I snort.

"You know what I mean! Seems like shopping is a team sport. What are you doing down here by yourself?"

I shrug and poke at a golden brown dough bubble on my crust.

"I don't know. I guess I don't really have anyone that I can ask to come with me. Matthew's a pain in the neck—he likes to hover over me when I'm browsing. I always feel rushed, so I just leave him at home now."

"What about Mila?"

"What about her?"

"I'll bet she'd go boot shopping with you."

God forbid!

"She might…" I start thoughtfully, "but, then I'd have to listen to her go on and on and on for hours—about the boots, about the cute guy selling the boots, about the cute guy's cute manager, about the manager's boots…"

He holds up his hands in mock surrender. "Alright, alright—I get the idea. And I see what you mean. That would suck."

"That would totally suck," I agree.

"What's up with her lately, anyway?"

"What do you mean?"

"I don't know…I have a good view of the cello section from back where I sit, and it seems like for the last few weeks, her body language is a little bitchier than usual. I thought maybe she's pissed about something and giving you the cold shoulder."

I stifle a laugh. Bitchy body language? I'm not even going to ask.

"Yeah, well, that's more about you than me."

"What?" He puts his pizza down and faces me. "What did I ever do to her?"

"Nothing. That's the problem."

"What are you talking about?"

"I mean that she likes you, Jeremy. *A lot.* And she doesn't like that you and I have been…talking so much."

"Seriously? Well, I have zero interest in her," he mutters, picking up his slice again and taking a bite.

"Oh, something tells me this isn't the first time a McInnes girl's had a crush on you," I tease.

"Maybe once or twice," he says sheepishly.

"Uh-huh. I'll bet."

He rolls his eyes and sighs in resignation. "Okay, maybe more than once or twice. There was Katie the bassoonist—she never said a word to me. Not one. But she followed me around all the time. The harpist, Shania, she was actually pretty cute, and we went out a few times. Let's see…" he appears to be thinking hard. "Oh! And the timpanist."

"Timpanist? I don't remember any girls who played the timpani…"

"That's because it wasn't a girl."

"Oh?" I say, needing a second to work that one out. "*Oh!*"

Jeremy pokes me in the ribs with his elbow. "Boy, can't get anything past you!" he teases.

I chuckle and take a sip through my straw. "So, does that mean you're between girlfriends?" I ask, and immediately wish I could stuff the words back into my mouth.

"Why, you interested in the gig?"

His grin is nothing short of brilliant. And obnoxious. I giggle a little before turning serious.

"Hey, thanks again...for the Rachmaninoff," I begin softly. "I can't tell you how helpful that was."

"Happy I could help," he replies, starting to gather his now-empty paper plate and cup. It takes him a few seconds to meet my eyes again. "I, uh, hope you didn't mind the..."

"The kiss?"

"Yeah... Sorry, I know it was a little impulsive. I just wanted you to feel what you had just played. You know? You already had it in you. The passion, I mean."

Now he shrugs and the edges of his mouth curl up just a bit.

My *God* this guy is hot.

"You just needed a little help to tap into it."

I feel the blush as it rises to my cheeks, giving me away. He pretends not to notice, but I'm sure I catch a wicked little twinkle in his hazel eyes.

"So, when do you need to play it for Dr. Sam?"

"Friday."

"Would you like me to come and accompany you?"

"Really?" I ask a little too quickly...and a little too loudly. "Really?" I try again with less enthusiasm. "You'd do that for me?"

"Sure." He shrugs. "Why not?"

I sit back, shaking my head at my good fortune.

"Wow, that would be amazing, Jeremy. But are you sure you have time for that with finals coming up?"

"I'll make the time."

"Okay...well, my lesson is at eleven in Dr. Sam's studio, up on the third floor..."

"I can be there then."

I put a tentative hand on his forearm.

"Thank you, Jeremy. I mean it. If you hadn't helped me, I wouldn't be playing that piece. And I've got my heart set on playing it."

He pats my hand on his arm. It's a warm, soft hand. I find myself wishing he'd leave it there for a little bit longer, but he pulls it away and slips off the stool.

"Really, it was no problem. Now, if you and your boots will excuse me, I have to get home to Brooklyn to teach a lesson. I hope to see both of you at orchestra rehearsal tomorrow. Oh, and you really should bring Mini with you."

"Mini? Who's Mini?"

"Mini Skirt! You, Mini, the boots, you'd be like this trifecta of sexy in the middle of the orchestra."

"You're awful!" I giggle. "No Mini, but Boots and I will be there with her more conservative cousin, *Midi*. Okay?"

"Midi skirt? Is that a thing?"

I roll my eyes. "God! You are *such* a guy!"

"And you are such a girl!" he counters, smiling. "But, I guess we all have to pick our own friends, don't we?"

Before I can answer, he bends down and gives me a peck on the cheek. I think maybe he just picked me.

Jeremy is out the door in a second, waving at me as he crosses in front of the window, and melts into the afternoon foot traffic.

12

I'm so startled by the vibration of the phone in my pocket, that I drop my bow. It hits the base of my music stand with a loud clang and several people turn to look, including the Maestro. We're all waiting patiently while he takes the time to work through a passage with the violin section. I mumble an apology for the disruption, feeling the familiar crawl of red from under my collar. Matthew would never text me during rehearsal. Not unless something was really wrong. I dig the phone out and take a peek at the screen.

I like your boots

I look down at the new brown leather boots without thinking. What kind of a message is that? It could be Jeremy, but I can't be sure… I take a closer look at the phone and see that I don't recognize the number that sent it. I type back as furtively as I can with a bow in one hand and a phone in the other.

Who is this?

Someone who can see your feet

I try not to be too obvious as I glance left and right. But, no one on either side is paying the least bit of attention to me. And, since no one in front of me can see my shoes without turning around, this has got to be someone behind me. It's got to be *him*. But how did he get my cell phone number?

"What is it?" Mila asks, jarring me out of my thoughts.

I lob the question back to her guiltily.

"What's *what*?"

"What's wrong with you? God, you're being so weird today!"

I'm saved from having to reply when the maestro taps his baton on the podium.

"Thank you for your patience, ladies and gentlemen. Please keep your voices down for just another moment while we sort out a bowing issue," he says, with a pointed glance at Mila. She shakes her head and huffs.

This time when the phone vibrates in my hand I nearly drop it.

Close call! Tell Motor Mouth to keep it down!

I can't stifle the snort of laughter that overtakes me, but I'm able to camouflage it by slapping a hand to my mouth and turning it into a fake cough. So it *is* him!

Stop it!

Make me

That's it. I nonchalantly knock the pencil off of my stand and 'accidentally' kick it behind my chair.

"Oh!" I exclaim, all feminine dismay, as I turn around and glance at the rogue No.2 longingly, as if the last morsel of food on earth is just outside of my grasp.

"I've got it," I hear Jeremy say from behind me.

In an instant, he's at my side, holding it out for me to take from his hand. When I reach for it, our hands touch briefly, and our eyes lock.

"Thanks," I whisper with a tentative smile.

"You're welcome," he says, flashing bright whites at me and winking.

"Ahem!"

Mila isn't amused by this interaction.

"What's the problem?" Jeremy asks, looking at her with a cocked eyebrow.

For once, I'm not the one turning a bright crimson color. She turns around quickly and makes a show of looking for something in her music folder.

"Nice boots," he says, turning his attention back to me. "Are they comfortable?"

"Uh…yeah, I suppose…"

"You don't seem so sure about that. Maybe we should go for a walk later. Then you can find out one way or the other."

Really? Did I just hear that right? Is this us moving further along into the *'Friend Zone?'*

"I…uh…okay…"

"Good! I'll meet you in the lobby after my counterpoint class. Five o'clock." He retreats back to the horn section before I can have second thoughts and back out.

I turn to Mila, who has witnessed the exchange with clear disdain on her face.

"So, what do you think of these boots?" I ask her.

"Tell me about you and Matthew," Jeremy says as we circle the Revson Fountain in Lincoln Center.

"What do you want to know?"

"Are you…?"

He lets the question hang out there, only half asked. But I know what he wants to know.

"No. Just very close friends."

"I've seen him around you. He's very possessive. If he's not sleeping with you, then he'd like to be."

As much as I'd like to dodge this particular topic, he's clearly waiting for me to elaborate.

"We grew up together in foster care, Jeremy. He was all I had for a very long time. No parents, no friends…no one. When we first met, I wouldn't even speak. But that didn't bother Matthew. He made sure no one teased me, and he helped me with my homework. And all the time he'd just chatter away about whatever. This went on for a long time. Like months."

Jeremy has stopped and turned to face me, a shocked expression on his face. "Holy shit. I had no idea."

I shrug.

"It's not something I tell many people about, you know? I don't need people feeling sorry for me, or thinking that I've gotten as far as I have because someone else felt sorry for me."

He nods his understanding.

"Matthew's the one who got a cello into my hands. He'd already been playing the viola a couple of years when he went into foster care. I don't know how he managed it, but he convinced one of the caseworkers to find a beat-up old cello for me."

I pause for a few seconds to toss some pennies into the fountain as we circle again.

"Jeremy, I never wanted to put the thing down. It was like…like the cello *spoke* for me. And then, one day, I finally spoke for myself. I swear, Matthew did for me what a bunch of psychiatrists, doctors and social workers couldn't do. He helped me to find my voice."

I've never talked about this with anyone. It feels good. So good.

"Jesus, Jules," he whispers, shaking his head in awe. "That's some unbelievable shit that you went through."

"*Jules?* Where'd you get *that* from?"

"You prefer Julia then?"

I suddenly find myself intrigued by this thing he's doing with his mouth. It's part smile, part smirk. And it's so sexy I can't stand it.

"Yes?" I mumble distractedly.

"You seem to be unsure of your name a lot," he mocks me openly now.

"Uh—no. I mean Jules is fine."

"It's a lot better than Mouse, right?"

"What?" All of a sudden I'm sharply focused.

"Hey, what is it? What's wrong?"

He's clearly confused by the change in my tone. I think I'm going to yell at him, that I'm angry with him for being the third person today to reference the moniker. But when I open up my mouth to speak, tears start to spill from my eyes and down my cheeks.

Oh, God, this is ridiculous!

"Hey, hey, hey! Don't cry!" He sounds really alarmed now. "Why does it bother you so much? It's just a name."

"You're right. And it's a name I've had for a long time, but it didn't start out nasty like that," I sniff. "But these idiots…they call me a mouse like I'm this weak little creature hiding in the corner, living on other people's crumbs. Like I don't deserve what I have."

"Just because they say it doesn't make it true," he soothes.

"Doesn't it?"

"Of course not."

"Jeremy, it's like I said that night at the diner. We've been in school together for years, and you don't know a thing—"

"I'll never forget anything about you again," he assures me.

I'm shaking my head. He doesn't understand and he's trying to placate me. "They call me Mouse."

"I know."

"I don't…I can't…"

Jeremy extends his hand. I'm not sure what it is he wants, but I take it and he pulls me up and into his arms, adjusting himself so that my head rests on his chest. He strokes my hair and speaks softly.

"You're not taking anyone's crumbs, Jules. You don't need them. You're a better musician than any of them can even dream of. They're just jealous, that's all."

I can't stop crying and it's absolutely mortifying. But he doesn't seem to be the least bit bothered. He just holds me for what seems like hours until, finally, I can look up at him.

"I'm so sorry," I rasp, "I didn't mean to dump all that—"

And then, he leans down and kisses me again, as if it's the most natural thing in the world. His lips are electric on mine, sending a delicious shock right to my core. I'm the one to cradle his face, this time. I breathe him in through my nose and drink him in with my lips. I can't even open my eyes until he pulls away and straightens up, gathering me back into his arms. I look up at him.

"Thank you," I murmur.

Confusion fills his beautiful face. "What are you thanking me for?"

"For being here. For listening. For the kiss. I know it's nothing, but it made me feel better..."

"Who says this has to be nothing?"

He pushes me away from him a little at the shoulders so I have to look at him.

"I don't know. I just assumed," I answer, pretending to examine one of his buttons so I won't have to look him in the eye. My voice is barely a whisper.

"Now, Jules, think about the conversation we've just had. You don't like it when people make assumptions about you. I think you should extend me the same courtesy," he chides me gently as he uses his thumbs to wipe the remnants of tears from my face.

He's right.

"So…" I start with a sniff, not really knowing what my next words are going to be.

"So," he picks up my unformed thought, "if this isn't nothing, then maybe it's something. Maybe not. But we won't know unless we try, right?" he suggests, locking his eyes on mine so I can't look away.

I nod.

"How about we start with some dinner, a bottle of wine, maybe another walk later on. We can see where things go from there. What do you think?"

"Yes," I reply hesitantly, "but, Jeremy…"

"What?" he asks before I can finish, concern clear in his voice. "What is it, Jules?"

"My feet are killing me. I've got to get out of these boots," I explain earnestly.

"Oh, well, we can't have you suffering." His brows knit together with exaggerated concern. "I think we'd better get you out of those as soon as possible."

He looks as if he's having a light bulb moment now.

"Say, isn't your building right around here?"

13

He steps forward, I move back. We repeat the process again and again like some sort of unidirectional tango until I find myself backed up to the wall in the foyer of my apartment. Jeremy steps toward me again. And again. And again, until he's so close to me, that I can feel his sweet, warm breath on my face.

"You appear to be out of floor," he murmurs, moving his mouth toward my ear.

"Yes, it would seem so…"

I close my eyes in anticipation of his lips on me. When I don't feel them, I open my eyes again and he's gone.

What? Where did he go?

I've no sooner formed the question then I feel his hands on my calf. He's pulling the long zipper down the left boot. When he's done, he looks up at me.

"Lift," he instructs.

I do, and he extracts my stockinged foot. After we repeat the process with the right side, he picks up the pair and tosses them into the living room, where they land on the carpet with a dull thud.

"Hey!" I protest with a laugh. "Those were expensive!"

In an instant, he's upright again, his face only inches from mine.

"I'm sorry, Jules, I cannot allow your tender little feet to suffer for fashion. The boots have to go," he informs me firmly.

"Is that so?" I ask, with a hint of a challenge to my tone.

"It is," he insists as he leans around me, rubbing his rough cheek against my smooth one and making me giggle.

The giggle turns to a sharp gasp the second he takes my earlobe into his mouth and starts to nibble gently. He has a perfectly sculpted chest. I know this because it is now pressed up against my breasts, and I can feel every contour as he breathes in and out. Now, he's kissing behind my ear, making his way slowly down my neck. I groan when he gets to the collarbone. Who knew it was such a hotspot?

I'm so enthralled by his mouth that I barely notice he's quickly unbuttoning each of the buttons on my blouse. In an instant it's off my shoulders and hitting the floor with a silky swish. With long, strong arms, he reaches around behind me, unzips my skirt and helps it along on its journey to join the blouse.

Who is this woman? Since when do I sleep with guys I hardly know? I guess since I have the opportunity to sleep with this guy. I can't deny it. I've been attracted to him since we were in freshman music theory together, but it never even occurred to me that it might lead to something like this.

"Jeremy," I say quietly.

He looks up from where he's kissing my shoulder and I touch the side of his face. My thumb rubs his cheekbone gently while my other hand brushes back the hair from his forehead. I feel his eyebrows with my fingertips and trace the curve of his mouth. He watches me in intense silence as I memorize each of his features by touch.

Finally, my gaze finds its way back to his, his face held gently in my hands.

"Jeremy, I…"

And again he grabs me and pulls my mouth hard into his. Until this very second I don't realize how hungry I am for this, for him. I wrap my arms around his neck and draw him even closer against me. I want to feel every inch of him against every inch of me.

Sex has never been like this before. Pleasurable, sure. Sweet even. But this heat—this longing. I've never wanted anyone or anything as much as I want this man right now. Even as his tongue is exploring my mouth, he's unclasping my bra. I'm impressed. I can't even get it undone that fast. He slides it off, and his hands immediately find my liberated breasts. His thumbs begin to draw slow circles around my nipples and there is an immediate jolt of electricity to my core.

"Ahhh…"

I have to break our kiss so I can speed this along. I unbutton his shirt as quickly as I can without ripping it off of him. Before it can even hit the floor, my hands are upon him. I'm desperate to feel the smooth skin over his taut muscles. First the chest, then I reach around to feel the ripple of his back and he grabs me again, pulling me into a tight embrace. I rest my head against him, every quickened beat of his heart echoing in my ears. I hear his breath as it moves from his lungs, and when he finally speaks again it is like a rumble from the center of the earth.

"I think maybe we should move this somewhere else. What do you think?"

I'm exhilarated and terrified at the same time. What if I disappoint? What if he thinks I'm ugly when he sees all of me? What if…

"Jules?" His voice is a concerned whisper close to the top of my head.

I don't look at him as I separate my body from his. It's my turn to make the gesture. I simply turn away, holding my hand out behind me. He takes it and I lead him down the short hallway to my bedroom. Once we're inside I turn to face him but he's already on me, lifting me, pushing me, steering me gently, but firmly, onto my bed. I don't bother to turn the lights on. There's such a delicious thrill in the unseen, the unknown. I'm actually trembling with the anticipation of it.

He straightens up long enough to unbuckle his belt and then his pants are gone in one swift movement. It's dark in the room but the moon casts just enough light through the windows that I can see his briefs. Then, they're gone too, and he's crawling onto the bed and over me.

He kisses me gently now, more sweetly than before. I don't even notice that he has hooked his thumbs into the waistband of my tights and is tugging them off. I instinctively arch up so he can slide them over my hips. The panties come with them. And then he's gone, following them down the length of my legs and finally separating them from my body. He tosses them to the other side of the room and I giggle.

My breath is faster and shallow now in anticipation of him taking me. Taking. Who says that? Well, Mila did. And now I do, too. Because I get it now. I'm his for the taking, and I want it. Oh, do I want it. But Jeremy knows exactly what he's doing and he obviously has no intention of rushing, no matter how much either of us wants this to be quick and dirty.

Back at the foot of the bed again, he doesn't climb up as I expect. He takes one of my ankles in each of his hands and pulls them apart slowly. Then he helps me to bend them up at the knees. I feel a sudden rush of panic. Oh, God. Really? Is he really going to go there? It isn't anything any of my previous lovers were especially interested in and, quite frankly, I'm not that comfortable with the notion of it myself.

I struggle to sit up but he holds my legs down firmly. "Jeremy, you don't have to…"

"Shhhh…" he says, looking up at me from between my legs with a lascivious smile.

"I have just ascertained that you are, indeed, a natural redhead, Julia James."

"Jeremy, really, let's just…"

"Please, I've got work to do down here," he admonishes. And before I can protest further he has my knees draped over his shoulders and I can feel his breath on my sex.

I want to let go so badly but this is just so…intimate. Ugh. Of course it's intimate! I feel so out of my depth. My internal conflict is cut short abruptly when I feel him pull my folds apart softly and snake his tongue all the way up.

"Oh. Oh, Jesus. Oh, God…" The words fly from my mouth involuntarily. I didn't know...

He licks again, following the same path but this time stopping just short of the spot that makes me want to scream.

"I want you to make me scream." Even as I whisper the plea, I can feel my face growing scarlet with my own boldness.

He looks up at me, and for the briefest of moments I'm afraid he's going to laugh at me. I close my eyes so I won't have to see him if he does.

But he doesn't.

"Yes, ma'am," he whispers into the darkened room.

And then he's there again and I can feel him everywhere all at once. He nibbles on my thighs and gets close, oh so close. He uses his tongue to trace an outline with painstaking softness that makes the pressure in me mount. The torture is exquisite. I feel his fingers on me again, opening my most intimate side to him and I think he's about to put me out of my misery. But there is no pressure at all. Just… What is he doing? I can hear him, now blowing gently.

"Ohhh…" I groan, with the sweet exasperation, as he excites me without giving me any relief.

"What's the matter?" he asks with mock concern.

"Jeremy…I don't think I can…"

Before I can finish he dives his tongue back in and starts to slowly circle me. It is maddening. Around and around. Almost making contact with…but no. So close. I can feel the pressure building, and then it quickly subsides as he pulls back again.

My breath is starting to quicken as I begin to lose control of my own body. With eyes still closed, I rock my head from side to side. My mouth feels so dry. I have to lick my lips. My hips twitch slightly, a not-so-subtle invitation for him to continue. Why has he stopped anyway? I open my eyes and he's watching me intently from between my legs.

God, he's so hot. He won't drop his eyes from mine as he renews his contact with just the lightest tip of his tongue. Not enough to bring me any satisfaction...just enough to get me more bothered. Yes, he knows exactly what he's doing.

I'm whimpering now in my frustration and it's time. He pushes my thighs apart roughly, obscenely wide and buries his face in me, nibbling, sucking and circling every square inch.

I'm moaning now, and it sounds sexy, to even my own ears.

Jeremy's assault grows vigorous as he finds the spot that makes me writhe around him. There's no controlling myself now, but he holds me firm, swirling and sucking with enough pressure to send mounting waves of pleasure through me.

"God, God, God. Jeremy..." I'm getting louder.

And then he pulls his face away. I start to whimper, thinking I will weep, literally sob if he leaves me like that. But he's only gone for an instant. He quickly pumps two fingers inside of me while working his thumb in fast, firm circles. I can feel his eyes boring into me as my head tosses from side to side on the pillow, beads of sweat on my forehead as I clutch and ball the sheets around me.

"Now, Julia. Come on, honey. Come for me." It's an order. A demand. He rubs me harder and faster.

"Yes! God yes! Jeremy…" And there is the scream. I can feel myself spasm around his hands and know he's watching my body writhing in its first unapologetic orgasm. Slowly he lets up the pressure and speed but continues his internal and external stroking until I'm shuddering from sensitivity. He crawls up next to me on the bed. I should be mortified, lying splayed out like that. But I'm too ecstatic to care. Never have I ever felt so much, so fast, in my entire life.

"Jeremy, that was…" I can't even get the sentence out before he's on top of me. Literally on top of me. I hear the rip of foil and realize he doesn't mean to waste any time. He bites my neck hard at the same moment that he plunges himself into me.

I gasp with the exquisite pain and sensitivity. He's so big. So hard. So…

I can't think. I can only feel.

He has my knees pulled back wide again and he moves in and out slowly while he kisses my shoulders. I didn't think I could take even a second's more stimulation, but he feels so amazing inside of me. Slowly, oh so slowly, he starts to pick up speed.

How on earth does he have so much self-control? Every other guy I've been with can barely hang on for five minutes after we get right down to it. He's got my hands pinned up on either side of my head now. I try to pull them away to touch him but he holds firm and that is sexy as hell. I'm starting to breath hard along with him.

"Julia," he whispers in my ear. "Julia James," he repeats. "You hear me? I'm reminding you now, because by the time I'm done fucking you, you're going to forget that's even your name," he says with a snarl that makes the hair on the back of my neck stand on end.

And, just like that, I'm on the fast track again. "Please..." I murmur.

He stops all movement suddenly and stares down at me "Please what?"

I pause for a long moment. "Please fuck me."

I don't have to ask twice. He plows in with a renewed vigor that has us both grunting with every rough thrust.

Again and again and again until, without warning, the most intense wave of pleasure that I have ever felt washes over me. I can feel him come inside me at the same moment. He holds me down tight until the last tremors have subsided from my body and I can open my eyes again. He rests his forehead against mine.

In that moment I know I am his, totally and completely. I will do anything this man wants for as long as he will let me.

It may not be love exactly, but it's pretty glorious anyway.

14

Somewhere, in the distance, my phone is ringing. It stops for a few minutes, and then starts again. I groan and pull a pillow over my head, but it just won't stop. A squint at the alarm clock tells me it's close to ten. A squint in the other direction tells me that I didn't dream the handsome man sound asleep in my bed.

I try not to wake him as I extract myself from the warm sheets. I have no clue where my robe is. I seem to recall wearing it at some point last night but the way clothes were flying around this place it could be anywhere. I spot Jeremy's T-shirt on the floor and throw it over my head as I move out to the hallway, closing the bedroom door quietly behind me.

Of course my cell phone is silent now and I have no idea where it is in this room. I turn over a few cushions and look under some papers. Nothing. I'm about to head back to bed when it rings again. I follow the chirping sound to the vicinity of my discarded skirt on the floor.

Aha! I glance at the screen and see that it's Matthew calling. I'd rather not take it, but I have a feeling he's not going to stop until he gets me. And if he can't get me, he might just hop on a plane and head home. *So* not worth it. I answer.

"Hello?" I ask in a scratchy voice.

"There you are!" he says, a little loudly for my sleepy ears. "God, do you ever check your messages, Julia?"

"Matthew, please, I'm fine. I've been living in the practice rooms and you know the cell reception there is awful. Please don't be upset…"

I hear him take a breath. When he speaks again, he's considerably calmer.

"No, I'm sorry. I was just worried because I thought you'd be at the practice rooms all night. But then, when you didn't leave the apartment, and you didn't answer your phone or your texts…"

"Wait, wait, wait," I stop him, pressing my palm to my forehead as if it will somehow help me to process. "How did you know I didn't leave the apartment all night?"

Suddenly Matthew has nothing to say. And suddenly, my conversation with Cal is making a whole lot more sense.

"My Orbit? That was you?"

Guilty silence.

I want to be angry, to be indignant about the violation of my privacy, but I can't. I know him well enough to know that there's love behind his neurosis.

"Do you realize how insane that is? Matthew, why would you want to track me on my phone?"

"I don't think it's insane at all," he says defensively. "It's one thing when I'm home, Julia, but when I'm away, I worry about you. Worry that something might happen to you."

"Like what, Matthew? What do you think is going to happen to me?"

"I don't know. Like maybe you could get mugged or hurt or…" his voice trails off.

"Or that I might spend time with someone else?" I finish the thought for him. His silence is the answer to the question. "You know, you don't have to spy on me. You can just ask."

"Okay, so, are you…spending time with someone?" he asks.

"Maybe. Yes, actually."

Long pause.

"Oh. I see. Well I'm sorry if I interrupted your date, Julia," he says softly, his voice dripping with disappointment thinly veiled as sarcasm.

"Matthew, wait…"

"No, I'd better get going. I'm glad you're okay."

"Stop it! Please, Matthew, can we just start again? Come on, let's talk about you. Tell me how the tour is going," I coax.

He clears his throat. I know he feels silly now, and is looking for a verbal olive branch. Finally he finds it.

"Well, you know Ingo Katz, the bassist? He's touring with us so we can do the Schubert Trout Quintet. Apparently he has a groupie."

"A groupie?" I snort. "Seriously? There are actually women out there who stake-out concerts to see a double bass player?"

"Who said it's a woman?"

This time I get it right away.

"Oh, wow!" I laugh. And just like that—just like always—we're back to our old selves.

"Where are you headed next?"

"Boston. Then Philly. Hopefully home after that but I'm not sure. It's not like this all the time, thank God. This tour will wrap-up right around New Years."

"Ah! Just in time to see me take the cello division at the Kreislers!"

"Oh. Is that still happening?" he asks, teasing me.

I feel better hearing him lighten up a little. "It is, and you'd better be here to cheer me on, mister!"

"Like I'd miss something that important."

"Hmm. Well, that still gives you plenty of time to get your own groupies!" I tease back.

"Not quite," he laughs. "The viola just doesn't have the same kinda sexy that the double bass does."

"So true," I say in mock agreement.

There is another long pause and I can tell he's working up to something. I can guess what.

"So…who's the guy? Anyone I know?" His tone is tentative.

"Maybe. But I don't want to talk about it till you get home. This may have run its course by then."

Matthew hates Jeremy's brother, Brett. Unfortunately, that puts Jeremy pretty high on his shit list, just by association. I'm not going to tell him about this until I'm absolutely certain there's something to tell.

He sighs heavily on the other end of the line. "You know I…" he starts.

"Worry about me. Yes, I do know. And I love you for that. Tell you what—let's make a phone date for when you get to Boston. I'll get a glass of wine, curl up on the couch, and you can fill me in on everything. It'll be just like you're home."

"Yes. I'd really like that," he says. "Oh, hey, before I forget, how's the Rachmaninoff coming along?"

"So much better. I think I've finally got it figured out."

"That's wonderful!" he says, and I can hear that he's genuinely happy for me. "So it'll be that and the Bach."

"Yup. If I win that, then the medal round is a month later."

"This is some exciting stuff, Julia. I'm really proud of you."

"I'm proud of both of us Matthew. Seems like all the things we dreamed about are starting to come true."

"Well, not all of the things…"

Ughh. He makes me crazy.

"You know what, my friend? You should seize this opportunity to have a fling."

"A fling?" he echoes incredulously.

"Yes, a fling. A one night stand. Go get laid."

Now he snorts. Loudly. "I'm sorry, did you just tell me to get laid?"

"I did."

He lets out a belly laugh that I haven't heard in ages. "Oh, oh God," he says when he finally catches his breath. "You have no idea how bizarre that sounds coming out of your mouth."

If only he knew the kinds of things that have been coming out of my mouth lately. He'd be stunned.

"Bye, Matthew. Love you."

"You too. I'll talk to you in a few days."

I end the call on my phone, and try not to think about how I'm going to explain all this to him when he gets home.

15

Jeremy is still sound asleep when I slip back under the covers next to him. He's lying on his side and I snuggle tight against his back. I'm starting to doze off again when I feel his hand come around behind him and stroke my leg.

"Good morning," he mumbles groggily.

"Good morning. Did you sleep alright?"

He rolls over now and I adjust so we are face to face on our respective pillows. He smiles at me sleepily.

"Oh, yes. I could stay in this bed all day."

"Then why don't you?"

His dark eyebrows rise. "Why, Julia James, are you asking me to spend the day in bed with you?"

"Maybe," I say coyly.

He gives me that wicked smile of his. "Nope. You're not a mouse. If you want to do it, you have to say it."

I shake my head, suddenly feeling shy again.

"If you want to do it," he says again, slower this time, "you have to say it."

I take a long, deep breath and roll over on top of him, wrapping my body over his, so that my face is barely an inch from his. I lock my eyes on his.

"I want you," I whisper.

"You want me to what?"

"I want you to make love to me all day long."

His arched eyebrows shoot-up...and so does his erection.

"Well then. I'm all for giving a lady what she wants," he says as he grabs me and flips me underneath him in one fluid movement. As he kisses me, he pushes my wrists up over my head.

"Though, I have to admit I'm more partial to fucking than lovemaking. Do you think you can work with that?"

I nod enthusiastically. I'll take whatever it is he wants to give me. I try to pull my hands free so I can touch him but he tightens his grip.

"Uh-uh," he says, dropping his mouth to my breast. "Don't you dare move an inch."

Until this very second, I hadn't realized how much I have wanted exactly this. For someone to take control and make me feel, make me experience, make me love against my better judgment. How ironic that his control makes me feel free.

He suckles first one breast, then the other. I sigh with the pleasure of it. Now he's kissing up my neck, nuzzling behind my ears.

"I want you so much," he murmurs in my left ear. Then he moves to the other side, nibbling the lobe of my right ear. "I'm not going to let you out of this bed all damn day."

Again, I try to wrest my hands away from his grip. I want to pull him into me.

Suddenly he stops. "What did I just say?"

I smile up at him sheepishly but he's not amused. I clear my throat and try to look contrite. "You told me not to move an inch."

"Hmmm. I don't like to be disobeyed, Jules. Do I have to tie you to the headboard?"

Oh, my dear good God. I'm not expecting the thrill that shoots through me at the mere suggestion of it.

"I just don't know if I can keep my hands off you…" I say noncommittally.

In an instant he's off of the bed, and me, rummaging around in my dresser. When he turns around he's holding a pair of my tights and there is a triumphant smile on his face.

"Well, well, Miss Julia James. I think you need to be taught a little lesson in…restraint."

And, before I can react he's upon me. He's got my left wrist stretched as far as it will go and is securing it to the bed frame with one leg of my tights. I just watch in fascination.

"Looks like you've done this a time or two before."

He ignores my comment as he pulls the other leg of the stockings across the headboard, and wraps it around my right wrist. And then he stops.

"What?"

He rubs the skin on my upper arm.

Oh. I know what.

"Are these scars, Julia?" The huskiness in his voice has disappeared.

He's rubbing his thumb on them. One, two, three…

"Julia?" he's looking at me, waiting for an explanation for the four perfectly cylindrical scars.

"They're burns."

He leans in to have a closer look. "But they're so perfect. They almost look like a car cigarette lighter," he says more to himself than to me.

Of course that's what they are. He can see that plainly. But now comes the part I dread. The part where I can see the wheels turning in his head. He's trying to figure out how I could accidentally burn myself four times with a car lighter.

I couldn't.

And now that realization is dawning across his face. He looks from the scars to me, and back again. "Who…" he licks his lips and starts again. "Who did this to you?"

The eyes look more brown than green today, and I notice tiny specks of gold in them that I didn't see before. They're boring into me, demanding an answer.

"My father."

His face is uncomprehending. "Your father did this to you? He burned you?"

I nod.

"But why would he do such a thing?"

Oh, you sweet boy, you have no idea the things people will do to one another.

"He did it because I dropped his six pack on the ground. I broke four bottles. One burn for each bottle. He wanted to make sure I never did that again."

"Holy shit. But…"

"You know, Jeremy, if you really want to have this conversation then I think maybe you should untie me."

"Oh! Of course!" He scrambles to release me from the headboard.

So much for my foray into bondage. It was pretty hot while it lasted, though. I sit up and pull the sheet up over my bare breasts then I hug my knees.

"My father beat me. When I was eight, a teacher realized what was going on and I was removed from his custody. That's when I went into the foster system, and when I met Matthew."

I can see he's still processing this information, so I wait until he seems ready to hear more.

"What happened to him?"

"My father? He got about nine months in jail. When he got out he stopped by the family courthouse on his way out of town to sign over his parental rights. I never saw him again."

"But your mother. Surely she must have…"

"She left us when I was five. That's when he started to hit me. I never heard from her again either."

"Jesus Christ. How did you survive that? How is it possible that you can live a normal life after that?"

I shrug. "I was lucky. But still, now you can see why I'm not the most outgoing person you've ever met. I really don't have any friends, other than Matthew, because I don't trust many people."

He's nodding his understanding. I can see he's tempted to scoop me up into his arms, but isn't quite sure how I'll react.

"You know what?" I say, swinging my feet out of bed once again. "I'm starving. Can you cook? Because, I can't. Maybe we can forage for something in the kitchen. And then I have to go work on that Rachmaninoff that you were so helpful with last night."

"Julia, we can talk about this more if you want…"

"We will, I'm sure. But seriously, do you know how to make French toast?"

16

Turns out that, like playing the piano, Jeremy Corrigan does, in fact, know how to make French toast—and well at that. After I've done everything short of lick the plate clean, I sip the outstanding cup of coffee he's made for me. Handsome, great in bed, an amazing musician *and* he cooks? I think I've died and gone to heaven.

After some light conversation over breakfast, I think I have successfully brought him back from the recesses of my deep, dark past. Bad enough I have to live there. No reason he should too.

"What would you like to do today?" I ask him.

"Well, I had my day planned out but it took a little detour back there in the bedroom," he says ruefully.

"Tell me about it." I let out a rather dramatic sigh of disappointment.

His left eyebrow shoots up.

Huh. Maybe I can get this train back on the rails after all...

Jeremy takes my breakfast plate from in front of me and sets it in the sink with his own. "So, now I'm thinking I'll just lay around in my underwear, scratching myself, drinking beer and watching baseball."

"Uh... I think it's a little late in the year for baseball. Football. That's the sport you're looking for," I offer helpfully, taking another sip.

"Are you correcting me, Julia James?" His mouth pulls down with an exaggerated frown.

Oh, yeah. I see where this is going, and I like it.

"Maybe," I say. "I mean, you obviously need a little guidance on the seasonal timetable of sports. But, no need to be embarrassed about that. Lots of men need guidance from time to time." I throw that last part in as the cherry on my sexual-fantasy sundae.

What's happened to me? In less than twelve hours this guy has not only managed to rid me of my inhibitions, but he's got me practically begging him for more. Now he's left the small kitchen and walked around to my side of the breakfast bar. I can feel his breath on my neck as he stands directly behind me.

"You'd best watch yourself, Miss James." The warning sends a delicious chill down my spine.

"Or what?" I ask, as I take a disinterested sip from my coffee cup.

He puts his left hand on my shoulder and reaches around me with his right to take the cup from my grasp. He sets it down on the counter and then guides me off the stool, so that I'm facing the opposite direction.

"Get into the bedroom." His tone is soft but with a firmness that implies I'd better not disobey him.

This is *so* hot.

I start to walk to my bedroom, looking over my shoulder to see if he's going to follow me.

"Face forward," he growls, eliciting a naughty pulse through my core.

I stop in front of the bed, listening as he closes the door behind him and locks it—I'm guessing more for effect than anything else.

And then his hands are on my shoulders, spinning me around to face him. He has lost his pants somewhere between here and the kitchen, and now I have an eyeful of gorgeous in broad daylight.

"You like that, do you?" he says, watching me intently as my eyes land on his nether regions. I nod. "I asked you a question," he says, his voice icy.

"Yes, sir."

"Then suck it."

"What?"

"You heard me, get on your knees and suck my cock."

Never in my life did I think I could be aroused by those words. Now I know better. I drop to my knees and look up at him expectantly. He puts one hand behind my head and guides it gently to his penis, which he's holding in his other hand. I'm tentative at first. I've done this before, but I don't especially like it. Though at this moment I'm not so much concerned about that as I am about doing a bad job. I'm certain he must have had hundreds of blowjobs by women a lot more experienced and efficient than me.

Still, I take him in my mouth and slowly start to circle with my tongue. I hear him suck in his breath as I barely brush his testicles with the tips of my fingers. His hand encourages me further forward and I allow him deeper into my mouth. He groans and I glance up to see his eyes closed and his head lolling back.

Now I have a better idea of what last night was about. It's not just giving pleasure to someone. It's about the power, the feeling of control you have while you're giving it to them. I could stop right now, and his reverie would be over in a heartbeat. But I want to keep going. I want to see just how excited I can get this incredibly sexy boy.

Did I say boy? At the moment he's all man.

"Get into the bedroom." His tone is soft but with a firmness that implies I'd better not disobey him.

This is *so* hot.

I start to walk to my bedroom, looking over my shoulder to see if he's going to follow me.

"Face forward," he growls, eliciting a naughty pulse through my core.

I stop in front of the bed, listening as he closes the door behind him and locks it—I'm guessing more for effect than anything else.

And then his hands are on my shoulders, spinning me around to face him. He has lost his pants somewhere between here and the kitchen, and now I have an eyeful of gorgeous in broad daylight.

"You like that, do you?" he says, watching me intently as my eyes land on his nether regions. I nod. "I asked you a question," he says, his voice icy.

"Yes, sir."

"Then suck it."

"What?"

"You heard me, get on your knees and suck my cock."

Never in my life did I think I could be aroused by those words. Now I know better. I drop to my knees and look up at him expectantly. He puts one hand behind my head and guides it gently to his penis, which he's holding in his other hand. I'm tentative at first. I've done this before, but I don't especially like it. Though at this moment I'm not so much concerned about that as I am about doing a bad job. I'm certain he must have had hundreds of blowjobs by women a lot more experienced and efficient than me.

Still, I take him in my mouth and slowly start to circle with my tongue. I hear him suck in his breath as I barely brush his testicles with the tips of my fingers. His hand encourages me further forward and I allow him deeper into my mouth. He groans and I glance up to see his eyes closed and his head lolling back.

17

He's carrying his horn case in his right hand, and my cello case in his left.

"You really don't have to do that," I insist for the fifth time.

"Yes, I do."

"But why? I've been hauling that thing around for thirteen years. I think I've got the hang of it by now."

He stops in the middle of the hallway and turns to look at me.

"You're not getting this, are you, Jules?"

I put my palms up towards the ceiling in a shrug. "What? What am I not getting?"

"It's like I'm sending a message. I'm walking into the rehearsal with you. I'm carrying your cello. I'm kissing you right smack in the middle of the hallway, so everyone will know you're mine."

"Wait a minute, back that up, please. First of all, I'm not anyone's. Second of all, you're not kissing…"

Before I can even finish the sentence he has dropped both cases to the floor and sweeps me up in his arms. I don't have a moment to protest before his mouth is on mine. Maybe I am his.

And then I'm spinning. Jeremy has actually picked me up by the waist and is spinning me around slowly, his lips never losing contact with mine. By the time he puts me down again, I'm giddy...and more than a little dizzy.

"See what I mean?" he asks, tilting his head to where several people have stopped to watch us with interest. A couple of violinists are actually whispering and pointing. "No one's ever seen me do *that* with a girl."

"Your point being what, Mr. Corrigan?"

"My point being, Miss James, that I'm planning on sticking around to see where this goes. As far as I'm concerned there are no other women in the orchestra, or anywhere else for that matter."

I can't help myself. I have to reach up and touch his face with my hand. I spent the rest of the weekend expecting him to vanish, certain he wouldn't be at the apartment when I finished practicing. Sure I'd wake up this morning and he'd be gone.

"Don't be late, Julia," Mila says snidely as she walks past us and down the hall.

"Someone's jealous," Jeremy observes.

"Maybe so, but she's not wrong. We *are* going to be late if we don't get moving. Come on." I grab the music folder that I dropped during our little spin cycle while he retrieves our instruments.

"Good weekend, then?" Mila asks once I'm settled in my seat next to her.

It's obviously a rhetorical question, but I decide to answer it anyway. "Yeah, actually, it was a great weekend, Mila. Thanks for asking."

She's glaring at me petulantly. But I ignore her–pulling out the music we're working on today before starting to rosin my bow.

"Oh, fine!" she huffs at last. "Fine. You and Jeremy, I get it. I don't like it, but I get it." She leans a little closer to me and drops her voice. "Can I just ask you something?"

I raise an eyebrow. It's all the encouragement she needs.

"Do you think maybe you could fix me up with his brother, Brett?"

I shake my head and laugh. "I'll see what I can do, Mila."

As it turns out, Mila isn't the only one who has issues with my new relationship status. When I get to my orchestration class later in the day, Cal Burridge is waiting in the hallway.

"Hi, Cal," I say, greeting him with a smile. One that he doesn't return.

"Julia, do you have a second?" He nods his head toward the end of the hall, which is deserted.

"Uh, yeah, sure," I say, glancing at my watch. "I have five minutes before class starts."

We walk a few doors down and stop.

"I, uh—I saw you with Jeremy earlier today. Kissing him," he begins quietly.

"You know, just hanging out. It's nothing serious."

"I don't really know how to get into this," he begins.

"Into what?"

He looks down at his feet for a moment, as if there might be some secret store of courage down there. I guess he finds it, because when he looks up, there is determination in his blue eyes that wasn't there a moment ago.

"What's bothering you, Cal?" I press, even though I think I already know the answer.

"It's like I said to you the other night in the diner, Jeremy is a complicated guy. He can be a difficult guy. He's dated a lot of girls here at McInnes and it never ends well. I'm just concerned that you don't know what you're getting into with him."

I lean forward and put a hand on his wrist. "Listen, I respect you, but I'm not going to get in the middle of whatever it is that's going on with you and Jeremy. Besides, we're just sorta spending time together right now," I say. "Hanging out."

Cal doesn't look at all convinced. "I don't know how to say this any other way, so I'm just going to say it. In my experience, Jeremy Corrigan never does anything for anyone unless it benefits him."

Okay, now I'm starting to get irritated. I get that he's disappointed that I'm more into Jeremy than him, but that's no reason for Cal to go around spreading lies like that.

"I think maybe we should just let this go right here," I say, softly but firmly. "I like Jeremy a lot, and I have no reason to stop seeing him."

"Believe me, you don't want to have a reason to stop seeing him. By then it'll be too late."

"Now you're just being dramatic." I straighten up and backing away a little.

"Does Matthew know you're seeing him?" Cal asks suddenly.

"Since when do I need Matthew's permission—or yours for that matter?"

He looks as if I've slapped him. This is exactly what I didn't want to have happen. I sigh and rub my forehead with one of my hands. After a moment, I make a concerted effort to soften my tone.

"You're a good friend, Cal, and I appreciate your concern, but it's just not necessary."

He shakes his head again, looking at me a little sadly now. "Please be careful, Julia," he says, just before he turns around and walks away.

18

"Jules, please stop worrying, it's going to be fine," Jeremy says, looking down into my fear-filled eyes with his calm, steady ones.

"But what if he hates it? What if he says I need to play a different piece? I know it sounds silly, Jeremy, but I just have my heart set on the Rachmaninoff," I say, trying to convey my concerns, without sounding whiney.

He smiles and shakes his head. "He's not going to hate it, Jules. You've got this. And you won't be alone in there, I'll be right beside you. We'll do it together."

Together. Now that's a nice word. And, it does the trick. I nod firmly, and give a rap on the studio door before opening it slowly. Dr. Sam looks up from where he's sitting at his desk, writing something in his notebook.

"Hello, Julia," he greets me. When the door swings open further to reveal Jeremy, his eyebrows go up in surprise. "And Mr. Corrigan. To what do we owe the honor?" he asks jovially.

"I'm actually here in my capacity as an amateur accompanist for the lady, Dr. Michaels."

"I see. So you've been working together on the Rachmaninoff then?"

"Yes, Sir," I say, with a nod, as I get myself settled in my usual chair.

Dr. Sam seems to consider this as he rolls his chair next to mine so he can watch the music on my stand as I play. "Alright. Mr. Corrigan," he says once he's situated, "help yourself to the piano over there, and you kids can get started whenever you're ready."

Jeremy does as instructed, setting up the piano part and watching me for the signal to start playing. I give him the slightest nod and we begin.

The piece is even more beautiful than when we played it together the first time. He starts, I join in. With our respective instruments we embrace, we whisper, we speak of love without uttering a single word. I realize as the movement ends that I haven't taken my eyes off of him even once. I've played every note from memory.

Now, dropping the bow to my side, I hesitantly turn toward Dr. Sam—almost afraid to see what his reaction is.

But he's just sitting there—chin resting on folded hands—as if he's contemplating the fate of the world. I guess he's contemplating the fate of my world. Jeremy and I both sit perfectly still and wait silently until he looks up. It takes him a full thirty seconds. And then he nods slowly.

"I have to admit, Julia, I didn't think there was any way you were going to come back with this thing ready to go. And yet, here you are..."

I squint at him quizzically. "Uh, I'm sorry, Dr. Sam, is that a yes or a no?" I ask.

His face erupts into the broad smile he reserves for only my most spectacular moments. "That, my dear, is a resounding *yes!*"

Out in the hallway later on, I throw my arms around Jeremy's waist and squeeze him as hard as I can. Which isn't very hard, but it still gets the point across. "Thank you, thank you, thank you!"

He pats my back and rests his chin on the top of my head. "Don't thank me. That was all you in there, Jules."

"Hey," I say, nearly knocking his teeth out as I look up at him excitedly. "Stay over again tonight?"

Yikes. Did that sound too clingy?

"Unless you want to spend some time at home..." I quickly qualify.

"Well, I'm out of clothes. I'm already wearing what I had on Friday. If I come in with the same sweatshirt and jeans again tomorrow people will really start to talk!" he says with a laugh.

"Oh, yeah, of course. No problem. You can stay another night..."

"I just need to go home and check in on a few things. Tomorrow night for sure, though, okay?"

I smile, trying not to show my disappointment. I guess it's just as well. A little sleep wouldn't be a bad thing.

"You bet. I'd say I'll cook for you, but then you might never come over again."

"Yeah, well, maybe I'll pick up a pizza on the way." He smiles and bends down to give me a kiss on the cheek. "I'll call you later. When are you going to be home?"

"Uh, well, I think I'll put in a couple hours here practicing. Then I think a nice hot bath and an early night in bed."

A suggestive smile crosses his face. "Hmmm. Don't tempt me, Jules."

I start to walk away from him, toward the stairs. "Maybe bubbles, too," I say over my shoulder. "Oh, and candles. I do love to bathe by candlelight..."

As I turn the corner he's still standing there, shaking his head and smiling at me.

I revel in my man-free house by taking a ridiculously long, hot shower and curling up on the couch with a glass of wine and the book I've been trying to start for months. Unfortunately, I'm so relaxed that I fall asleep before I can enjoy either. When the phone rings, just after midnight, it takes me a while to find it under me, in between the cushions.

I knew it! I knew Jeremy couldn't go the whole night without calling.

"Hello…?" I say, in what I hope will pass for a sultry tone.

Silence.

I look at the phone, which is what I should have done in the first place. This isn't Jeremy at all. Damn! I really need to give him his own ringtone. "Matthew? You there?" I ask in a more normal voice.

"Yeah, sorry. I, uh, I didn't mean to call you so late. Did I wake you?"

He sounds a little off.

"That's okay, I fell asleep reading on the couch," I say gently. He sounds a little off.

"I was just missing you," he replies softly.

Ah, so he's homesick.

"I miss you, too. How was the concert tonight in—where are you again?"

"Boston. I got here last night. You were supposed to call me, remember?"

Crap! How could I have forgotten? Jeremy, that's how. He has a way of making me lose track of time.

"Oh, Matthew, I'm so sorry—it just totally slipped my mind."

I wait for his irritation, but it doesn't come. "I thought maybe you were pissed about the other night, and you didn't want to talk to me," he says with an odd tone to his voice.

There's definitely something going on with him.

"No, it wasn't anything like that! I swear, I just forgot. Tell me about it now. How did the concert go?"

"It went pretty well, actually. We've got another one here tomorrow night and then we move on to Philly. I was thinking I might try to come home this weekend. "But I'm just so damned tired, I think I'm going spend it sleeping in the hotel room instead."

"Oh, that's a good idea," I agree, trying not to sound relieved. "Hey, I got the okay from Dr. Sam to do the Rachmaninoff."

"Of course you did," he says, as if he never had a doubt. "And how's it going with…who did you say you were seeing?"

"Nice try, Sherlock. I *didn't* say."

"But you thought I was him calling, right?"

Busted.

"Maybe."

"I'm sorry I was such an ass on the phone the other night. All I want is for you to be happy, and if that's with someone else, then so be it. I'll always support you no matter what, Julia. You know that you can count on me, right?"

He's sounding sentimental now. I wonder how many little bottles are gone from the minibar in his hotel room?

"Of course I do."

"Please, just promise me you'll be careful."

"I'm always careful, Matthew."

"No, actually, you're not, Julia. You lead with your heart. I'm just afraid you're gonna get hurt."

Oh, yeah. We're talking at least three shots of the vodka. Maybe four.

"I just think you want to live happily ever after," he's saying.

Four. Definitely four shots.

"And what's wrong with that?" I ask.

"Nothing. But it's not always reality."

"Can we please not do this right now?"

"What?"

"This. This lecture on the darker side of human nature and how fragile I am."

"Fine," Matthew says flatly. "I'll spare you the lecture then."

Damn! I've offended him now. "Matthew, wait…"

"Goodnight, Julia."

I start to say something but he has already hung up on me. I think about calling him back, but I know he won't pick up. Instead I poke out a text on my phone and send it with a swoosh.

I'm sorry. I love you. Good night.

I take a deep breath and pull the covers over my head, but somehow I don't think sleep will return anytime soon.

19

"Come with me," he says, staring at me intently from the other end of the couch where my feet are in his lap.

"What? To Denmark?"

"Yeah, why not?"

"Jeremy, you're crazy! You're talking about going there to take an audition. That's not the time to be playing tourist. You need to be focused and I'd just be a distraction."

"Exactly! Don't you see? You'd take the edge off my nerves. You're so stable, Julia. There's something very… calming about you. I think it would be a good thing for me to have you around. And, when I'm done, then we can play tourist."

I don't know what to say.

"Can I think about it for a little while?" I ask finally.

He smiles smugly, as if he's already won the battle.

"Only if you think about it in bed."

Oh my. Now that's a tempting thought, as always.

"Hmmm…" I say, putting a finger under my chin and looking up at the ceiling as I pretend to ponder.

"Yeah, you're taking too long," he informs me, getting to his feet and coming to where I'm sitting on the couch. He takes the wine glass from my hand and sets it on the table before bending over and literally tossing me over his shoulder.

I shriek in surprise and start to kick. "Hey! Put me down!" The delight in my squeals belies my demand.

Jeremy ignores me as he carries me easily over to the kitchen and sets me on top of the breakfast bar so that we are face to face.

We our lips are connected as he manhandles my clothing. "Hey! Don't pull it, I like this sweater!" I protest as it gets stuck around my ears.

"I'll buy you a new one," I hear him say through the cashmere blend as he frees it with a yank.

And then he's onto the bra, slipping the straps from my shoulders and dipping his hands into the cups. He fondles both sides at the same time as he leans against me for a kiss. Did I just gurgle? Who knows? When Jeremy touches me my body does all kinds of unexpected things. I'm wearing a skirt and he's hiking it up and up and up until I feel cold granite on my backside.

"You know, I do have a bed…" I mutter.

"No time," he says.

"What do you mean 'no time'?"

He tugs my panties down roughly and his jeans hit the kitchen floor a few seconds later.

Ah. That's what he means.

As he leans into me, I wrap my legs around his waist and he pushes forward with so much force that I gasp loudly.

He groans his approval of both the gasp and my body.

I have to place my hands behind me to keep from sliding back on the slippery surface.

"God, I love you like this. Just like this," he murmurs, as he grabs me from behind and pulls himself harder into me.

I can't even formulate words at this point. I don't want him to stop. Ever. But this is that incredibly satisfying little carnal encounter known as the quickie.

"Oh, God. Oh, God..." I'm moaning loudly and he's picking up the pace that pushes me right over the edge.

My orgasm comes with such intensity that I find I'm digging my nails into his back, holding on for dear life. Apparently the nails do the trick for him, too.

"And you said you were no good in the kitchen," he teases, as we both struggle to catch our breath.

I start to giggle. He starts to chuckle. Within a few seconds the two of us, sweaty, half-naked and still on the breakfast bar are laughing so hard that neither of us hears the key in the front door.

20

When I see Matthew standing there, I freeze, mid-laugh. Jeremy can't see him, but he can see the look on my face and turns his head. The three of us are frozen in a horrific tableau. I hop off the counter and quickly pull my skirt down while Jeremy awkwardly grabs his pants from around his ankles. I want Matthew to turn around, to at least give us a second of privacy, but he refuses to look away—his eyes moving from me to Jeremy, and back again.

His face is expressionless.

Shit. This is bad. This is really, really bad.

"Uh…Matthew, I didn't expect you till tomorrow afternoon," I say, as I fumble with the buttons on my blouse.

"Clearly."

"Matthew…" Jeremy starts to speak, but the glare that Matthew levels on him stops him cold.

I put a hand on Jeremy's shoulder. "I think you'd better go home for tonight. I need to talk to Matthew alone," I say softly.

He shakes his head. "Uh-uh. No way."

"Please, Jeremy. Please do this for me. I promise, I'll call you later tonight."

Reluctantly, he picks up his keys from the counter, pausing long enough to glare at Matthew before he opens the door and walks out, leaving me alone with the one person I love most in this world. Only, he doesn't look like he loves me very much right now. In fact, he looks like he might actually hate me. I lick my lips nervously and come around the counter so we are standing face to face. When he finally speaks he spits the words out of his mouth in the most frightening tone I've ever heard.

"Really, Julia? *Jeremy Corrigan?* That's who you bring into our home?" He points at the door through which Jeremy has just exited the apartment. "That's who's been sleeping in your bed?"

"Matthew..."

His face is getting redder by the second, and he won't let me get a word in. "I don't believe you. Here I am thinking that maybe you've finally met the guy. Afraid you've finally met the guy. The one who's going to give you whatever it is that I don't seem to be able to give you. But it's him."

He stomps past me and into the living room, raking his hand through his light brown hair.

"And what is so wrong with him?" I demand from his back.

"I can't believe that you don't see it."

"See what? Matthew, is this about his brother? About you and Brett? Because I know the two of you don't get along, but Jeremy isn't his brother, you know."

He swivels around to face me again, looking even more agitated, if that's possible. "No. This has nothing to do with Brett, though he's just as bad. Julia, Jeremy isn't the guy for you. And you're definitely not the girl for him."

I shake my head at him in disbelief. "What has he done to make you hate him so much?"

He has no response. I watch him, lips pursed, arms folded across his chest. I take a step toward him, to touch him but he recoils. Suddenly my concern morphs into irritation. "Look at you. You're so jealous you can't see straight. You can't stand the idea that there is another man in my life. Someone else who wants to take care of me. Support me. Love me. I never lied to you, Matthew. Never. You've always known the way it was between us."

"You're right, I'm jealous. And you're right, I have always—I *will* always want more from you than you are able to give. But this isn't that, Julia. If it were someone else—anyone else I wouldn't be this angry."

His face softens and he comes toward me again, putting his hands on my now-crossed forearms. "Julia, I just need you to trust me on this," he says quietly.

I stare into his eyes for a moment before speaking again, my tone icier than I thought possible. "No," I say simply.

His eyebrows shoot up and he cocks his head to the side if he's misheard me.

"Julia…"

"No. I do not trust you on this," I repeat.

"Please listen to me. I'm only thinking about…"

"Yourself. You are only thinking about yourself and how my relationship with Jeremy is going to affect you."

I can feel my heart rate start to pick up, and I'm breathing heavier now. "What did you think, Matthew? That if you chased away every man in my life I'd have no choice but to be with you?"

He's taken aback as I go on the offensive. "Julia, the only thing I want is for you to be happy."

"I am. So please, get the hell out of my way."

All of a sudden, my voice sounds loud in my own ears. I'm done. I turn and go to my bedroom, slamming the door behind me. As I collapse on the bed in a heap of tears I half expect to hear his soft knock. But it doesn't come.

21

When I wake up, alone in my bed for the first time in weeks, it takes me a minute to recall the events of the night before. I'm still dressed in the same skirt and blouse. My makeup is streaked all over the pillow. Whether it rubbed off or I cried it off, I can't say. In the bathroom mirror, I confirm my suspicions that I look a fright. Under a hot, steamy shower, I let the remnants of yesterday wash off my body and down the drain. Time to start fresh today.

On my dresser, Matthew's face stares out at me from the old photograph. Maybe it's guilt, but it seems to be taunting me. I move it face down, so I won't have to see it anymore. And then, there's the other picture. The one with my parents. I run a finger over the glass above my father's young, strong, handsome face. He didn't look like that the last time I saw him, the only time I've seen him since…well, since I was eight years old.

It was the day of high school graduation, a chilly day for June on Long Island, and I was wishing I'd worn something a little warmer under my graduation gown. There was a big reception after the ceremony, and I knew I'd be miserable if I didn't go and get my sweater from Matthew's car. By then, it had been nearly a decade since I'd seen my father and I almost walked past him. Actually, I did walk past him. I was coming back from the parking lot, he was going towards it. I stopped and turned slowly and found that he had done the same. We were staring at one another, separated by only five feet.

The man who stood before me at that instant looked shockingly different than the man I'd known ten years earlier. He just seemed tired, like a man who had been beaten down by life. There was no trace of anger in his eyes then, just sadness and resignation.

For his part, my father took one long look at me, head to toe and offered a small smile.

"You're beautiful," he said softly, "just like your mother."

Until that very moment I didn't know you could be drawn to and repelled by a person at the same time. I couldn't stop myself—I took a step toward him.

"Daddy…"

But, he turned his back to me and started to walk away before I could say another word. When I started to follow him I felt a strong hand on my shoulder. I tried to shake it off but I couldn't. It was Matthew pulling me back.

"Let go!" I said with irritation.

He shook his head silently.

"Matthew, let me go!" I yelled louder as every second my father was moving further away. I don't know what I wanted to say to him or what I wanted him to say to me. I only know that somewhere deep inside me, there was this longing for him.

When I gave one more violent push away from him, Matthew wrapped his arms around me. I tried to wriggle out of his grasp, pounding on his chest with my fists and cursing him. But he only held me tighter. Over his shoulder I could see my father getting into his car.

"Daddy!" I screamed. "Daddy, come back!"

He put the car into reverse and drove away. It was like my mother all over again.

Long after Rex had disappeared around the corner, I stood there, sobbing in Matthew's unyielding embrace.

Pathetic, inconsolable wailing that eventually lapsed into gasps and hiccups and silent retching. And then, I was sliding, slipping toward the ground into a puddle of tears.

Now, I sigh and fight back the urge to cry now, putting on clean clothes, applying fresh makeup and preparing myself to face the light of day…and Matthew. But the apartment is eerily quiet. I stick my head into his room and find that the bed hasn't been slept in. Out in the living room. I spot a sheet of paper on the coffee table with my name on it.

Julia, I'm sorry, I just can't be here right now. Good luck with your audition on Monday. I love you.
-Matthew

This time, when the tears spring to my eyes, I don't fight them. I let them pool and slip down my cheeks, leaving long tracks in their wake. This feels so wrong and off-balance. Sure, we've argued before. But nothing like last night. He looked so hurt when I said I didn't trust him. Why does it have to be so complicated? Why can't I have them both in my life? I shouldn't have to choose. In fact, I refuse to choose. Not now, at least.

I blow my nose and splash some cold water over my face. Matthew is everywhere in this apartment. I can see his figure, I can hear his voice. I just can't be here right now either, so I grab my cello and head over to the practice rooms, which have been abandoned for the weekend.

There, in my safe little cubicle, the music comforts and soothes me. I run the lines again and again, eyes closed, breathing in time with the music. All of my frustration and anger pour out of me, and into the cello.

"It's okay," I whisper to myself. "You can do this."

I've been there close to two hours when the sound of the heavy, soundproof door opening pulls me from my musical reverie. Jeremy lets himself in and closes the door. He leans back against it and looks at me expectantly.

"Well?" he asks when I don't immediately offer comment.

"Well...it got ugly. Really, really ugly. We both said some things we didn't mean. I went to bed and he left. I think he's gone back to the Walton Quartet tour."

"How are you feeling?"

I shake my head sadly. "Like my heart is breaking. I love him but I also love…" I stop myself right before I can say it, but it's obvious to us both where my sentiment was headed.

A slow smile spreads across his lovely face, and his eyes do that crinkly thing again. "I love you, too," he says softly. And then he seems to have a thought. "Come on. Let's cheer you up. There's this great little bakery that I know you're going to love."

"Really, Jeremy? You think some muffins and a cookie are going to take my mind off of this?"

Now he draws his eyebrows together, looking rather stern. "Miss James, if you don't behave yourself I might have to discipline you later." His tone promises anything but punishment.

I give a half-hearted smile. "Let me put my cello in my locker. I'll meet you in the lobby in ten minutes."

"Sir."

"What?"

"That's *'I'll meet you in the lobby in ten minutes, Sir.'*"

I have to bite my lip to keep from snickering. I put on my best fake-contrite face and nod solemnly. "Of course. Sir. May I go now, Sir?"

"Get outta here," he says, holding the door open for me as I pack up. "I'll deal with you later!"

"I certainly hope so," I mutter under my breath as I pass him in the doorway. He swats my backside and I jump with a giggle. I do love him. I think. Maybe.

He's chatting with Gordon the security guard when I make my way down to the lobby.

"Hi, Gordon," I say with a wave.

"Hi there, Julia. Word has it you're the one to beat this week!"

I shrug my shoulders. "I don't know, it's anyone's game. Besides," I say, putting a hand on Jeremy's arm, "this guy is the best horn player I've ever heard. Wouldn't surprise me if he took the whole thing."

I catch Jeremy looking at me a little oddly. He seems surprised. Maybe a bit touched? I get the distinct impression I've pleased him with my comment. Maybe I need to compliment him more often if it makes him that happy.

He takes my hand and pulls me out the lobby doors, out into the bright, Saturday morning sun. It's chilly, but we move briskly down the block to the subway station. We get off at Thirty-fourth Street, I assume, to transfer to another line. But he leads me off the platform and downstairs to the heart of Penn Station. It's still pretty early and the terminal is relatively quiet, with a handful of travelers waiting for trains eastward. I look up at the huge wreaths hanging from the ceiling and the shiny gold garlands that are draped everywhere. I can barely keep up with Jeremy as he walks purposefully toward the Long Island Rail Road tracks.

"Jeremy, where exactly is this place?" I ask, starting to become suspicious.

He stops in the middle of the grand hallway and faces me. "Do you trust me?"

I wince a little. The question takes me back to the night before, with Matthew. But I know the answer to it now, just as

I did then. "Yes." I say this simply and confidently. I'm rewarded with that smile.

"Good." He takes a quick look at the huge board listing the outgoing trains. "Okay, come on." He snatches my hand and pulls me along with him.

"What? Where are we going? You can't mean to get on a train…"

But if Jeremy hears my protests he doesn't respond. We dart through the terminal and he leads me down the steep steps onto the platform of track nineteen.

"All aboard!" the conductor hollers.

I try to get a glimpse of where the train is going but Jeremy pulls me into a car just as the doors are closing.

"Jeremy! Where are we going?" I demand when he has situated us in a pair of seats.

"Nine-fifteen train to Ronkonkoma!" the speaker crackles.

"Ronkonkoma? Are you crazy? We've got to get off at Jamaica and go back."

"I love going through the tunnels. Don't you?"

"What?"

"The tunnels. They're cool. And then you come up and out into the daylight."

"Jeremy…"

"Jules, you said you trust me. So trust me, okay?"

How can I possibly disagree with that chiseled, slightly stubbly jaw? He's gorgeous. And he wants to spend time with me—to take me on an adventure. So I nod my head and sit back to look out the window.

He's right, the tunnel is kind of cool.

22

Clearly Ronkonkoma isn't our final destination as we get off on the B track and walk right across the platform to an old diesel train sitting on the A track. "I really wish you'd just tell me where we're headed," I mumble.

His only reply is an enigmatic smile—yet another in his "sexy smiles" repertoire.

As our second train pulls out slowly, I nestle into Jeremy's chest and the landscape flit past the window. This is close to where Matthew and I grew up—and area considered by many to be "Old Long Island." Mainly quaint hamlets separated by family farms, this area is a throwback to a time before suburban sprawl brought strip malls, packed parkways, and big box stores.

But now, facing backwards on the chugging diesel of the LIRR, I see all that melt away. Passing through some of the smaller towns I spot houses covered in bright, blinking holiday lights. Some have huge blow-up snow globes and reindeer on the front lawn. It makes me smile.

"What're you thinking about?" comes Jeremy's voice in my ear.

"Hmm? Oh, just how nice it would be to have family around this time of the year," I explain distractedly.

"How do you usually spend your holiday break? That is, when you're not being hijacked by a crazy horn player?"

"Hijacked. Yeah, that feels about right," I chuckle. "Uh…I don't know. Matthew usually cooks a big dinner. Sometimes we have friends over."

"Sounds nice."

"It is. Relaxed, low-drama. Hey..." I turn to face him. "You know, I'm so sorry, Jeremy. It's been nearly three weeks, and we've never talked about your family. I don't even know where you're from."

"Illinois. A little town about an hour out of Chicago called Owl Bridge."

"Are your folks still there?"

"As far as I know."

"Not so close then?"

"Not really."

I nod as if I understand. But I don't. Not really.

He reaches over and pushes a strand of hair off my face and tucks it behind my ear. "My mom calls your color strawberry blonde."

"Tell me about her," I say on impulse.

He screws-up his face as if he's thinking hard. "Ah, well, her name is Trudy and she's a kindergarten teacher. She's a great cook and a terrible driver."

"And your father?"

"Oh, Danny Corrigan is a good Irishman. Works hard, drinks harder. He's a mechanic. Taught us all about cars when we were little. I was helping out in his shop by the time I was fourteen. He wasn't thrilled when both of his boys went into music. He was hoping at least one of us would take over the business."

"Is that why you're estranged?"

"I don't know. I guess that's part of it. Seems like he just never got me. Things are better with my parents and Brett. He's sort of the lifeline between all of us."

"Huh." I don't mean for the single syllable to come out sounding so...judgmental. But it does. And he notices.

"You don't approve?"

"Oh, no. I mean it's none of my business either way. I just wish I had family to spend the holidays with. Now it looks like I won't even have Matthew. He's so angry I don't know if he'll come back at all."

I don't realize until just this moment that I really believe this. Jeremy kisses the top of my head.

"It's going to be alright, Jules. He'll come around."

I don't ask any more questions, and he doesn't offer any more details. Instead, I rest my head on his shoulder, and we spend the next half hour in companionable silence.

"Next stop, Montauk! Montauk is the final stop on this train. Please be sure to take all your belongings and watch the gap when exiting the train. Next and final stop, Montauk!" the speaker crackles.

"I guess we're headed to Montauk, then?" I ask with a hint of sarcasm.

"Smart ass," he mutters, getting to his feet and offering me a hand up.

The second we step off the train we're met by the smell of the sea. Montauk appears to be sleepy—at least for the moment. Come spring, the city folk and tourists will descend upon the tiny beach town, filling its shops and restaurants, snatching up exorbitantly priced hotel rooms and rental properties. The locals will complain bitterly amongst themselves, and breathe a sigh of relief when the last exotic car rolls out onto Montauk Highway headed west. By the time the daffodils are out, they'll be ready to do it all again.

But right now, on a Saturday morning in December, it's as if we have the whole place to ourselves. Granted, there isn't a whole lot open for us to enjoy, as most of the boutiques and restaurants close in the off-season. Still, the whitewashed charm of this casual community speaks to me. The Pine Barrens give way to the sand dunes, which give way to the inky blue waters of the Atlantic. And it's stunningly beautiful.

The main drag isn't especially big but it has everything one might look for during a leisurely week at the beach with family and friends. A pizza parlor, an ice cream shop and a pancake house are all within walking distance. Jeremy leads me through the crosswalk, picking up the pace excitedly.

"This is the place," he says as we reach the bakery, housed in an unremarkable storefront.

"Long way to come for a cup of coffee," I mumble as I peer into the window.

"Well, first of all, it's not just any cup of coffee," he says, pointing to a sign that reads *'Best Coffee in Town!'* "And we're not just here for the coffee. I've been dreaming about this place for months, and you're about to find out why."

We escape the chilly morning air into the warmth of the tiny shop. There's barely enough room for half a dozen people. Wide plank oak floors and paneling serve as backdrop for a vintage cabinet filled with pastries, cakes and cookies. The wall behind the counter is lined with shelves holding huge baskets. Nestled inside of them are loaves of bread in every size, shape and color.

Jeremy sidles up to the counter and a man emerges, wiping floury hands on his apron.

"Good morning," he greets us cheerily. Then he seems to recognize Jeremy.

"Hey, I know you!" he points a finger at Jeremy. "Back again for the croissants, eh?"

Jeremy shrugs sheepishly. "What can I say? I'm about to prove to this young lady that they're worth the two and a half hours on the train."

I practically melt when he puts his arm around me possessively. Now Baker Man is beaming at me. "Ah, well, you're in luck, miss. I just happen to have a batch coming out of the oven right now! Why don't you kids get yourselves some coffee and I'll pull the tray."

"Can you tell I love this place?" Jeremy asks as he fixes two cups of coffee and hands one to me.

"Just a little," I say with a giggle, watching him bounce excitedly from one foot to the next. Damn he's adorable like this—like a little kid in a candy store.

"It's just so nice to see you outside of the city. You seem so much more at ease here."

"I am. And I want you to be too."

"How many?" the baker asks as he sets a huge tray of croissants on the counter.

Jeremy considers for a second. "We'll take two now and we'll probably stop by later to get a couple for the ride home."

With a nod, the gentleman puts the two pastries into a white bag and hands them to Jeremy. When he takes out his wallet to pay, the older man waves his money away.

"These are on the house. My treat for the lady."

"Thank you!" I exclaim with delighted surprise.

He waves as we leave his shop.

"Let's sit over there," Jeremy says, using his chin to point out a wood bench, faded by sunlight and time.

When we're seated, I take a long sip of the hot coffee. Apparently they're not lying about it being the best in town. It really hits the spot, especially on a chilly day like today.

"Here," Jeremy says, handing me a pastry wrapped in a napkin. "This needs to be eaten while it's still warm."

I hold it up to exam it. "What is it exactly again?"

"It's a jelly croissant. A butter croissant fried like a donut, filled with strawberry jelly and sugared. You won't believe how good these things are."

I nibble a corner off, and then take a larger bite. "Oh. Oh, God, that *is* good…" I manage to say with a full mouth.

"Now, sip the coffee. They're amazing with the coffee."

I do as instructed, and know exactly why he wanted to come to this place. We chew and sip quietly for a bit, savoring the treat. Finally, Jeremy speaks.

"Did you mean what you said to Gordon?"

"What?" I squint at him trying to remember.

"That I'm the best horn player you've ever heard? That you think I could win the Kreisler?"

I nod adamantly. "Absolutely. And not just because we're…you know…"

"Sleeping together?"

"Exactly," I say, taking another bite. "I've always thought that, Jeremy."

He seems to consider this for a moment before popping the last of his croissant in his mouth. Then he leans toward me over his coffee.

"You are just all sweetness and sunshine, aren't you?"

"Well, not *all*…" I say suggestively. Now he's smiling from ear to ear. "What?" I ask, suddenly defensive. "What? Did that sound ridiculous coming from me?"

He shakes his headed slowly. "Not the least little bit."

"Then what?"

"Nothing. You're just amazing, and I can't believe it took me so long to realize that."

I can feel that old blush starting to rise again and I look down at the coffee cup in my hands. "Thank you," I murmur, without looking up.

He nudges my shoulder with his to break the awkward moment. "Eat that thing before it gets cold, will you? They're not nearly as good when they're cold."

23

"I—I don't think I can do this," I gasp, hugging the side of the steep circular stairway. I was fine on the way up to the top of the lighthouse, but returning back to solid ground is proving to be a bit trickier than I'd anticipated.

"Why not?" he asks.

"There's no railing!"

He chuckles, clearly amused by my predicament. "There wasn't one going up, either," he points out.

"Jeremy..." I whine.

"I'm not going to let you fall," he assures, sandwiching me between himself and the wall so I can feel a little more secure. We move like that, slowly downward, until my feet feel the lighthouse's floor.

"You okay?" he asks, when I breathe a sigh of relief.

"Yeah, well, apparently I have a fear of heights I didn't know about."

"Not to worry, it's all ground level from here on out."

We've hitched a ride to the very tip of Long Island's south fork where the Montauk Lighthouse stands, proud and tall. I've learned, from the small museum attached to it, that it was the very first lighthouse in New York State and is the fourth oldest functioning lighthouse in the country.

Outside, we take a walk down and around the back of the lighthouse, our feet crunching on a sandy path. After several hundred feet there is a break in the bluff and an opening to one of the most spectacular views I've ever seen.

The locals call Montauk 'The End.' Now I see why. The beach, littered with quartz, granite, and other rocks gives way to the inky blue sea. The long, narrow waves roll in, crest, and crash with a thunderous sound. Above, the sky is a perfect shade of blue. Sky blue. The gauzy clouds are motionless, hanging there as if they've been painted on with a brush.

I start to shiver as the biting wind comes off the water, ripping right through my lightweight coat. When he notices, Jeremy takes his own jacket off and lays it over my shoulders. Standing here, looking out at the vast and icy Atlantic, it's easy to pretend we're the last two people on earth.

I turn to face Jeremy and impulsively throw my arms around him, almost knocking him to the sandy ground.

"Whoa!" he laughs, trying to stay upright. "What's that about?"

"Thank you," my muffled voice says from against his chest.

"For what?"

Still clinging to him tightly, I look up at his handsome face. "This is just what I needed, Jeremy. The change of scenery, the beach...you. I don't know how you knew, but you did. Thank you."

He leans down and kisses me softly. I want this moment by the cold, briny water to last forever. But it can't. Not if we're going to catch the last train home this afternoon. With a little help from Uber, we manage to make it back to the center of town without much difficulty.

"We have a little time," Jeremy says, looking at his watch. "Did you want to look in some shops?"

I glance around us. My earlier impressions were accurate. The town is nearly deserted and most of the storefronts have 'Closed for the Season' signs hanging in the windows.

"I don't think there are any shops to look in," I say skeptically.

"How about that one?"

Jeremy is pointing to a window with a large awning and it does appear to be open. He takes my hand and we walk over to the large shop window where beautiful holiday decorations have been hung stylishly. Several gift-giving ideas are on display from hand-knit scarves, to fine leather bags and jewelry. One piece in particular catches my eye—an emerald pendant on a delicate gold chain. Jeremy follows my gaze.

"Let's go in and have a look," he says, pulling me toward the door.

I follow him inside and am immediately struck by the sweet smell of apples and cinnamon. The shop is warm, and cozy, and I can hear the soft strains of Christmas music on Celtic harp playing somewhere. He reaches into the window display and pulls out the blue velvet box where the necklace is nestled.

"Here, let's see how it looks on you." He carefully pulls the necklace out and affixes it around my neck before standing back to admire his handiwork.

He stands back to admire his handiwork, and I gather he likes what he sees.

"Oh, I love that piece!" Someone says from behind me.

I'm fingering the emerald as I turn back around, toward the friendly, welcoming voice behind me. It belongs to a pretty, middle-aged woman with auburn hair and eyes the same color as the stone hanging around my neck. My hand drops from the pendant, and I feel the blood draining from my face. I sway unsteadily, and Jeremy grabs my elbow.

"Are you okay?" he asks, leaning close to my ear.

But I can't speak. I'm frozen, fixated on this woman's kind, concerned face in front of me.

"Hey, you're shaking." Jeremy's tone is till soft but now it's edged with alarm. "What is it? What's wrong?"

Am I shaking? I hadn't noticed.

"Sweetie, you look as if you've seen a ghost," the woman says to me, her face furrowed with worry. "Come. Come over here by the counter and sit down."

When she takes my clammy hand in her soft, warm one, the room starts to spin around me. Oh, God. I'm going to pass out right here, in the middle of this cozy little shop, in the middle of this cozy little town.

"Mom, where should I...."

The second female voice startles me back to my senses, and the vertigo subsides. She can't be any more than fourteen or fifteen—a brunette version of her mother's fine features.

"Oh, I'm sorry, I didn't know you were helping someone," the girl apologizes.

"Corinne, honey, would you please get this young lady some water?" her mother requests, as she guides me the final few steps to a folding chair.

"Sure," she replies, dropping the box she's carrying onto the counter with a dull thud, and heading into the back again.

Jeremy is squatting down in front of me. He's saying something, but I can't hear him over the sound of my heartbeat pounding in my ears. I close my eyes until I sense someone close to me. When I open them, the teenager is there again, holding a bottle of water out for me. I accept it with trembling hands.

"Jeremy, would you please take the necklace off?" I look at him and whisper.

"Of course," he murmurs, reaching around my neck to unclasp it. His face is only inches from mine. "What is it?" he asks again, very softly, so only I can hear him. "Are you sick? Should I call an ambulance?"

I shake my head, and he stands up to put the emerald on the counter. When he moves, I realize that the girl is staring at me. What is she looking at? The answer comes in an instant.

"You have eyes just like my mom's," she says with some interest, like I'm a science experiment or something. "Hey, mom, look! This lady has the same eyes as you. That really, really green color. Daddy told me that only two percent of the population has green eyes, and that no one else has eyes like yours. Hey, we should take a picture!"

She's already fussing with her phone when her mother comes around in front of me to shoo her away. "Corrine! Leave the poor woman alone! She's trying to catch her breath, and she doesn't need you…"

As she's speaking, she glances at me quickly, and then back again immediately, more critically this time. I watch as it all unfolds in her mind. I see it so clearly. First a curious glance, followed by a moment of confusion, which gives way to sudden recognition. The entire gamut of emotions wraps-up in total, absolute, unadulterated horror.

Yes, at this very second she and I both know it without a doubt. I'm looking at my mother.

24

It's been eighteen years since Kelly James walked away from her life, from her husband and her only child. Eighteen years without so much as a glance in the rearview mirror at what lay wasted behind her. And now, here she is, standing so close that I could touch her if I wanted to. Which I don't.

As we stare at one another in stricken silence, the nausea passes. I've stopped shaking and I feel the warmth of blood returning to my hands and my face. I close my eyes to break the intensity between us and I take a few long, deep breaths until finally, I feel as if I can speak again.

"You're very sweet," I begin softly, "but I think I'm okay now. I just got a little light headed there for a minute." I set , the water down on the counter and plaster a smile of gratitude on my face. When I reach out for Jeremy's hand, he helps me to my feet, a bewildered expression on his face.

"Julia, I really think you should sit for another minute," he suggests.

I see my mother wince at the mention of my name. It's the confirmation she didn't want.

"No," I say a little too firmly. "Really, I'm fine. I've taken up enough of these lovely ladies' time."

It requires every ounce of determination I have to get across the shop floor and to the door. But I can't help myself. I pause for a split second with my hand on the knob, holding my breath. This is her opportunity to run after me, but she doesn't take it. I think I'm going to step outside, just keep going and never look back, like she did all those years ago. But I can't. My shock is turning to something else now. Something darker. I turn around and face her, still staring at me with wide eyes and a pale face.

"How long?" I ask in a voice I don't recognize.

She blinks hard and her brows knit together in confusion. "How long what?"

"How long have you been here? In this perfect town, raising your perfect new family?"

She doesn't reply.

"Mom?" asks the teenager standing behind her mother. Our mother. "Mom, what's going on?" I can hear the fear creeping into her voice.

"Aren't you going to answer her?" I ask when Kelly remains silent. "Or are you going to ignore your child? You're good at that, aren't you?"

My mother stands up and extends a hand out towards me. I don't know what she's expecting. Does she want me to take it? Shake it? Hold it? What? No. I realize with sudden clarity that she's reaching for me.

"Julia…" When she speaks my name, it is barely the shadow of a whisper on her lips.

"Mom!" Corinne sounds more insistent as she grows more alarmed.

But Kelly doesn't move. Her arm remains outstretched, her eyes brimming with tears.

I look down at the hand with disdain, shaking my head. "Too late," I say simply.

"Who the hell are you?" Corinne demands. "What do you want?"

My eyes meet hers—my sister's eyes. I'm surprised she doesn't see it. "I'm her daughter," I say. "And nothing. I want absolutely nothing from her."

When I turn back my back on them and return to the door, This time, keep moving this time—without so much as a glance over my shoulder. Once we are a safe distance away, I throw my arms around Jeremy's strong chest. It's as if his entire body envelopes mine as I sob, wordlessly, inconsolably.

The ride back to the city feels unbearably long. The only thing I want to do is go home. Jeremy is very respectful and doesn't ask any questions when I explain what has just transpired. He takes my hand and leads me gently from train to train to subway until we are in the lobby of my building at last.

"You don't have to stay," I say, dropping my hand from his.

He looks a little hurt. "Do you want me to leave? Because I'm not so sure you should be alone right now."

"Jeremy, this isn't what you signed on for. I have a lot—and I mean a *lot* of baggage. Too much to dump on you. I think this might be a good time to just call it quits. We can stay friends..."

"Friends?" He snorts. "I don't think so."

He grabs my hand firmly and pulls me toward the elevator. When we get to my door I unlock it. He's in motion before I can push it all the way open. He shuffles me into the foyer, closes the door behind us and pulls the coat from my shoulders in what feels like one fluid movement.

"Jeremy, I'm really not in the mood to..."

"Julia, get out of those clothes and meet me in the bathroom. I'm going to go get the shower running," he instructs, even as he's walking down the hallway towards my room.

I'm too tired to argue so I strip down to my underwear and pad down the hall behind him. The bathroom is steamy by the time I get there and Jeremy is testing the temperature of the water with his hand.

"Okay," he says, reaching around me to unhook my bra. "Let's get you into a nice hot shower, shall we?"

I step out of my panties and allow him to help me over the side of the tub and into the soothing downpour.

"I'll be back to check on you in a few minutes," he says, pulling the shower curtain closed.

Music starts to play softly as he switches on the radio I have by the sink. Then I hear the bathroom door close behind him. Once I'm alone, I replay it all, every awkward, horrifying moment, over and over again in my mind. Walking into a random shop in a random town...running into the mother who abandoned me nearly twenty years ago. The chances are infinitesimal.

After she first left, I waited for her to come back for me. I just knew that if I were a good little girl, she'd rescue me from my hellish life. But she never did. And I blamed myself for that. Then, as I grew older I allowed myself to believe that she didn't come back because she couldn't. After all, she had been an alcoholic and a druggy. Maybe she was destitute or sick or in trouble. Maybe she was in jail. Maybe she was dead.

But this...to know that she could have and didn't... I can't finish the thought. I start to cry. Loudly. I think wailing might be the best way to describe the sound that is coming from me. In an instant he's there, pulling back the shower curtain and climbing in with me. He's fully clothed as he wraps his arms around me. And then we are sinking, sliding down until he's sitting up against the back of the tub, my face buried in his chest. He's rubbing my back and shushing me as the water pours down on us from above. We stay like that for a long time until finally I look up at him.

"She didn't want me, Jeremy. She left me there with him and forgot about me. She has a brand new family. It's like I never existed…" I break down in sloppy sobs and he pulls me back into him.

He doesn't try to make excuses for her. He just holds me and listens and whispers comforting things in my ear until, finally, there is no cry left in me. When I look up again he strokes the sides of my face.

"You are so beautiful," he says softly, drinking me in. To have someone look at me with such intensity is both uncomfortable and mesmerizing at the same time. But I don't have the energy to respond. I'm physically and emotionally exhausted. After a time he maneuvers us both into a standing position and turns the shower off. "Stay there just a sec," he murmurs as he steps out onto the bath mat and shucks the soaked clothing from his body. He wraps a towel around his naked waist and pulls another one off the rack for me.

"Okay, come on," he beckons, holding out his hand to help me from the shower. I take it and allow him to envelop me in the fluffy towel. Then his hands are on my shoulders and he's pushing me gently out of the bathroom and into my connecting bedroom.

We pause at the dresser and he rummages around, eventually pulling out a nightgown. He gently pulls the towel from my body and has me raise my arms up so he can slip the gown over my head. I'm visibly trembling, but I'm not sure if it's because I'm upset or just cold. Either way, it's not pleasant and Jeremy steers me to the bed as quickly as possible. He holds the covers up and I slip underneath them. Now he finds a pair of socks and, lifting just the very bottom edge of the comforter, eases them onto my ice-cold feet.

"I'll be right back," he says as he leaves the room.

When he returns a few minutes later he's wearing a pair of Matthew's pajama bottoms. "I don't think Matthew will mind, do you?" he asks with a little smirk.

I give him the barest of smiles and slightest of nods before he turns out the light and crawls in next to me. Under the covers he spoons me from behind, surrounding me with his warmth and his strength. I feel safe here with him. He doesn't talk, just holds me. But suddenly I realize that I want more. I need more.

"Jeremy," I whisper into the darkness.

"What is it, Jules?"

"I want to forget. I want to feel good for a little while."

I can tell he immediately comprehends what I'm asking. "Okay," he says softly.

I feel him reach under the hem of my nightdress and his hand finds my breast. He traces my nipple with his thumb. Slowly, oh so slowly. He kisses the side of my face and the back of my neck and finally my shoulder. This isn't passionate, so much as nurturing. He's tender and gentle, deliberate as he moves his hands across my body. I gasp softly. Yes, this is what I want right now more than anything. He maneuvers his right arm underneath me, using it to draw me even closer and embracing me from behind. The right hand picks up with my other breast while his left gently caresses my side and the curve of my hip. When he slips his finger between my legs I cry out and arch my head back onto his shoulder.

"Ata girl, that's it," he whispers right in my ear as he gently, slowly moves his hand up and down the length of my sex.

I'm breathing heavily as he takes his time. Up and down, pausing just long enough to tease and nudge the tiny bundle of nerves at my center. Something unintelligible comes out of my mouth and he slides his hand down, dipping first one then two fingers into me.

"God, you are so wet," he murmurs next to my ear. "That's for me. All for me and no one else. You understand?"

I nod enthusiastically and feel him shifting behind me. I'm not sure what he's doing until I feel his huge erection pressed against my back. Then there is the tear of the foil.

Ah, so the pajama bottoms are gone now.

I whimper when he pauses his languid caressing but it is only a second before his hands are on my waist, pulling me back even further to him. And then I feel him against me, pushing, prying, looking for the spot. When he finds it he wastes no time. He pushes into me with a guttural grunt that sends shivers through my entire body. He pulls out all the way and slams in hard again, eliciting a groan from me. And then he reaches back around and his fingers are on me again, pushing, teasing, circling even as he's thrusting. It is more sensation than I've ever experienced at one time. I'm writhing against him and moaning.

"That's it," he whispers in my ear. "That's it, baby. Come for me. I want to hear you come loud, Jules."

It's out of my control at this point. I hear myself getting louder and louder as he delves deeper and deeper into me until finally, with one rough stroke, he sends me right over the edge. He's only a few seconds behind me. Afterwards, I lay in his arms, panting heavily as he reaches around to brush the hair from my sweaty forehead.

"A little better?" he asks.

I nod and he kisses the back of my head, pulling me in close, my back to his chest. I drift off feeling the beat of his heart against me. Until I don't

I wake myself up with a strangled scream in the middle of the night. Jeremy scrambles to turn on the light in the pitch-blackness of my room as I sit bold upright, panting and gasping.

"What? What is it? Bad dream?"

I nod, unable to speak because I'm breathing so heavily.

"Okay, you know what? You need something to help you get some rest."

He climbs out of bed as I draw my knees up to my chest and rest my head on them. When he returns it is with a glass of water and a bottle of pills. "Here, take one of these," he says as he pops the top off the prescription and hands me a small white oval to swallow.

I don't ask him what it is. I don't care. I just want to sleep. I want to feel…nothing. All I want is to be numb and that is exactly what washes over me. Within moments everything fades away.

25

It's taken every ounce of physical and mental strength I have to get me up on this stage. I'm not sure if it's the emotional rollercoaster of my mother's reappearance, or that little white pill that Jeremy gave me last night so I could sleep, but right now I feel as if I'm walking around in a dream. And not just any dream, either. This is one of those dreams where you're late for the final exam and, when you finally get there, somehow you've forgotten to put on any clothes. I'm clothed and on time, but I can't seem to pick up my bow and play.

The accompanist is hissing at me from over his piano.

"Pssst! Are you okay?"

I look over at him blankly, then back to the music sitting on the stand in front of me.

"Miss James?"

That's Nick Lautner, the highest paid cellist in the country. He's sitting in the middle of the judges' table. I'm not certain, but I don't think this is the first time he's called my name.

Jeremy was right when he tried to talk me out of this earlier today. I'm not up to it. And if I play poorly because I'm distracted…play poorly in front of these people, my career is over before it's begun. The only thing I can think about right now is my mother. And, really, it's the only thing I *should* be thinking about right now. I clear my throat and meet the perplexed stares of the committee.

"I'm sorry...I can't do this right now," I say, standing up, taking my cello and bow and walking off the stage. I keep walking until I'm safely on the other side of the auditorium door. That's when I hear a familiar voice.

That's when I hear a familiar voice. "Julia! How'd it go in there?"

Apparently Sam Michaels has decided to surprise me. Well, turns out he's the one who's about to be surprised.

The smile fades from his face very quickly as he gets a good look at me. Pale, drawn, dark circles under my swollen eyes.

"What is it? What happened?" Dr. Sam asks, gently grasping my arm above the elbow.

I can only shake my head. I'm afraid if I open my mouth I'll start to cry and if I start again, I might not ever stop.

"Did you play?"

I shake my head again.

"Are you sick?"

I shrug.

He lets go of me and takes the cello from my hands, gesturing with his head for me to follow him down the hallway. Jesus, what have I done? What am I doing? When he finds an empty room a few doors down, he holds the door open for me and I go inside. He sets the cello on the floor and turns to face me.

"Talk to me, Julia." I start to shake my head once again, but he holds up his hand to stop me. "Talk to me," he repeats.

I sigh, and take a seat at one of the desks. "I couldn't play," I tell him softly.

"Why not? You're more than ready for this."

"No, it's not that…"

I put my head in my hands.

"What, sweetie? What is it?"

He's next to me now, down on one knee. Anyone peering through the window in the door would think he was about to propose.

Dr. Sam Michaels was the first cello teacher I ever had. It was rare for him to take a student as young as I was, but when he heard about my situation—the fact that I was a mute, abused, and abandoned child—he made an exception. At this moment, it's a relief that he knows all of the ugly details of my past. Because, when I finally look up, the tears and the words start to spill out in one unstoppable wave.

It takes several minutes to get the whole sordid story out but he listens intently, nodding and sighing and keeping eye contact with me through every bit of it. When I've finished, he stands up and puts a firm, reassuring hand on my shoulder.

"Stay here. I'm going to take care of this."

Take care of what? My totally screwed-up life? Sam is good, but he's not that good. Before I can voice an objection, he's gone, leaving me alone in the empty classroom. When he returns twenty minutes later it is with Cal, who's carrying the case and music I left behind when I bolted from the hall.

"So, kiddo," Dr. Sam begins, leaning up against the teacher's desk in front of me. "The committee has agreed to hear you in the last slot, tomorrow night at six."

I look at him and wonder how he can possibly believe I'll be able to play. I mean, right now I have to remind myself to breathe in and out.

"You can do this," he says, guessing my thoughts. "And you will. Do you know how I know this?"

"No," I reply dispassionately.

"Because I have been teaching you for a very long time, my dear girl. And over the years, I've watched you leave a horrific past behind you and find joy in your life—joy that came to you through music. You'll find it again. Don't be afraid of the emotions that you feel while you're playing—lean into them. Let them wash over you and carry you."

He means well. And on some level I know he's right. But at this moment I'm so exhausted I can't even think about it. I just want to go home. I just want to go home and curl up in Jeremy's arms so he can tell me it's all going to be okay.

"Listen, Julia, Cal here is going to see you home. You get a good night's sleep and meet me in my office at two o'clock tomorrow afternoon. I'll take you through your warm-up and we'll ride over here together. Sound like a plan?"

I shrug, noncommittally

Dr. Sam nods at Cal who has packed up my cello while we were talking. When I stand up, Sam Michaels breaks the rules—scooping me up in a big, warm hug, the way he did when I was a little girl. It feels good. It feels safe.

"Are you…will you be home alone?" Cal ventures once we're tucked away in a cab headed back downtown.

I nod. "Matthew is back on tour."

"And...Jeremy?" he asks cautiously.

"He's rehearsing at McInnes with his accompanist but he'll be over as soon as he's done."

"Has he been supportive about this?"

"Yes," I assure him firmly, wanting to prove to Cal that Jeremy has my best interests at heart. That he loves me.

"He must be worried about you," Cal pushes a little further.

"He is. That's why I don't think he's going to be thrilled that Dr. Sam wants me to play again."

"Huh."

"What?" I ask. "What's that supposed to mean, Cal?"

"Julia, if it were me…"

"Which it's not," I interject petulantly.

"Which it's not...I think I'd put more stock in what my teacher tells me than what a…friend…tells me."

I sigh heavily and shake my head. Cal is never going to be able to get past this competitive thing he has going with Jeremy. He wisely drops the subject and we ride the rest of the way in silence. When we pull up in front of my building he makes a move to get out with me.

"I've got this, Cal."

"I promised Dr. Michaels I'd get you all the way up to your apartment," he protests.

"You know what? I'm sick and tired of everyone questioning every decision I make. And how interesting that it's always a man. You, Matthew, Sam. Get back in the cab, Cal. You're not setting foot in my building."

He nods silently and sits back as I take the cello and turn my back on him.

26

He fills the frame of my door as I open it—all lanky, scruffy, and crinkly. He's a sight for my incredibly sore eyes.

"Hi." I feel suddenly shy as his hazel eyes settle upon me.

"Hi," he replies, stepping forward to hold me close to him.

"I'm glad you're home," I murmur.

He gives me a sweet smile.

"Home. I like the sound of that."

I reluctantly extricate myself from him, and he follows me inside and drops his horn in the foyer.

"How was your rehearsal?" I ask.

"Seriously? You're going to ask me about my rehearsal before you tell me about your audition?"

He takes a seat at the breakfast bar and watches as I open a bottle of wine and pour out two glasses for us.

"There's nothing to tell. I walked off the stage without playing a single note," I explain as I set the glass down in front of him and take a long sip from my own.

"I knew it. Jules, I wish you had just listened to me. You could have spared yourself all this heartache."

"Well, it's not over yet."

"What do you mean?" He's leaning forward now, suddenly very attentive.

"I mean that Dr. Sam convinced the committee to give me one more chance, tomorrow night."

He puts the glass down hard—wine sloshing over the side and onto the granite countertop. "Do you really think that's a good idea?"

"I don't know," I admit with a sigh as I take a seat on the stool next to him. He puts a hand on my wrist.

"Jules, I'm going to respect whatever decision you make. But you need to give this careful consideration. You've already sent up a red flag with the committee by walking out. It doesn't help that your teacher had to ask for a special favor to get you back on the roster. If you go in there and you have a meltdown in front of these world-class musicians, well…I'm just afraid your reputation might take a blow that you can't come back from."

I look down at the wine in my glass and swirl it a little, creating a blood-red mini-vortex. He has a point. A very good one, in fact. I'm off my game, and there's no telling how badly I might play. That is, if I can make myself play at all.

"You know what, why don't you sleep on it? Besides, there's something else I want to talk about." He gets up and mods toward the couch. "Come on, let's sit."

"Okay…" I follow him into the living room, perching on the cushion next to him. "What is it?"

"Jules, I think we should move in together."

Surely I've misheard him. "What?"

"Seriously. Matthew's on the road all the time, right? Let's stay here together and give it a trial run. I think it'll give us a better idea of where this relationship is headed, and then maybe we'll get a place of our own. Of course it wouldn't be as grand as all this…" he holds up his hands and gestures around the apartment.

I don't know what to say. I mean, I know what I should say: Are you out of your mind? Only that's not really what I want to say. Right now, there is no place I feel safer than here, with him.

"What are you thinking?" he asks.

"I–I don't know. It seems a little soon, no? I mean we just started to date. We don't even really know each other..."

"Here's the thing," he begins, eyes intent on mine. "I've been in a lot of relationships, with a lot of women. And not one of them has felt this way, this stable and secure. Julia, all I want to do is spend time with you. When I'm not with you, I'm thinking about being with you."

As nice as it is to hear, I know in my heart that what he's talking about is insane. He sees me wrestling with this.

"Okay, I'm just going to say it out loud," he says, putting his wine glass on the coffee table in front of us and facing me.

"Say what?"

"What we've been hinting at for weeks. I'm falling in love with you, Jules. And I think you're falling in love with me, too."

Well, maybe just a little. But still…

"Jules, you're not like any of those other girls I've dated. There's so much more…substance to you. You're so strong, so caring. Not to mention the fact that you're beautiful and sexy as hell," he says with the hint of a naughty smile.

Really? My eyebrows go up.

"And," he continues before I can comment, "I think I might like to spend the rest of my life making you happy…" Wait. What? Is he talking about marriage now? "But I know it's a little soon for that. So how about if we start by moving in together and see how it goes from there?"

I don't know what to say. I was already on unstable ground before, but now I'm afraid I might be headed for a total emotional overload. My head is spinning with the torrent of feelings running through my body—the competition, Matthew, finding my mother…and now this. I just stare at him and try to process.

"Tell you what, this isn't something you have to decide right now either. Let's have some dinner, go to bed early, and see how you're feeling about everything in the morning, hmm?"

"Okay…" I say softly, looking up at him with an appreciative smile.

He leans in and kisses me. "Of course," he says, between nibbles on my lip, "we can always go to bed and have a late dinner…"

The bed is warm and soft. It's as much a haven for me now as it was when I was a child. I hear the phone ringing out in the kitchen and I pull the pillow over my head to block out the sound until it has stopped. I know it's daytime because there are chinks of light slipping past my blackout shades. But somehow the bedside clock has come unplugged and I'm not sure exactly what time it is.

Should I get up and see? Do I really care? No, not really. The heaviness that started in my heart a few days ago has spread throughout my body. I can't seem to get comfortable no matter what I do. Sit, stand, play, walk. I just want to crawl out of my own skin. The only relief I can find comes in Jeremy's arms.

He's sleeping next to me, and I pull the pillow away so I can watch his well-defined chest rise up and down with each deep, dreamy breath. He looks so serene. I wish some of that peace would rub off on me. Maybe it will, I think, as I snuggle up to him, draping my arm over his chest. He stirs just enough to pull me closer against him. Yes, this is where I need to be today. Maybe every day. Nowhere else.

When I wake again, it's with a start. There are loud voices in the hallway outside my room and they're growing closer. The other side of the bed is empty. Who is Jeremy talking to? Almost before I can form the question in my mind, I know the answer.

"You'd better get out of my way, Jeremy!"

"No. I'm not going to let you go in there so you can bully her into doing something she's not up to."

"I'm not going to tell you again. Get the fuck out of my way," Matthew says in a tone I've never heard him use before. It's almost…deadly.

Without warning, my bedroom door swings open with so much force, that I'm certain the doorknob has pushed a hole into the wall. And then he's standing there staring at me. Jeremy tries to follow Matthew in, but he's a split second too late, and the door is slammed and locked in his face.

"Get up," Matthew commands flatly.

I sit up in the bed and rub the sleep from my eyes. "What do you want?"

"I want you to get your ass out of bed. You were supposed to meet Dr. Michaels over an hour ago."

Oh, so that's what time it is. I shake my head at him. "No. You don't get to do that. You don't get to walk out on me then come waltzing in here making demands when it suits you."

He comes closer and sits on the bed next to me. "You're right, Julia. And I'm so, so sorry. But I'm here now."

"No. Jeremy is the one who is here now. He's the one who was here when it all went to hell. He's the one who's been holding me while I cry myself to sleep at night. He's the one who is worried about what it might do to my career if I go in there and bomb because I'm half out of my head."

Matthew breaks his stare to close his eyes for a long moment. It's as if he's closing them against something he doesn't care to see.

"Julia, I'm not going to argue with you about Jeremy. I'm here because I know you better than anyone else, including him. Dr. Sam filled me in on what happened to you out in Montauk and hell, I'm even glad that son of a bitch was there so you weren't alone when you came across her."

Well, now, that gets my attention.

"But goddammit," he continues, his voice becoming softer and more intense at the same time, "you are *not* made of glass. I don't know where you ever got the idea that you are. Julia, you are strong. You are determined and you are independent. She isn't your mother. She's just the woman who gave birth to you. You are so much stronger than she is, because you stayed. You endured. You thrived, in spite of what your parents did to you."

He looks tired as he pauses to rub the bridge of his nose with his fingertips.

"But you know what," he resumes, "you can sort through all the emotional baggage later because, Julia, I'm not going to let you throw away this opportunity. I will not let her ruin your life a second time."

I look at his face, so different from the last time I saw it, when he was wounded and furious and jealous. Now I only see love, and a little bit of fear. That, more than anything, is what sets me in motion.

I nod my head. "Okay."

He tilts his head a little, as if he's surprised that I agree with him. "Okay?" he echoes.

"Would you mind letting my boyfriend in please?" I ask, gesturing to the door where I know Jeremy is trying to eavesdrop.

"Only if you stop calling him that." Matthew sneers.

"You'd prefer I call him my lover, then?"

He grimaces. "God, no. Boyfriend is fine."

He gets up and reluctantly unlocks the door. Jeremy pushes it open, almost knocking Matthew in the face. For a brief second I'm afraid they are going to grab each other and drop to the floor in a tussle. But the moment passes. Matthew leaves and Jeremy enters. The symbolism isn't lost on me.

I'm on my feet before he can even get all the way into the room, pulling open dresser drawers, throwing clothes onto the bed. He doesn't look happy.

"I guess this means you're going to the audition then?"

I stop what I'm doing and wrap my arms around his waist, hugging him hard before looking up at him. His eyes are colder than I think I've ever seen. No, he really is *not* happy at all.

I smile, coaxingly. "I have time for a quick shower. Why don't you come soap my back for me?"

His demeanor doesn't soften. "I think I'll pass, Jules. You might change your mind halfway through, and ask Matthew to join you."

Oh, now that's really not fair. But I ignore the tone. "Please don't be like that. Matthew's right. If I can do this, I should do this. And I can, Jeremy."

He looks away, refusing to return my embrace. "Is this the way it's always going to be?" he asks.

"What do you mean?"

"I mean you running back to him every time you have a problem. You listening to him over me."

He pauses and the eyebrow goes up. But it's not quite so sexy this time. "Maybe it's time for you consider the possibility that Matthew isn't the only one who feels more than friendship."

I push back from him. "Stop it."

"Excuse me?" Now his brows draw down into an irritated frown.

"You heard me, Jeremy. You know how I feel about you. Right now I'm scared as hell, and I need you. I need you to have my back. I need you to support me…and love me. Please?"

I think I see the edge deteriorating, but I can't say for sure. He can be so hard sometimes. Not to mention hard to read.

"Jeremy, after everything that's happened, I don't think for a second that I'm going to win this thing. And, the truth is, I don't even care at this point. But Matthew is right about one thing—I have to try, if for no other reason than to show myself that I'm more than an abandoned, abused little girl. That woman ruined my life once before, I'm not going to give her the power to do it again." I put my hand on his chest and give him a tentative smile.

After a long, hard look into my eyes he sighs, and pulls me in so I'm against him again. He rests his chin on the top of my head.

"I can't say I agree. I don't think you have anything to prove to her, or Matthew, or anyone else. I saw you the other night after Montauk. I held you while you cried. Jesus, Jules, how much more are you going to put yourself through?" he asks from above me, his voice laden with concern.

I look up into his hazel eyes.

"I don't know. All that I do know for now is that I can't do it without you. I won't do it without you, Jeremy."

He is looking at me intently, searching my face for something, but I'm not sure what. Finally, he sighs and shakes his head. "I won't lie to you, I think this is a mistake, Jules, but I love you, and I've got your back no matter what."

I smile and he puts his hands on my shoulders, gently pushing me away. "Go get ready, you're going to be late if you don't get moving."

I stand on my tiptoes and kiss his lips lightly. There is nothing I can't do with this man behind me.

Part Two: Jeremy

Manifesto

There is an art to destroying a life. If you're going to do it right, it's not something to be rushed. It requires research, planning and patience. A lot of patience.

Once you have determined to do this, you will become a private investigator. You must carefully chart your subject's routine and personal connections. Discretely examine every smile, every toss of the head, every slouch and stretch. Drink in each action, because everything means something. It won't be too long before you are an expert in reading body language and facial expressions

After the legwork is done, you should have a fairly complete external picture of your target. The next step is to assemble the internal picture. What makes her tick? Watch for signs of insecurity, arrogance, loneliness and other characteristics that you can use to your advantage later. Try to ascertain what she's looking for in a man and become exactly that—because your best chance of success lies in your ability to transform yourself into the man that she has been dreaming of all her life.

The first step is to insert yourself into her life. Your encounters must appear to be totally random, completely coincidental. Here and there, allow yourself to be "spotted" at her favorite coffee shop or bookstore. Pretend not to notice her at first. Act genuinely surprised to see her when you do. Make each subsequent encounter a little friendlier.

A word of caution here—once you've actually made contact, it's in your best interest to move quickly. Don't give her time to question your motives or to be influenced by suspicious friends and relations. You can camouflage this expedited timeline with charisma and charm. Make yourself irresistibly free-spirited and spontaneous. In short, sweep her off her feet and don't let her touch the ground again.

You know that expression "Go big or go home?" Embrace it. Think grand gestures and whirlwind relationship. Shower her with what she's been missing—usually things like security, romance and intimacy. This is not the time to be cheap—even if money is what you're after at the end of the day. Think of it as an investment.

If seduction is part of your grand plan, then having an idea of her ideal partner will come in very handy here. If she's longing for security, go slow and be tender. If she's shy or self-conscious, be especially attentive and make her feel special/beautiful/sexy—whatever the situation calls for. The objective here is to guide her to the point where she is dependent upon you, both sexually and emotionally.

And this, my friends, is where the real fun begins. You have collected all the tools you need to get the job done, so roll up your sleeves and let's get down to business.

This is the time when you start to erode her self-confidence.

Start with little contradictions. For example, invite someone over, and don't tell her. Become irritated that she didn't remember. Become possessive. Demand to know where she has been and who she's been with when she's not with you. Isolate her from friends and family. Become enigmatic. Leave without telling her where you'll be or when you'll return. For as much as you demand she tell you everything, you tell her absolutely nothing. And when she does inquire, accuse her of being clingy or desperate.

Reinforce her insecurities. Make comments on her appearance or the way she performs a job or task. Hit with something close to home here. If she's an artist, make a snide comment about one of her paintings. Is she self-conscious about her nose? Ask her if she's ever considered surgery to correct the problem. Show interest in other women right in front of her. Make comments on how hot/sexy/beautiful your former girlfriends were. These are all loose little threads to be picked at and pulled until the final unraveling.

Now, if you're really lucky, you'll have stumbled upon an "old wound" during your prep. Some skeleton buried deep down in the closet—maybe even a person who has caused her pain in the past, such as a parent or former boyfriend. Nothing will set someone off-kilter faster than coming face to face with something…or someone they believe to be safely relegated to the past.

So, if the goal here is to destroy a life, how do you know when you have succeeded? Quite simply, when you have reduced her to a quivering mass of insecurity, unable to trust her own instincts, incapable of functioning independently. You have taken away her self-esteem, her security and her very sense of wellbeing. None of these losses is easy to come back from.

Congratulations, you have ruined her.

If any of these actions raises even a pang of distaste, dismay or disdain, then you might as well just hang it up right now—because you're not wired for manipulation on this scale. Your conscience, no matter how small it may be, will always get in your way. Never once should you consider something to be too much, too far, too dangerous or too destructive. It can be a painstaking, labor-intensive process. Because, to thoroughly and completely eviscerate a person, without actually killing them, is no easy task.

27

There are only a handful of other horn players in the warm-up room when I get there, and I spot Cal Burridge right away. Sure, I could go to another part of the room where there isn't anybody else playing. But what fun would that be? So instead I make a beeline towards him, setting my things down right next to his. He doesn't stop playing scales. In fact, he doesn't even acknowledge the fact that I'm standing there. But that doesn't bother me in the slightest. I start to unpack and assemble my instrument.

"What're you playing? The Mozart again?" I ask casually, unzipping my case and pulling out the pieces of my horn one by one.

Cal just keeps on playing, pretending that he can't hear me. I know better. C Major. C-sharp major. D major. All the keys go by in a blur, one by one go, as his fingers fly and his breath pours through his horn like its lifeblood. I screw the bell flare onto the body of my horn and pop the mouthpiece into the lead pipe, all the while chattering away at him.

"Now the Beethoven Sonata, you do a decent enough job of that most of the time, but I've heard you get a little flat in that center section. If it were me, I'd…"

He stops playing G-major and glares at me. "Shut the fuck up, Jeremy."

I smile at him broadly. I can't help myself—I just love getting under Cal's skin. Now, I put my own horn to my lips and start with a slew of scales that are faster, higher and louder than his. He begins to gather his music from the table, shaking his head and mumbling something under his breath. I stop playing.

"Time to go already? Too bad. Sounds as if you could've used a little more warm-up. That's okay, I'm sure you'll do fine anyway."

"Stop wasting your breath," he snaps, not even bothering to look at me anymore. "There isn't anything you can say that's going to get you into my head. I'm going out onto that stage to kick your ass, so I suggest you start thinking about what you're going to say to everyone when you lose."

I shake my head, still smiling at him. "Dude, you're a good player—I'll give you that. But I'm better. And that's not ego talking, Cal. That's just observable fact."

His face reddens and I think he's going come back at me, but we're interrupted before he has the chance.

"Jeremy?" comes Julia's tentative voice from behind us.

I spin around to face her, holding up my arm. It's an invitation, and she accepts it, slipping in and wrapping her arms around my chest. Her expression is impassive, so I'm guessing her performance was less than stellar but better than catastrophic.

"Hey, Jules! How did you do?" I ask.

She turns those big eyes up at me and shrugs. "I did okay. I'm glad I did it, but I'm glad it's over," she says. "I just wanted to come by and wish you luck."

"I appreciate it, but I don't believe in luck. Just talent," I inform her with my most confident grin.

"Well, you've certainly got that covered," she says, stretching to give me a quick kiss on the cheek. "I'd better go. I'll be watching up in the balcony with your brother."

"Good. I'll be able to look up and see you," I say softly. "Cal's up next, and then it's my turn."

The look she gives Cal is chilly. No, more like frosty. There's definitely something going on between the two of them.

"Good luck, Cal," she mutters quietly, before leaving us alone again.

When I glance back at him over my shoulder, he's shaking his head slowly. "What the fuck was that, Cal? Did you say something to upset my girl?" He snorts. "Something funny?"

"Your girl? Is that what she is?"

I ignore the comment, and step a little closer to him. "Seriously, man, Julia's nice to *everyone*. What the hell did you say to piss her off?"

"I tried to warn her about you," he explains flatly. "But she wasn't interested in hearing it."

"And that just makes you crazy, doesn't it?" He's glaring at me, and I see in his face what I have suspected for some time now. "You have a thing for her, don't you?" I ask with a teasing smile.

Cal doesn't say a word, only stares at me with sheer, unadulterated hatred. I give him a playful punch on the arm.

"Well, I get it, believe me. I mean, how could I not? She's beautiful, she's sweet and she's sexy as hell..." I just can't resist winding him up a little more before he has to perform.

He's trying not to show any emotion, but I notice his jaw clench.

"Burridge? Calvin Burridge?"

One of the competition pages is standing in the doorway with a clipboard.

"Oh, Cal, you didn't even get to finish your warm-up," I say, with a little too much sympathy. He grabs his music and stomps off toward the door. "Break a leg!" I call after him with a chuckle.

28

"Are you ready, Mr. Corrigan?"

A pretty young page is holding the door open for me to enter the auditorium. I nod and follow her, watching her ass under an exceptionally short plaid skirt. Nice.

And there they are—five of the top horn players in the world, all of them waiting to pass judgment on my playing. Well, they're in for a treat, that's for sure. Especially since I'm following Cal. I'm about to make him look like a total amateur. I smile at the committee, seated at a long table in the middle of the house. This is where the last round of auditions was held, so I'm comfortable getting myself situated on the stage.

"You may begin whenever you're ready, Mr. Corrigan."

The Kreisler accompanist has set up my music on the piano and he watches me for the signal to begin. One nod, and we're off.

The Villanelle by Paul Dukas is everything a horn player could want in a situation like this. It's a showcase for tone, range and finger work. It requires technical, as well as musical skill. And from the opening call, I own that theatre. It is flawless, and I can't help but smile when I take the horn from my lips and rest it on my lap.

While the committee is conferring, I glance back at the accompanist. He gives me a big grin and a thumbs-up. I squint out into the concert hall beyond the stage. From where I'm sitting I can just make out Julia in the balcony, leaning forward over the rail. My brother is sitting next to her. I wait until all five sets of eyes are on me again.

"Very good, Mr. Corrigan. May we hear your Mozart Horn Concerto, please?" asks a woman who I recognize as the principal horn player from Detroit.

"Of course, Miss Kutter," I respond in a loud, clear voice that carries back to their table. She smiles because I know who she is. Who doesn't? Not only is she a striking looking woman, she's a notorious diva. A little ego stroking couldn't hurt.

Again, I confer with the accompanist, and we're on to the Mozart. Nothing flashy or fancy here—it's written in what they call the 'meat and potatoes' range. Not too high, not too low. What's tricky about all of his horn concertos is the degree of delicacy required to play them well. You have to make it sound light, bright and effortless.

I wait for the piano to play its introduction, take a deep breath and close my eyes. I don't need to read the music—I know this one inside and out. Another brilliant performance. I'm breathing heavily as the committee members put their heads together. After only a minute or so, Louise Kutter is smiling up at me from her place in the center of the judge's table.

"Mr. Corrigan—Jeremy—that was some really lovely playing. I look forward to hearing more from you."

I stand up and nod.

"I look forward to that too, Miss Kutter," I say with what I know is too much innuendo, but I can't help myself. Even from here, I can see her cheeks flush, and she quickly busies herself with the papers in front of her.

When I get out into the main hallway Julia and my brother, Brett, are waiting. She's hopping up and down excitedly while he stands back, looking on with amusement.

"Jeremy! That was brilliant! Amazing!" she exclaims, throwing her arms around my neck.

"Whoa! Hold on, let me put my horn down." When I do, she jumps up into my arms and showers my face with kisses. "Okay! Okay!" I laugh, and set her back down on the floor.

Over Julia's shoulder I see Brett. He steps up and slaps my back. "You nailed it, man."

Brett doesn't lie to me, so when he says this, I know he means it.

"Thanks!" I say, putting an arm around Julia's shoulder and picking up my horn again. "I'm starving. How about a burger at the place around the corner?"

I see a flash of disappointment in Julia's eyes. She isn't a fan of Brett's. We haven't really spoken about it, but she becomes noticeably uncomfortable every time he's around. As for his part, my brother couldn't care less either way. He knows better than to get attached to any of the women I bring home because most of them aren't around for very long.

Brett and I weren't always as close as we are now. In fact, we hated one another for years. Or, at least, he hated me. I liked him fine, because he made for such a convenient scapegoat. I'd break, steal, hide, hurt and destroy, then put on the face of an innocent little lamb. No one, including my parents, suspected for even an instant that an average six-year-old could be capable of causing the kind of malicious damage I committed on a daily basis. Of course, I wasn't your average six-year-old, and I watched with delight as he took the blame and the beatings and the punishments. Oh, he'd protest his innocence, until he realized it would get him in worse trouble for 'lying.' After a while, he just kept his mouth shut and took it. Until, one day, he didn't.

"I'm going to tell Mommy that you tried to touch me last night," I said to Brett, never taking my eyes from the television set.

"What?" he asked, looking up from his bowl of cereal at the kitchen table.

"You came into my bedroom last night after everyone was asleep and you touched me on my privates," I said casually, popping an Oreo into my mouth. It was something I'd heard on one of my mother's afternoon talk shows. She had been so scandalized that I couldn't resist.

Brett stared at me incredulously.

"I heard them talking you know," I told him, spraying crumbs out onto my pajama top. "They're going to send you away to a special school for bad boys. You'll only get to come home for Christmas."

It was brilliant. And I'm sure it would have worked too, had something totally unexpected not happened. My usually passive brother got up from the table, stomped over to where I was sitting on the floor and dragged me to the kitchen by my hair. I screamed and fought, but Brett was bigger and stronger. And with our parents out for the morning there was no one to come to my rescue.

"I'm telling Mommy!" I wailed.

"No you're not," Brett assured.

"I will! And you know Daddy will…"

Before I could say another word my brother slammed me down on the hard linoleum floor. I tried to get up but he just kicked me back down. When I tried a second time, I found a size nine sneaker pressed hard against my spindly little arm. As crafty as I was at that age, there was no getting around the fact that Brett had fifty pounds and five inches on me.

"You want me to break it?"

I refused to respond.

"Do you?"

Finally I shook my head and glared up at him with a look that made him recoil. I saw Brett swallow hard, before continuing.

"I have never told Mom and Dad you're a liar, have I?" he asked.

My eyes turned into suspicious little slits. I didn't answer.

"Have I?"

Finally I shook my head.

"So cut it out, or else!"

"Or else what? You think they'll believe you? I'll just cry and Mommy will tell Daddy to send you away," I threw back up to him defiantly.

"Or else I'm going to tell them what really happened to Coco."

I froze. I didn't think anyone knew about what I had done to the neighbor's cat.

"I saw you do it. I know where you buried her. But I didn't say anything, did I?"

How could that be possible? Why would he wait so long to squeal on me when that had been months ago?

"No," I spit at him finally.

"So stop telling them I did stuff that I didn't. I don't care what you do to the kids at school."

"I don't do anything to the kids at school," I insisted stubbornly.

"Will you shut up and listen to me, dummy? I see what you do, and I. Don't. Care. I just want you to leave me alone."

I couldn't believe what I was hearing. A slow smile started to spread across my face as I began to understand what this meant. I wasn't invisible, as I'd always assumed. There was someone who could see who I was and what I was doing, and he didn't care. I could just be myself and he wasn't going to do a damned thing about it.

"You won't tell Mommy and Daddy?" I asked suspiciously.

"Not if you leave me alone," he assured me.

"Okay," I said, my whole demeanor turning amiable in a split second. "Now let me up."

"I will. There's just one more thing."

"What?"

He lifted his foot off my arm and brought it down so hard you could actually hear the bone splinter. I screamed for real this time.

"That's what will happen to you if you ever mess with me again," Brett informed me calmly as he went into the living room and changed the channel, leaving me to writhe on the floor.

And just like that, my brother and I forged a very unique relationship. So unique, that when I left home at eighteen, I followed him to New York City, where he was already a student at McInnes. I was accepted too, and we've been sharing an apartment ever since. It's easy being around him because I don't have to pretend to be anything when I'm alone with Brett. Now, there may come a day when he outlives his usefulness to me, but I'll just burn that bridge when I come to it.

29

It appears to be raining condiments as small packets of ketchup, mustard and mayonnaise fall off the shelf above us. It's the waitress—her foot is knocking against the rickety metal shelving as I fuck her in the restaurant pantry. She's trying hard to be quiet but she's not doing a very good job of it. If this girl still has a job by the end of the night it'll be a miracle. Her black skirt is hiked up around her waist and she's spilling out of the half-open white blouse. I love this shit—a good, hard, anonymous screw in a public place. This one is done as quickly as it started, and she smoothes her skirt down while I pull up my pants from around my ankles.

"You've got something…" she reaches over and plucks some debris from my hair. The wrapper from a straw. Her girly little giggle that irritates me.

The tall, leggy brunette had her eye on me the second we walked in the door. When she handed me the menu, she let her finger brush against my hand. Less than five minutes later we were getting to know each other a little better.

"You go first," she says, buttoning her blouse. "I'll come out of the kitchen with your drinks in a sec. What's your name, by the way?"

"Does it matter?" I ask, as I tuck my shirt back into my slacks.

She blushes crimson at the inference that she'd fuck anyone. "I guess not…" she mutters, as I slip out the door and into the hallway.

When I get back to the booth, there is an uneasy silence between Brett and Julia.

"Sorry," I say, slipping in next to Julia and draping my arm across her shoulders. "I stepped outside to get a little fresh air. I think all the stress is finally catching up with me."

Brett lifts a disbelieving eyebrow. Clearly he has his suspicions about my recent activities—which are confirmed when Katie or Carrie or whatever her name is, comes by with our drinks. She doesn't realize her lipstick is smudged. My brother stifles a snort and pretends to be interested in the menu. Julia notices, too, but she has a very different reaction.

"Karen..." she whispers, leaning across me to put a hand on the girl's wrist.

That's it! Karen.

"You should have a look in the mirror. I think you need to fix your lipstick." Julia's thoughtful discretion and sweet smile make the girl blush all over again. She mutters her thanks and moves away quickly. I see her stop and say something to another server, a guy, who comes to take our food order.

"So what have you two been discussing?" I ask, genuinely curious.

"I was telling Julia that I sat in the balcony for her performance," Brett informs me.

"And how'd my girl do?" I give her a proprietary squeeze that makes her smile. If only she knew what—or rather—who, I'd been doing just a few minutes ago, she wouldn't be so pleased with me.

"She was amazing," he says more to me than to her. "Jeremy, the judges couldn't take their eyes off of her."

"That's great, Jules!" I say with practiced enthusiasm. "And Cal? Did either of you hear him?"

"Yeah, actually, I did," Brett replies as Julia shakes her head no. "I don't know what you said to him back in the warm-up room, but he looked really pissed when he came on stage. I thought he was going to have an aneurysm right there in front of the committee."

I can't hide the smirk that creeps across my face. "And…?" I ask, gesturing for him to tell me more.

"I have to be honest with you, Jeremy. I thought he was going to blow it, but he didn't. If anything, he was more solid than before. It was like he was going to play great just to spite you."

"So what are you saying? Do *you* think he played better than me?"

"Not possible," Julia proclaims.

"I can't tell." Brett shrugs. "The judges definitely liked you better. That much was clear from their body language with you, versus Cal."

Then I remember my earlier conversation with Cal. "Julia, what's going on with the two of you? How come you're so cold with him all of a sudden?" I ask.

"It's nothing," she says, taking a sip from her glass of ice water. "He doesn't like you very much. And now he doesn't like that I'm seeing you."

"Okay. And what was your response to that?"

"I told him to mind his own damn business."

"Good girl, you tell him!" I grin and watch as Brett takes this all in from across the table.

"So, Julia," he says, changing the direction of the conversation. "I noticed Matthew didn't stick around for long after your audition. Where's he off to?"

She clears her throat, obviously reluctant to give my brother too many details about Matthew—*her* friend and *his* archenemy. "He had to get back to the Walton tour for a master class they're doing at the Massachusetts Conservatory tomorrow morning."

Brett nods. He and Matthew Ayers have been rivals since their first day at McInnes. There simply aren't that many paying viola jobs in this town—or anywhere for that matter—and the two of them have been taking the same auditions for years. By all accounts, Matthew just barely beat out Brett for the viola spot in the Walton Quartet. My brother doesn't complain much, but I know it pissed him off.

For her part, Julia comes down squarely on the side of Matthew. And that competition makes it awkward for her to be around Brett, especially now that she and I are together.

"How's that going? Matthew and the Walton Quartet?" he fishes, trying not to sound too interested.

"He's doing great, Brett, thanks for asking," Julia responds with a little too much enthusiasm. "He loves the tour, and they think he's fitting in great."

"Great!" Brett echoes, mimicking her animated tone.

Julia is not amused.

"What about you, Brett?" she asks, with a little more snark than I'm used to hearing from her. "Doesn't seem as if you've gotten anything big in a while. Still filling in on the off-Broadway circuit? Maybe you should cast your net a little wider. I hear the Guam Philharmonic is looking for a new viola player."

He smiles slightly and arches an eyebrow. "Thanks, Julia. I'll be sure to keep that in mind."

"Now, now..." I say, making an effort to appear as if I care enough to try and smooth things over.

I know very well that my brother could cut her off at the knees in a heartbeat—he's holding his tongue on my account.

After a long moment, Julia sighs. "I'm sorry, Brett," she says softly. "I don't mean to be so...nasty. You're Jeremy's brother and I'd like it if we could get along."

Now my brother's other eyebrow goes up. Well, this is an interesting turn of events. I don't think I've ever seen anyone actually apologize to him before.

"Alright, fair enough," he says slowly with a nod.

Obviously, he's not used to it either.

"Great!" I exclaim with faux pleasure. "Because you're the two people I care about most in this world."

The irony of this entire exchange is that it was in this very diner, in this very booth in fact, that Brett first warned me about Julia. I didn't believe him when he told me. How could I? She was so shy and unassuming. Four years of undergrad and one year of master's studies together and I didn't even know her name. I couldn't remember ever having heard her utter a single word. So when Brett pointed to her as the biggest risk to my Kreisler Competition gold medal, I practically laughed at him.

"You cannot *think I should be concerned about the little cellist. What do they call her? The Mouse?"*

"Her name is Julia. Julia James."

"Whatever."

"You asked me what I think. Do you really want to know? I mean honestly?"

I took a deep breath and nodded.

"Have you ever heard her play? I mean outside of the cello section?"

"Actually, I haven't," I had to admit.

"I think it would be a big mistake to underestimate Julia."

"Uh-uh," I shook my head. "No way she could be that good, I would have noticed her by now."

"How do you think she got to be principal cello at one of the top conservatories in the country? Do not count her out," my

brother warned. "I'm not kidding, Jeremy. You'd be a fool to assume she's not a threat."

And there it was, just like that. I have no doubt that as soon as the word 'threat' was out of his mouth Brett regretted saying it. With six letters he had activated my keen instinct for self-preservation.

30

"Morning, Matthew."

Matthew turns around and nearly spits his coffee all over when he sees me standing in his kitchen in nothing but my boxers.

"Aren't you going to offer me a cup?" I ask. "Oh, I'm sorry. Maybe you weren't expecting me to be here, I was Julia's guest last night. Actually, I'm surprised you didn't hear us…"

"Shut. Up." He grits out between clenched teeth. I smile. "Don't you have a home of your own?"

"Aw, Matthew, don't be like that…" My voice drips with insincere disappointment.

"Why don't you find your pants and get the hell out?" he suggests in a deathly quiet tone.

I don't move. He's finally returned from the Walton Quartet's holiday tour, and that means he's going to be around a lot more. I don't like that one bit.

"Seriously, Matthew. We're going to be seeing a lot more of each other, you know? So maybe you should just accept this now instead of dragging it out—"

In an instant, he's in my face, but I don't so much as blink.

"I'm not going to say it again. Get the fuck out of my apartment."

"Ahem." Julia has come out of the bedroom and is standing there, in her robe, watching us. "If I'm not mistaken,

Matthew, it's my apartment, too," she reminds him. "I mean, that's what the rent check is for every month, right?"

I look from her back to him with a smile and one cocked eyebrow. Oh, bad timing for you, Matty boy.

"And you," she turns to me. "This is his home and he's my friend. Please be respectful of that."

I pretend to be chastened.

"Julia, I'm going to rehearsal. I'd appreciate it if we could have a little…privacy this evening," Matthew says, angling himself so he's facing her with his back to me. "I thought I might make us a special dinner."

Julia meets his gaze and holds it. "You know what, Matthew? Why don't you make yourself some dinner? I'll stay at Jeremy's. That should give you plenty of privacy."

I try to keep from snorting with laughter.

He's shaking his head. "That's not what I meant…" he starts to protest.

She holds up a finger and he stops, mid-sentence. "I know exactly what you meant."

He doesn't say another word, just grabs his jacket and walks out the door, letting it slam hard behind him.

"Well, that didn't go especially well, did it?" I chuckle.

She walks toward me, wagging that same finger. But her irritation has passed and the scowl on her face has been replaced with a smile.

"Does this mean you've given more thought to us moving in together?" I ask hopefully.

She shrugs a little and smiles a little more. "Maybe…"

"I've got to warn you," I say, looking around the apartment, "my place is a little less impressive than this. I'm not sure how comfortable you'll be there."

Julia wraps her arms around my waist and presses the side of her face to my chest. "I don't mind. Is that okay, though? Will Brett have an issue with me being there?"

"Brett doesn't care. It won't be the first time he's had to share the bathroom with someone I'm sleeping with. One morning he walked in on me in the shower with Deb Kaufman."

"Wait, wait, wait…do you mean *Doctor* Kaufman? The Early Music History professor?" She's tilting her head up, trying to gauge whether or not I'm kidding.

I'm not.

"Let's not worry about her or Matthew right now, okay? I'm much more interested in you."

She opens her mouth to say something but I lean over to nibble her earlobe as I reach down and find the sash on her robe. With one tug I pull it open and it slips to the floor into a puddle of satin.

"I'll bet the sheets are still warm…" I whisper, scooping her up like a newlywed about to be carried across the threshold. Julia throws her head back and squeals.

The apartment that Brett and I share is a narrow two-bedroom housed over a pizza parlor in one of Brooklyn's less gentrified neighborhoods. It always smells of garlic, and when the locals gather on the street corner on warm summer nights, it can be hard to get an hour's sleep. It's hardly an apartment at the Strathmore, but it'll do for now.

"How long is she going to stay here?" Brett asks, glancing down the hall toward my bedroom, where Julia is clearing a drawer and some closet space for herself.

"Not sure. Why, is she in your way?"

"Nope. Just wondering. They're usually here for a night or two at most."

"She'll be here for as long as it takes," I reply quietly, taking another swig from the bottle.

Brett nods his understanding, and we continue watching television in silence. It's nine o'clock when she walks into my living room, setting her cello case on the floor so she can cram assorted odds and ends into her purse.

"Where are you going?" I ask from the couch, where Brett and I are watching *The Godfather* for about the fiftieth time.

"I'm going to head up to McInnes. I've got a lot of work to do," she says.

"Oh," I say, sounding very disappointed. "I was just thinking about ordering some Chinese. And I'd hoped you would join us for the movie..."

She gives me a sad smile that says 'no' before her words do. "Jeremy, that is so tempting...but I can't. I've already missed too much practice time, and Dr. Sam is starting to notice. He'll have my head if I don't work through some of those tricky passages that have been tripping me up."

I get up and walk to her, putting my arms around her waist and pulling her close to me. "Jules, I totally get that, but you have to understand that you're not at the Strathmore anymore. This isn't the safest neighborhood, and I'm really not comfortable with you walking to the train station by yourself and then standing on a deserted platform with your cello."

"I love that you worry about me, but this seems like a perfectly safe neighborhood," she says, giving me an extra hard squeeze. "I'll be fine!"

I give her my best look of stern concern. "Just because it looks safe, doesn't mean it is, Jules. I've lived her a long time.

There have been two rapes, three muggings and a shooting in this neighborhood, and that's just in the last six months. I've never worried too much about it, because Brett and I can both take care of ourselves. But you…"

I leave the sentence hanging out there, and watch as a cloud of concern rolls across her face.

"Then what do you suggest?" She's looking up at me with raised eyebrows. "I mean, I can't *not* practice."

I shrug. "I'll go with you…when I can. And sometimes Brett has rehearsal up that way."

"I have a lesson tomorrow. Can one of you go with me now?" she asks.

"Oh, Julia, any night but tonight… *The Godfather* trilogy is on!"

"But, you guys can stream that any time you want! Do you really have to watch it now?"

I shake my head. "No, no, no. That would be sacrilege, Jules! It's a family tradition. Our folks are probably home watching it now, too."

She rolls her eyes at me. "Jeremy, I have a feeling that if I wait for you to go to McInnes with me, I'll never get to practice."

I separate from her and hold up my palms to the ceiling. "Jules, I don't know what to tell you. Like I said, this isn't a great neighborhood, and I'm only thinking about your safety. I couldn't sleep knowing you were out there in the middle of the night. Of course, if you'd rather go back to your apartment in Midtown, then you can be in the practice rooms at all hours of the day and night. Maybe that's what you should do…"

"No!" she says a little too quickly and emphatically. "No, I want to be here, close to you. I can make it work…I don't suppose I could practice here?" she asks hopefully.

I shake my head. "Nope, sorry. The landlord owns the restaurant downstairs, and he doesn't like any noise from up here. Brett tried it a couple of times and we got a nasty note."

"Well, I guess it can wait until the morning, I'll just go in early, before rehearsal."

"Good idea!" I say, and watch as she unpacks her things and disappears down the hall.

Brett cocks his head and looks at me. "Since when does Sal have a problem with us playing up here?" he asks quietly enough so she won't hear. "And, I guess it's time to move, sounds like the neighborhood's gone to shit!" he stifles a laugh. "Jesus, you make it sound like we live in a war zone!"

I shrug sheepishly and smile. "It was all I could think of. Scared her though, didn't it?"

"Are you serious? You even had me scared!" he laughs. "I'm thinking we should be looking for an apartment at the Strathmore ourselves!"

"Maybe after I win that prize money." I smile.

"Yeah, well, I'm not holding my breath," he replies, shaking his head.

"You know, I haven't seen that little flutist of yours in a while…the one with the nice ass. What's her name? Jennifer? Janine?"

"Jessica," he corrects me, knowing full well that I know full well what her name is.

"That's the one. And, man, she's got some rack too! Where've you been keeping her?" I ask, watching as my brother shifts ever so slightly on the couch. Someone's uncomfortable with this conversation.

"Not here," he mumbles.

"What's that? I couldn't hear you, Brett," I say with an innocent smile.

"We've been staying over at her place," he tells me coolly, all traces of amusement done from his tone now.

"Have you?"

"Jeremy, this is the first night I've been home all week," he says incredulously.

"Huh, I hadn't noticed. Well, I don't see what the problem is…you used to bring the other one here all the time…Wendy."

"Wanda," he corrects me, a little too sharply.

Sore subject, party of one!

"Right, right. Wanda. Whatever happened to her?" I ask nonchalantly.

Brett glares at me. I love this game. Push, push, push those buttons and watch his blood pressure rise.

"You mean after I came home and found her screwing you?" he asks in an equally casual manner. "I'm not sure. We just kind of fell out of touch after that."

And to think, the stupid bitch thought it was *her* who I wanted to fuck that night! Brett's no dummy, but he does forget the cardinal rule sometimes. What's mine is mine, and what's *his* is mine…if I want it. It's the rule he's always lived by to keep the peace between us. I didn't particularly want Wanda—I just thought my brother needed a little reminder.

"Too bad, that girl gives great head," I say regretfully. "But, I guess you already knew that." There's the slightest hint of a smile playing on my lips. "Now, by the sound of your sleepovers with Jessica, I'd say that girl has some skills, too…"

"Fuck you, Jeremy," he spits before I can even finish my sentence. Then, he's up and headed down the hall, slamming the door loud enough that Julia comes out to see what happened.

"Everything okay out here?" she asks, her face scrunched up with concern.

"Yeah, we're good, Jules. Brett just gets choked up every time he sees the part where Sonny gets ambushed at the toll booth." I pat the seat next to me. "Come and watch with me," I say, holding up an arm for her.

"I hadn't didn't realize Brett's so sensitive," she replies as she snuggles into me.

"Oh, he'll get over it," I mutter. "He always does."

31

Julia is sound asleep when I get up for a glass of water and silently snatch her cell phone from the nightstand. I slip out of my bedroom and into the kitchen. When I turn it on, its bright white light displaces the dark, and I have to blink until my eyes adjust. A few swipes and pokes later, I find several text messages from Matthew that she's neglected to tell me about.

I miss you. Please come home.

You'll be home for Christmas, won't you? I miss you.

Can we talk? Please call me.

Cal says he hasn't seen you in the practice rooms for a while. Are you okay?

I'll be at the Kreisler finalists' announcement because I know they're going to call your name!

No responses from Julia to any of these, and further inspection shows me that she doesn't return his calls either. Good for her. Good for me. If she doesn't place in the final round, then my job is done and I can concentrate on myself. But, if it turns out that we're up against each other, well, that's when the big guns come out.

For now, I'll just do what I can to keep her more attached to me, and less attached to Matthew, and to her cello, for that matter. I glance at the time on the microwave. It's a quarter till four. We have orchestra rehearsal at nine, and I know she set her alarm for five, so she could be up at McInnes by six. With a single swipe, I ensure that little alarm will never see the light of day. I return the phone to its place and climb back into bed, careful not to wake my sleeping beauty.

By eight-fifteen, she's neither sleeping nor beautiful as she wakes with a start and proceeds to fly around the apartment in a panic. She doesn't live around the corner from the conservatory anymore, so last minute isn't an option.

"I don't understand!" she whines as she rummages through my closet, looking for the clothes she's hung in there. "How come my alarm didn't go off? That's never happened before!"

I shrug as I sit on the corner of the bed, fully dressed and ready to go, sipping a cup of coffee.

"And why didn't you wake me?" she asks, stopping to turn and shoot me a glare.

"Jules, how was I supposed to know? When I got up, you were still in bed, so I figured you'd decided to sleep in this morning. It wasn't until it got later that I realized something might be wrong."

"Oh, God, I am so screwed," she is mumbling from inside the closet.

I smile a little into my coffee cup.

"Okay, well, I'm going to get going," I say, standing up.

Julia stops what she's doing and pulls out of the closet to stare at me, incredulously. "What? You're going to go without me?"

“Well, there’s no sense in both of us being late, right? And besides, how would it look if we both came in late. Together.”

“Like we spent the night together. Like we’re dating, Jeremy. That’s what we’re doing isn’t it? Or are you having second thoughts already?”

“No, Jules, no second thoughts I’m just thinking that there’s no point in both of us getting into trouble…”

“Fine, you go on ahead,” she says in her best ‘don’t you dare leave me here’ tone. But I pretend to be just another oblivious guy.

“Alright, then. See you there,” I say, ignoring her anger and frustration as I walk out the door.

When she finally does make it to rehearsal, Maestro Hagen is in a foul mood. He has one of the flute players on the verge of tears just as Julia appears and slips silently into her chair. Unfortunately for her, she is not invisible. Hagen spots her and stops, mid-sentence, to level his steeliest stare on her.

“Miss James,” he says. “You are aware that rehearsal started fifteen minutes ago, no?”

“Yes, Maestro,” she whispers, so quietly that I don’t think even Mila can hear her.

“What was that, Miss James? I cannot hear you. Speak up!” he demands, his own volume rising considerably.

With her hair high on her head in a bun, Julia’s neck is bare. Even from back here I can see the crimson tide that’s creeping steadily up toward her face.

“Mouse!” comes a catcall from somewhere in the violin section. The Maestro doesn’t take notice as he waits for Julia’s response.

“Yes, Maestro,” she says, louder this time.

“Miss James, do you believe that, as a Kreisler competitor, you no longer have to follow the same rules as everyone else?” he asks her in his German accent.

“No, Maestro,” she says, shaking her head.

“I’m not so sure about that, Miss James. This is incredibly rude and unprofessional behavior. Please stand and apologize to your colleagues,” he orders.

Julia sets her cello down on its side on the floor and stands up. She is visibly trembling, and there is a quaver to her voice when she speaks.

“I—I apologize for being late and disrupting the rehearsal. It won’t happen again,” she says, clearly close to tears.

The Maestro gives her a ‘humph!’ and continues to glare, still not satisfied. “Miss James, I believe you should pack your cello and go. I do not wish to see your face again today. And next time you are late, I will not wish to see your face again ever. Do you understand?”

She nods silently, presumably because she’s unable to speak at this point. I watch as she snatches her music off the stand and tucks it under her arm, grabbing the cello and bow with her hands. She slips off the stage and into the wings as quickly and quietly as she entered.

“Miss Strassman, today you are principal cello!” Hagen declares. But Mila isn’t paying attention—she’s looking back over her shoulder to where Julia has just exited. “Miss Strassman!” he repeats, with an edge, and she turns around quickly.

"Yes, Maestro. I'm ready," she says in a voice that lacks the confidence to back up that statement.

From next to me, I sense the eyes of Cal Burridge.

"What the fuck are you looking at?" I ask him.

"I'm pretty sure I'm looking at the reason Julia just got her ass handed to her," he replies flatly.

I snort. "Seriously, Cal? Is that the best you can do? Don't be such a pussy. The best man won, and it's my bed Julia is sleeping in tonight. I suggest you get used to disappointment, man, because you're looking at the winner of the horn division, too."

Cal is staring at me with such loathing, like he'd douse me with gas and set me on fire right now, if he thought he could get away with it. I just smile sheepishly and shrug.

"You know, she's a natural redhead, too," I say, matter-of-factly. "Yeah, I had to see it to believe it. So many girls get their color out of a bottle these days..."

"Horn section!" the Maestro yells at us. "Is there a problem back there now, too?" he demands.

We both look at him and shake our heads.

"No, Maestro," we say in unison.

32

"Shit!" Brett says, leaning toward me across the table. "He threw her out of the rehearsal? I don't think I've ever seen him do that. Hell, he didn't even kick out the trombone section after he threw his toupee at them!"

As a recent McInnes grad himself, Brett knows Maestro Hagen very well.

"How upset is she?" he asks.

I shrug and squirt a line of ketchup on my burger. "Well, she was crying when she left. After that, I don't know."

"You didn't bother to check on her?" he asks, even though he already knows the answer.

"No. Why do you think I texted you to have lunch? I want to be MIA when she has to face Sam Michaels in her lesson today."

"Jeez, you are really committed to this thing, aren't you?"

"I have to be, Brett. Julia's a lot tougher than I thought."

"The mother, that was no accident, was it?" He's shaking his fork at me. "That was all you, right?"

I smile proudly. Brett can spot my handiwork a mile away. "Fuck, yeah!" I say, brandishing one of my French fries.

Brett is shaking his head, in awe. "Shit. That couldn't have been easy to arrange."

"God, no. I can't tell you how much time I spent online, researching birth records, marriage certificates, business licenses. And then all the trips to Montauk. I had to be sure.

And then, I had to decide the best way to bring mother and daughter together again."

"Jeremy, you never cease to amaze me with the lengths you'll go to get what you want. Did you track down the father, too?"

"Yeah. He wasn't much help, though. He's buried out at Pinelawn Cemetery. Killed himself a few years back."

Brett leans forward. "Really? Jesus Christ, that is so fucked up! Does she know?" I shake my head. "Are you going to tell her?"

I shrug. "I'm not sure yet. He did a real number on her. You should see the burns on her arm, even I was impressed."

We chew in companionable silence for a few moments.

"And what are you planning to do about the more…immediate problem?" he asks me.

"What, you mean Cal?" My brother nods. "Yeah, well, I've got a few ideas," I say, downplaying the situation.

"Shit, Jeremy. All this for a gold medal? It seems like an awful lot of work."

That's my brother, shortsighted, as usual. He never has his eye on the long game, and, one of these days, that's going to cost him.

"Dude, it's what comes with the gold medal that really matters—like the money, the world concert tour, and the recording contract," I explain. "Not to mention the career opportunities. Every Kreisler gold winner has gone on to either big solo or orchestral careers. Man, if I win this thing, I can have my pick of gigs anywhere in the country. Hell, around the world!" I stop to take a swig of my own beer. "I can tell you one thing for sure, I'm not going to let Cal Burridge steal this thing out from under my nose."

"Well, I'm curious to see how this one plays out, Jeremy," Brett says. "I guess we'll know more tomorrow when they announce the finalists."

"No guesswork about it, Brett."

"Jeremy, how can you be so calm?" Julia asks from the seat beside me.

"What have I got to be nervous about?" I chuckle.

She shakes her head and punches me playfully. "God, I wish I had just a little of your self-confidence. Life must be so much easier."

"You have no idea," I say with a grin.

"Ugh. It's like a sauna in here." I pull on the collar of my shirt, trying to loosen it a little "There must be close to a thousand people in this hall."

"You're probably right," she agrees, craning her neck to look around us. "There are a hundred of us semi-finalists in this section alone. Then there are the families, the Kreisler judges and staff, music teachers… And every one of them hoping to hear a familiar name called."

"Well, most of them are going to be disappointed," I observe. "Four names out of a hundred isn't great odds for anyone."

"Except you, maybe," she says, poking me in the ribs. "You have *so* got this. Everyone's been saying you're the horn favorite by far."

"That's the plan…" I mumble. "Have you seen Matthew?"

She shakes her head. But I know he's here, somewhere. He can't stay away from Julia, and she hasn't been home in nearly a week. It must be making him crazy.

When the house lights start to dim, a hush falls over the crowd. If you didn't know any better, you'd think you were waiting for the conductor to come out on stage and lead an orchestra. Only this time, there is no orchestra. And it isn't a conductor who enters from stage left, but a tall, fifty-something-year-old man who strides out.

He's impeccably dressed and groomed. Everything about him screams 'Old Money.' I recognize him as Lester Morgan, a regular in the society pages, one of the biggest supporters of the arts in New York City, and Director of the Kreisler International Music Competition. Lester. Of course his name is Lester. Christ, all that money and you can't buy yourself a better name? Lester's shoes, which are worth more money than most musicians earn in a year, do not make so much as a click as the hand-tooled Italian leather soles glide across the stage floor. He stands easily in front of the mic, looking from one side of the audience to the other and then up to the balcony, smiling broadly as he does.

"Good evening," he says in a soft, genteel voice. There is a collective mumbling of 'good evening' back at him. "My name is Lester Morgan. For the last decade it has been my honor and my privilege to stand on this stage and announce the four brilliant young musicians who will perform head-to-head, shoulder-to-shoulder in the quest for classical music's highest honor."

Lester looks down for a second, clears his throat and looks up. "I won't lie to you. I'd give my right arm to be able to do what these men and women do every day. They give life to all of the musical geniuses who have walked this earth before us—the Bachs and the Prokofievs, the Coplands and the

Beethovens. In the hands of these amazing young people, the life's work of these composers is reborn every day. And they do it with an ease and effortlessness that belies the years of sacrifice and dedication needed to perform at this level."

He pulls a small envelope from his coat pocket and pulls out a slip of paper. He holds it up for us to see while he speaks. These dilettantes and their ridiculous appetite for drama. Just make the Goddamn announcement already.

"And now, I'd like to introduce you to this year's Kreisler International Music Competition finalists. If I call your name, please join me on stage."

Next to me, Julia grabs my hand and squeezes anxiously.

Lester smiles as he looks at the list. "In the piano division, Lucy Kim from the International Conservatory in China."

No surprise there, the girl is flawless. She's the hands-down favorite for the next Tchaikovsky competition, too. But a pianist has won the last three Kreisler Competitions and rumor has it they don't plan on choosing a pianist this year, no matter how good she happens to be. Sorry, Lucy. Better luck next time. The tiny girl, who looks like she's about twelve, stands to acknowledge the applause before climbing the steps onto the stairs. Lester shakes her hand.

"Next, in the violin division, our finalist is...Mikhail Fedoseyev of the Moscow Academy of Music."

Now that one is a surprise. He's quite good, but he's got a nasty disposition. Idiot can't hold his temper long enough to win anything. Usually by this point in a competition, he's already had a meltdown that's gotten him booted. Right now, he's practically sneering as he stomps heavily to Lester and offers him a hammy hand.

"Okay. Now for our two rotating divisions," the older man says, glancing down again at the card. "Please join me in congratulating our cello finalist..." He pauses and Julia grips my hand like a vice. She's pretty strong, considering her size. "Miss Julia James of the McInnes Conservatory here in New York City."

The applause is huge, and Lester peers down at our section, waiting for someone to standup and claim the honor. Julia doesn't move.

"Julia, stand up," I whisper loudly. "Stand up!"

I let go of her hand and give her a push forward. She stands up, clearly stunned, and gives a small smile to the audience around us. I can actually see her trembling as she takes the stage next to the other two. The concert hall is deathly silent now as everyone waits for the last name to be announced. I lean forward in my chair a little and straighten my tie.

"Our final division is the French horn," Lester continues, "and I understand this was an incredibly close call. The judges spent hours deliberating over the winner before finally coming to the conclusion that the fourth and final Kreisler competitor will be…" I take a deep breath. Julia is smiling at me from the stage, just waiting for them to say it. "Calvin Burridge, also of the McInnes Conservatory!"

I have to physically stop myself from getting to my feet. Did I just hear that right? Did he just say *Cal* is the winner? He must have, because from behind me, there's a disturbance, and I look back to see Cal making his way out of the row. As he passes my chair, he puts a hand on my shoulder and gives it a squeeze. I suck in my breath. On stage, Julia looks stricken. Cal shakes Lester's hand and offers his ridiculously goofy smile to the applauding audience. He looks down and scans the rows of seats until his eyes settle on mine. And then he winks.

Wait. What? What the hell just happened?

I've been blindsided, that's what happened. And I don't do blindsided.

33

I've managed to make myself scarce for a few days, not wanting to hear any bullshit from Cal. Unfortunately, there's no avoiding him tonight at our year end concert—a conservatory tradition that draws a huge audience. While the other college orchestras around town are doing the usual 'holiday pops' themed concerts—complete with schmaltzy, sentimental Jingle Bells sing-a-longs—we've got a whole different kind of schmaltz happening at McInnes. Each year they put together an impressive program of compositions. Audiences have been known to demand multiple encores at the end.

When Julia finally emerges from our tiny bathroom, she's wearing the traditional all-black uniform of an orchestral musician—long black skirt and silk blouse. Black heels give her a bit more height than I'm used to seeing. She's actually managed to wrestle all of her hair into submission with a bun at the nape of her neck.

"Is this okay?" she asks, giving a little twirl so that her skirt flares out around her.

"Here," I say, reaching around to fix the collar of her blouse. I step back and look at her, head to toe and back again. "Hmm."

I can see the self-consciousness as it creeps up Julia's entire body. She slouches a little, runs her fingers through her hair and looks down at her feet, as if to make sure her shoes aren't scuffed.

"What?" she asks nervously. "What's wrong?"

"Isn't there anything you can do about your nose? You know, with makeup or something? I thought you girls could camouflage anything with that stuff you plaster on your face."

She puts a hand to her face and instinctively covers the offending feature. "What's wrong with my nose?" she asks from behind her five-fingered shield.

I shake my head. "You know what, don't worry about it," I say with a pitying smile. "Nothing you can do about it now anyway."

She's still standing there in a daze when I get up and grab my horn case from the hallway.

"Coming?" I ask over my shoulder.

She looks up. "Oh. Yes, sorry," she says, hurrying to sling the cello case over her shoulder.

She clops down the stairs behind me, trying to keep up. Julia hasn't had to carry her own case for a while now, and I see she's struggling with the weight of it in combination with her shoes and the stairs. No elevator here, baby. And certainly no doorman to hold that heavy door open for you. I've already got a cab when she finally pushes out of the building and steps onto the sidewalk.

"Come on, slow poke!" I tease.

She gives me a half-amused, half-irritated look. "You could help me, you know," she calls back to me.

I could. But what fun would that be?

"Nah, you seem to be doing fine all on your own."

34

"Oh, my God, oh, my God, oh, my God! Julia! You made it!"

I think that Mila Strassman communicates on the same frequency as the dolphins. Her voice is shrill enough to shatter glass, and I watch Julia actually cringe as her stand partner comes running up to us back stage.

"I'm so happy for you! Who'd have thought it? Who'd have imagined it'd be you? I can't believe it! Can you believe it? I mean this is so crazy!"

Julia levels an irritated glance at her, but Mila is, as always, oblivious.

"Thanks for the vote of confidence," Julia says with a bit of an edge.

Somebody's a little grumpy this evening.

"Oh, no! I'm sorry, but you know what I mean! I just think it's so fabulous that it's not just one, but two musicians from McInnes in the final round! That's like half the finalists! I just know that you and Cal are gonna nail it…"

Her voice trails off and I catch her darting a glance my way. Motor Mouth Mila realizes that it's me she's offended now. I think that bothers her more than the prospect of hurting Julia's feelings. She's just another little tart who wants to bang me. I'd do it too, if I could gag her first. I mean, she never shuts up. Never.

"Jeremy, I'm sorry. Jeez! I keep sticking my foot in my mouth. I really need to talk less, you know? That's what my mom tells me all the time, anyway. Okay, well, I'm going to go warm-up on stage. I'll see you in a few minutes, Julia. Sorry again, Jeremy. It definitely should have been you. Too bad about that woman."

"What woman?" Julia asks before I have a chance to.

Mila claps a hand over her mouth. "Oh! I wasn't supposed to say anything!"

She looks from me to Julia and back to me again.

"Not supposed to say anything about what?" I demand in a loud hiss that stops her cold.

She's flustered. "Uh...well... I—I heard that the committee was a split between you and Cal and they were deadlocked half the night. Finally, it came down to the one woman to make the decision."

Why am I just hearing about this now? And why am I hearing about it from this crazy chick? I take a step closer to her and she instinctively steps back, her widening eyes locked on mine.

"Who told you that?"

She shakes her head. "I... I can't say... I shouldn't have mentioned it..."

"Who?" I demand.

She squirms. "Umm... really, I don't..."

"Mila, was it a professor?" Julia asks as she puts her hand on my forearm and gently guides me back a step.

She's right, I'm scaring the little blabbermouth.

"No. I'm really sorry," she says imploringly to Julia. "I wasn't supposed to tell anyone that. I wasn't supposed to say..."

Julia smiles at her comfortingly. "Mila, Jeremy isn't going to say anything to anybody. He just wants to know," she says, looking back at me over her shoulder. "Isn't that right, Jeremy?"

I take a deep breath and put a forced smile on my face. "That's right, Mila. I'd just like to know. You'd want to know if it were you, right?"

She seems to relax a little. "Yeah. I would," she nods.

We're waiting for her to say something else, but she doesn't. I raise my eyebrows expectantly. She gets the idea.

"Um, yeah, so I know one of the pages for the competition, right? And it was his job to collect the final decision from the horn committee and bring it back to the office in this sealed folder thingy. It's all very official the way they do it, you know?"

I feel one of Mila's epic digressions coming on here.

"I mean, did you know that there is one person whose only job is to open the sealed results and write each of the winner's names on one of those tiny slips of paper? You know, the paper in the little envelope that that guy Lester has in his pocket on stage?"

"Mila, please just get to the point," Julia says before I can interrupt with something a little less civil.

"Oh, yeah. Sorry," Mila says, sounding a little flustered. "Uh, anyway, so he says he waited for almost two hours—that's my friend the page, not the person who writes the names. Anyway, he told me he could hear them arguing. Finally it came down to this lady. She said she was voting for Cal. They argued some more but she wouldn't change her mind."

I'll be damned. It was that bitch Louise Kutter. I should've known.

"I'm really sorry, Jeremy…" Mila says.

"Why don't you take your mediocre ass over to the cello section and keep your mouth shut for a change?" I hiss so softly that only the three of us can hear.

"Jeremy!" Julia exclaims in an equally quiet voice.

Mila's chin starts to quiver, and tears spill from her eyes and down her cheeks. For once, she has nothing to say. I stand aside and hold my hand out in the direction of the stage in an "after you" gesture. It's her cue to get the hell out of my sight. She takes it.

When I turn around Julia is glaring at me. "Jeremy Corrigan! How could you do that?"

"Do what?" I ask defensively.

"You're not a child, Jeremy. You can't just say whatever you want. You have to filter sometimes."

"Why would I do that?"

"Because you can't just go around saying things like that to people. She didn't do anything to you."

I roll my eyes at her. It's so pathetic, this need to worry about hurting other people's feelings. "Don't be so fucking naive, Julia." I walk away from her out onto the stage.

When I saunter back to the horn section, there are a few other musicians gathered around Cal congratulating him. They scatter awkwardly when they spot me approaching. I'm playing the principal horn part on this concert and he's my assistant. I take my seat ahead of him, waiting for a snide remark about the competition, but there isn't one. For now, he seems content to tune up quietly and run a few passages under his fingers. The other three players in our section make a point of not looking our way. They're probably afraid something ugly is going to happen between us up at the head of the section. They don't know the half of it.

"Hello! Hello!" Maestro Hagen dashes out to his podium from back stage. He looks like a chubby little penguin in his tuxedo. The toupee appears to be anchored tightly to his head. Hair glue, perhaps? Thumbtacks? Who the hell knows what the batty old coot does. At any rate, he's been in a much better mood for the last week, much to Julia's relief, I'm sure.

"Well," he begins, looking around the orchestra, "we're running a bit short on time this evening. They will open the doors in about fifteen minutes and it is a full house. Let me just take a couple of minutes to go over a few things. First, please watch the tempo on the Hebrides overture. Bassoons, you tend to rush us a little bit so please keep an eye on me. The Tchaikovsky is going to require every bit of stamina every one of us has. So please, pace yourselves accordingly! That goes for the brass in particular. Jeremy, let Cal do some of the heavy lifting so you can be fresh for the solos. Finally, I'd just like to take a moment to acknowledge our Kreisler finalists. I could not be more proud to have Cal and Julia representing us."

Applause and hoots from the orchestra. Then the Maestro looks back at me. "And Jeremy, while I'm sorry you are not among them, we are all aware of what a brilliant horn player you are. Your success will most certainly not be defined by any competition."

There's some scattered applause for me as I give him a forced smile and nod.

"Please do not forget that I will be offering a few comments to the audience before the Tchaikovsky. Alright then. Backstage with you!"

The little penguin-man shoos us off the stage so they can let the audience take their seats. I see Julia in a corner putting rosin on her bow. She's doing her best to disappear. I must have really upset her earlier when I snapped at her. Better do some damage control. She has her back to me, and doesn't notice my arrival.

"I'm sorry," I say contritely as I wrap my arms around her from behind. I push my nose into her hair and take a deep breath. She smells good.

Julia leans back against me. "No, I'm sorry. You're a grown man. It's not my job to tell you how to act. It's just that

Mila...well, she's a little clueless. She doesn't mean any harm. Please don't be angry with her. She just thinks you're the hottest thing on two legs, and it would break her heart if she thought you didn't like her."

I don't like her, but I do like that Julia has come to her senses and backed down. "You're right," I say in a simulation of sincerity. "I'll apologize to her later. I was just upset about the Louise Kutter thing."

She turns around to face me. "Louise Kutter? How do you know it was her?"

"I just know."

In fact, there's no doubt in my mind.

"Oh. I'm sorry, Jeremy," Julia says, reaching up to touch the side of my face. "Are you going to say something to her?"

I'm going to do more than that.

"Nah. I'll let it go. She has a right to her own opinion."

The noise from out in the audience is getting louder as patrons find their way to their seats.

"Please take the stage, everyone! Tuning in five minutes!" the stage manager calls out.

Julia stands on her tippy toes and kisses my cheek. "You go out there and show them what a mistake it was not to pick you," she says firmly.

I have to smile. Sometimes Julia comes out with exactly the thing I want to hear. This is what I've tried to explain to Brett when he wonders why I haven't dumped her yet. Not only is she a good lay, but she really believes I'm as great as I know I am. Why not keep her around a little bit longer?

"Thanks for the vote of confidence," I say. "How about we grab a nightcap after the concert?"

"Oh, I was planning on sticking around to get an hour or two of practicing in after the concert tonight..."

"Hey, didn't you say Matthew is out of town?"

"Yes, he's in DC for the White House Christmas party tomorrow…"

When Matty is away, The Mouse will play…

"Perfect! Let's go to your place then."

She looks skeptical. "Jeremy, I really need to put in some more time on my recital music."

I pretend I haven't heard her, and drop my voice so only she can hear. "What do you say we spend tonight in that big old bed of yours? Take advantage of a little privacy, hmmm?"

The pink rises to her cheeks at the suggestion behind my suggestion. She nods shyly.

"Good. Now get out there and tell Mila to stop crying already. I'm not mad."

Julia gives me one of her impulsive, hard hugs where she throws herself against me. She may be small but this girl has a way of knocking you off your feet if you're not careful, good thing I'm careful.

35

The applause dies out as Maestro Hagen takes the stage and walks to a microphone that has been placed in front of his podium. He addresses the audience.

"Tchaikovsky described the opening of his fourth symphony as: *'that fateful force which prevents the impulse to happiness from attaining its goal, which jealously ensures that peace and happiness shall not be complete and unclouded.'*"

Hagen speaks the quote and pauses to let it resonate.

"As you hear the brilliant brass fanfare, listen for the dark undertone and remember the composer's words: *'that fateful force which prevents the impulse to happiness from attaining its goal.'*"

With that, the penguin hops up onto his podium to face us, his hair flopping ever so slightly. Maybe it's not anchored as well as I first thought. He raises his baton and, for one brief moment, time stands still. One hundred pairs of eyes are glued to him, one hundred people hold their breath in anticipation of what is to come next. The maestro gives us a smile and a wink before dropping his arm into the powerful swooping downbeat that sets the tone for the entire symphony.

The horns are in motion, starting the fanfare alongside the bassoons. In an instant, the trumpets are there, too. Together we create a splintering wall of sound. But Hagen was right. This is no light little regal fanfare. It is a proclamation of the inevitable darkness that eventually envelops us all. You'd think there'd be no place to go after such a powerful opening.

Ironically, the movement grows even more intense as the theme is deconstructed. It breaks down and spreads across the orchestra, infiltrating every voice of every section. Yes, it is the same theme as in those stirring opening notes, but now bits and pieces of it surface and unfurl in melodic fronds.

The second movement is as powerful in its understatement as the first movement is in its grandiosity. It is ushered in by a single oboe, a nostalgic voice of pining for days long gone. From there, the symphony dovetails into a coy scherzo of plucked strings, until finally the fourth movement washes over us in a wave of triumph, punctuated by the fateful theme that started it all.

Maestro Hagen doesn't even conduct the last several frantic measures. He extends his baton outward in front of him, the way a sorcerer might aim his magic wand. He holds it there, pointed at us, beckoning, challenging us to play to a speed and intensity which even he cannot direct, until the last roll of the timpani and ring of the brass die away into the rapt audience.

It's as if they are paralyzed for a split second, but then the spell is broken and a sea of people, row after row, are on their feet. They applaud and cheer, hoot and whistle. Hagan points to the horn section. My section. We stand and I bask in the swell of applause that greets me. It's a good night. Five curtain calls and three encores later, I find Julia backstage, waiting by my horn case.

"Jeremy, that was amazing!" she says. "The horns were brilliant, Jeremy! You were *unbelievable!*"

"Thanks, Jules," I say, starting to pack up. She just stands there watching me, a strange expression on her face. "What?"

She smiles.

"What?" I ask, with just a hint of irritation.

The color is creeping up again, from under her collar, up her neck and to her cheeks. She drops her voice. "It's just…you're so good, at everything—and so sexy I can't stand it," she says in a low voice that gets my attention. "You're right. I'd rather be with you tonight than practice. I can't think of anything but going home and getting into bed with you."

I arch an eyebrow at her.

"Oh, yeah?"

She nods.

I smile.

The good night isn't over yet. "Come on," I say.

"Where?"

I give her a lascivious smile and she follows me out of the concert hall stage door and through the intricate series of corridors that brings you back into the main part of McInnes. Just as I suspected, the practice rooms are deserted at this hour, especially just after the last concert of the semester. I pull Julia along behind me and into the room at the end of the hallway.

Once we're inside, she reaches for the light switch but I put a hand over hers and we stay mired in the pitch black of the tiny space. I have a vague idea of where the piano is, and the music stand and chairs, so I drop my horn and aim for a clear patch of sound-insulated wall paneling to the left of the door. Julia is giggling a little.

I pull her into a tight embrace and lean down to kiss her. Her tongue meets mine hungrily and she's making soft little happy noises. I drop my hands from her without losing contact with her lips. I'm not sure if she's even aware that I've loosened my belt and dropped my tux trousers to my ankles along with my boxers. I'm good and hard already.

I separate from her just enough to pick her up, put her back against the wall and step into her, so she has to wrap her legs around me to secure herself. When I reach down to pull her panties aside, they are soaked. I run a finger up and down her length and she lets out a garbled cry when I find her clit. I nudge it from side to side. Her legs are locked around my back now and she's holding on for dear life.

"Uh..." she moans every time I make contact.

When I start to work it with my thumb she practically screams. She's ready and so am I. I position my cock at her sopping entrance and slam into her with a force that pushes her hard against the wall.

"Oh… Oh, God…Jeremy, you make me so wet…"

I know I make her wet, but the fact that she knows it is more exciting to me than the actual fact of it. Now, I push her hard against the wall, pulling back and slamming into her again and again until it is clear she's close. I pull out and wait several delicious seconds, running the head of my cock up and down, getting her more and more excited.

"Please…" she begs. "Please, Jeremy, now…"

I oblige with one final stroke that brings her to a frenzied climax.

She's loud. And I like that, too. I enjoy that fact that I can make her come, or not, whenever I want to. I catch up to her with a few quick strokes that send palpable shivers of sensitivity through her body as I come. She clings to me, her head on my shoulder, her arms wrapped around my back.

"No one…" she whispers into the darkness. "No one makes me feel the way you do."

That's exactly what I'm counting on.

36

"Jeremy, I'm telling you, I don't cook," Julia repeats for the third time, as I look through the kitchen cabinets and jot down items on a shopping list.

"Don't, or *won't*, Jules?" I ask, shooting her a dirty look over my shoulder.

"Can't, Jeremy. I can't cook. And even if I could, how could you expect me to pull together a fancy dinner when you never even mentioned that we're having company?"

I open up the refrigerator and examine some of the condiment bottles on the door. "I don't need excuses, Julia," I mutter without looking at her. "Maybe if you'd pay attention, you wouldn't miss stuff like this."

"Pay attention to what? You haven't spoken more than ten sentences to me all week!"

"Maybe not, but one of those ten was 'we're having company Saturday night.' What the hell is wrong with you, Julia?"

She shakes her head at me in disbelief. "Nothing. There isn't a thing wrong with me. It's you, Jeremy."

I close my eyes and stand very still, giving her the distinct impression that I'm trying to control my anger. "Julia, things are not going to go well for you if there isn't a respectable meal on that table for Christmas."

"Jeremy, you have to understand. I haven't missed a holiday with Matthew in over fifteen years. I'm not going to start now. He's my family. Besides, I haven't seen a practice room in days. I'd planned to spend most of Christmas Eve at McInnes—"

I cut her off.

"First of all, you and Matthew are not family. I've told you before, it's him or me. You can't have it both ways."

"You never said that!" she protests, putting her hands on her hips.

"And as far as the practicing goes," I continue as if she hasn't spoken, "I wouldn't worry too much about that. There's no way you're going to beat out any of the other finalists. Don't bother trying to practice your way up to their level. It's nothing but sheer luck that got you this far. Wouldn't surprise me if Sam Michaels told the committee all about you. They probably felt sorry for you, threw you a bone."

The pain I have inflicted is written over every square inch of her face. She has grown a chalky white color and I see her start to tremble. It's been a slow, even progression to this point over the last couple of weeks. I'm going out more and more, telling her less and less. I ignore her attempts at affection, rejecting her again and again. We barely speak. And sex? Well, lets just say I've changed the whole tone of that. Not so much romance as mechanics. My needs, my desires are the only ones that matter from here on out. Julia is off-balance all the time. And that's just how I want it.

"So, turkey. What, like fifteen pounds?" I ask her, returning to the list that I started earlier.

I think she's going to say something but she makes the wise decision to refrain. After a long moment she simply nods her head.

"Good. And sweet potatoes, not that candied crap but real potatoes…"

"Can I…" she starts to ask quietly.

I give her a look that stops her mid-sentence. "Can you what?" I put the list down and take a step closer to her.

"I just wondered if maybe…if I could ask Matthew to come here for dinner since you don't want me to go there?"

I don't need to say a word. The look I give her says it all for me. Julia simply hangs her head down and walks back to my bedroom. Brett has heard the whole conversation from where he's sitting on the couch, making notes in the score he's playing for the Big Apple Ballet next week.

"Harsh," he says, once she's gone.

I shrug. "She'll never learn if I don't teach her."

"Jeremy, the final round is in two weeks. I don't see Cal backing out. Maybe you should just..."

"What? What should I just do, Brett?" I cut him off. "Accept defeat and let the moron steal my gold medal? My career? Uh-uh. Not going to happen. He'll back out."

"Dude! I was just going to say maybe you should cut Julia loose. She's a distraction. Breaking it off with her will push her over the edge. Just do it, so you can focus on...other things."

"No. Matthew brought her back from the dead once before, he can do it again. I'm not taking that chance. She stays right here where I can keep an eye on her."

He shakes his head and looks back down at the music. "How much more of this do you think she'll put up with?" he asks as he erases a notation.

"Oh, Brett, you have no idea what a girl like that will take. Don't you get it? This is like going home for her. She's like me. She had to learn to live like a normal person, but she isn't a normal person. Now, all she wants is approval. All she wants to do is please me. What she doesn't know is that I can't be pleased."

"I don't see why she doesn't know, the rest of us sure do," he smirks.

I laugh as I head toward the bedroom myself. He's right. When I open the door, I find Julia sitting on the bed, looking distantly out the window. There isn't much of a view, just the alley behind the building. But she's focused on it intently, lost in thought. So much so that she jumps when I come to stand next to her.

"I've finished the list. You can go to the market whenever you're ready."

"Aren't you coming with me?" she asks, without turning away from the window.

"Nope. I'm going out."

I wait for her to ask where, but she doesn't. She catches on fast, I'll give her that. "What time do you want dinner on Christmas?" she asks softly.

Good girl.

"I think five should be fine."

She nods, still not so much as glancing my way. "I miss you," she says.

"What?"

"I miss being with you. I miss your company. I miss your…attention."

"That's your problem now, isn't it?" I say coldly.

"I suppose it is," she mutters.

"Are you trying to be a smart ass, Julia? You know I hate that."

It's clear when she looks up at me, that this was not her intent. But I don't care. It's fun to fuck with her. And I'm quite sure part of her gets off on a little forced submission.

"No," she says, shaking her head.

"I think you are. Perhaps you need a refresher course in good manners?"

She blinks hard, trying to work out what I mean. She knows.

"Stand up."

She does.

"Take your blouse off."

She does.

I reach around behind her and unclasp her bra, and pull it free of her shoulders. I cup her breasts in my hands and she gasps. She reaches out to pull me to her but I step back.

"Uh-uh. You don't get to touch me."

Her eyebrows knit together in confusion. "I don't... what do you want me to do…"

"I want you to shut the fuck up and do what I tell you to do. Is that so hard?" She shakes her head slowly. "Lie back on the bed," I say sternly.

She does, and I join her, pulling her skirt up to her waist. I love skirts. They provide such easy access. Once the panties are off, I'm all hands, fingers, tongue and teeth. She's writhing, mewling for release.

"Please…please..." she murmurs.

"Please what?"

"Please, Jeremy. I want you."

That's all I need to hear. I stop what I'm doing abruptly and stand up and walk to the door. When I look back she's sitting up, naked above and below the skirt that is now twisted around her waist.

"Wait…" she says.

"What?"

"I haven't...I mean we didn't…don't you want to finish?"

"I am finished, Julia," I say as I turn my back and walk out the door.

Get used to it, you're going to be abandoned again, and again, and again. If you thought your nightmares were bad before…

37

I am an exceptional creature in an unexceptional world. Don't get me wrong, as liberating as it is to be free of emotional baggage, it's not without its difficulties. I mean, people tend to notice when you're not sad at a funeral or ecstatic at the birth of your first child. What comes naturally to everyone else is a carefully practiced craft for someone like me. My face is a permanent mask. On the plus side, I've learned that the people all around me are my teachers. From them I can assess what fear looks like, what grief sounds like or how I'm expected to respond to exciting news.

So if I want to move freely among the "normal" people, I have to appear to be one of them. In other words, if you really want to know your enemy, you must become him. Think like him, act like him, be him. It's what I do on a daily basis. I assimilate mannerisms and body language. I mimic speech and mirror expressions.

With Julia, it's been easy, no digging required. She wears her insecurities like a tattoo across her forehead. No, more like a bright, flashing neon sign. The girl was abandoned by her mother and abused by her father. She grew up in the nurturing arms of the state foster care system with that pussy Matthew as her only friend. By the time I took notice of the shy Miss James, she was desperate for security and hungry for unconditional love. Talk about low-hanging fruit. And now she's mine. Emotionally, sexually, intellectually. Completely.

I can see Matthew's frame filling the doorway of her practice room when I come down the hall to find her. He doesn't go to school here anymore, the son of a bitch should just mind his own goddam business.

"What's wrong with you? Mila told me you were late for rehearsal," I hear him say to her.

"I overslept," she replies with some irritation. "It happens, Matthew!"

"Julia, Dr. Sam actually called me because he's worried about you. He says you're not putting in enough practice time and he's concerned you won't be ready for your final recital..."

She says something that I can't hear.

"It's him, isn't it?" Matthew demands. "Is he keeping you from practicing? You know he's afraid you're going to beat him out..."

"Stop it! You're just being difficult because I've been living with Jeremy."

"Don't say that. You're not living with him, you're just...fucking around with him for a while."

"I think what you're trying to say, is that she's fucking me, Matthew. And yes, she is, on a regular basis. Which is more than you can say."

Matthew turns around. "Nobody's talking to you, Jeremy," he hisses.

"I am!" I hear Julia from inside. "Jeremy?" she calls out and I push past Matthew to take my place besides her.

"Are you coming home for Christmas Eve dinner?" he asks her, ignoring me.

"We have plans already, Matthew, but thanks anyway," I answer for her.

"Please, at least come by on Christmas morning," he implores her softly.

"I...I don't know, Matthew," she says, looking up at me nervously. "Maybe. I'll let you know."

The poor fuck looks devastated. This is probably the first Christmas he's spent without her since their pathetic little orphanage days. Christ, between the two of them, I feel like I'm in a Dickens novel.

"Is Dr. Sam wrong? Are you ready for your recital?" he asks her.

She shrugs. "Well, I guess I haven't gotten as much playing time in as I probably should."

"That doesn't sound like you, Julia," he says, looking more concerned. "Not at all. This recital is coming up fast…"

"Come on, Jules," I cut him off. "We've got to get home," I say, taking the cello from her and putting it in its case. Matthew actually flinches when I refer to my apartment as her home. Still, he's standing in the door, looking back and forth between the two of us. "Was there something else you wanted?" I ask him with an arched eyebrow.

"Yes, actually, Jeremy. I'd like very much for you to go to hell," he spits back at me.

I give him my shiniest smile. "Now, now, Matthew, just because she loves me more than she loves you doesn't mean you have to get all nasty."

He's fuming.

"Matthew…" Julia starts to speak, but stops abruptly when she sees the look on my face.

"What? What is it, Julia?" he's asking now.

She shakes her head. "Nothing," she says quietly.

"Julia, if you're in trouble… if you don't want to be with him… Don't be afraid. Just say the word and I'll take you back home right now. To *our* home."

"Matthew, I'm not afraid!" she stresses to him firmly. "I–I love Jeremy, and he loves me. I wouldn't be with him if that wasn't the case."

There it is. Matthew gives a curt little nod and leaves the practice room without further comment.

"I don't like you talking to him, Jules," I say to her as she packs up her music.

"He's my best friend."

"I don't care. He upsets you every time you talk to him lately. It's not good for you. I think you need to take a break from Matthew for a while."

She stops and looks at me carefully, trying to assess my mood. In the end, she doesn't say anything, just stands up and takes the cello case from me. Once we're out on the street again, headed for the subway she takes my hand.

"I've been thinking a lot about my mother," she says.

"Yeah?"

"Yes. And I don't think it was an accident that we met like that." Shit. If she thinks I was involved with that, we might have a problem. "I think we were meant to find one another again. I mean, how else do you explain the sequence of events that brought us together?" she finishes.

Unbelievable. This is just too easy.

"And what does that mean? Are you going to get in touch with her again?" I ask.

She shakes her head slowly.

"No, I don't think so. Just because we were meant to see one another, doesn't mean we should have a relationship. I don't think I'll ever forgive her."

"You can't make people love you, Jules," I say, knowing I'm hitting a sore spot here.

"You don't think she loved me? Like ever?" she asks, almost begging me to assuage her insecurities.

"Probably not," I say in my most therapeutic tone. "How could she? She abandoned you. She knew what kind of a man your father was, and she left you with him anyway. She knew he'd take it out on you and she didn't care. She could have taken you with her but she didn't want you, Julia. I think the sooner you accept that fact the easier it will be."

Out of the corner of my eye, I see her surreptitiously swipe at a tear rolling down her cheek. I cough into my hand to hide my lips, which are twitching up into a smile.

38

She's standing in the kitchen, hopping up and down, excitedly, holding a flat box wrapped in gold foil paper with a bright green bow on it.

"What's this?" I ask her, once I've straightened up from basting the turkey.

"It's your Christmas present, silly," she says with an excited smile. "Go on, open it!"

I pull the bow off and peel the wrapper from a black box. When I pull the top off I find and envelope. I take it out and open it. There is printed receipt for two plane tickets inside.

"Surprise!" she squeals. "They're for the International Horn Conference in Miami this April. You said you'd never been…and since it's here in the US this year…I thought it would make a great vacation for us. It falls right over the McInnes spring break."

Wow. These weren't cheap.

"Thanks, Jules," I say, giving her a peck on the cheek and closing the box up again. "Okay. We've got company coming in less than hour. Where are we on the potatoes?"

But Julia is looking at me expectantly.

"What?" I ask.

"Well?"

"Well what?"

"Oh, come on, stop teasing! Where's mine?"

"Where's your what?" I ask with genuine confusion on my face.

"My Christmas present!"

I stare at her blankly and watch as the excitement vanishes from her face.

"You..." she begins softly. "You didn't get me a Christmas present, Jeremy?" she asks, sounding more than a little hurt.

"Uh, actually, no. No, I didn't, Julia. Sorry, I didn't realize you were expecting one," I say with a disinterested shrug.

Julia doesn't say anything else—she just nods and gives me a tight smile. She picks up a stack of dishes and sets them out on top of the dining room table. But she doesn't stay there for long. I hear the sound of the bedroom door clicking shut.

"Do you want me to check on her?" Brett asks when I tell him what's happened a half-hour later.

"Nah, I'll do it. I think we need to have a little talk about the Christmas spirit."

When I open the door to the bedroom, I find Julia lying face down on the bed, crying softly into a pillow. I close the door quietly behind me and take a few steps toward the bed.

"Okay, enough of the theatrics. We've got company coming in about fifteen minutes."

She sits up and glares at me, as she uses her sleeve to dry her eyes and cheeks.

"Company?" she whispers angrily. "You had me thinking half the brass section was coming. It's just Brett and that ass, Tom Carson. You know I hate him. Why would you ask him to spend Christmas dinner with us, but not Matthew?"

I sit down on the edge of the bed.

"Hey, this is my home, Julia. I get to decide who is and isn't invited. Tom is a welcome guest so I suggest you get off your high horse and start treating him like one. As for Matthew fucking Ayers, he's definitely *not* welcome in my home, so that was never gonna happen."

She's fuming. "You've got a lot of nerve..."

I hold up a finger and stop her mid-sentence.

"No, *you've* got a lot of nerve. You want to go back to your swanky digs in Lincoln Center? The door's right there. But you won't be seeing me again anytime soon, if you do."

"What? Why are you being like this?" she asks, her eyes welling with tears again. "Jeremy, I love you! This is what you wanted, isn't it? The two of us living together? Why are you being so mean to me all of a sudden? What did I do to make you so angry with me all the time?"

"Julia, I'm done with this discussion."

"Well, I'm not," she says, her dismay turning to irritation.

I give a heavily annoyed sigh and stand up.

"Get up," I say in a cold, flat voice.

She doesn't move.

"Julia, so help me God, if you aren't out of that bed in ten seconds I'm going to drag you out by your hair."

This time there's something more in my voice. A serious threat.

"Don't you dare speak to me like that!" she spits back at me, still not moving an inch. So, I make good on my promise, grabbing a handful of her long, red hair and yanking her up to her feet.

"Ouch! Jeremy, you're hurting me!" she howls.

From the living room, I hear the sound of the intercom and then Brett buzzing Tom upstairs. "Keep your fucking voice down," I snarl.

She wipes the tears from her face and straightens up. Oh, so the Mouse is going to try and stand up to the lion. Good luck with that, sweetheart.

"I will not. I don't care who hears me. If you think for one second that you can treat me like this, then you are very much mistaken!"

I move even closer until my face is only inches from hers. She tries to push around me, but I block her. "Julia, I'm in no mood for your pouty little girl bullshit. So get into that bathroom and wash your face. Fix your makeup, put on a smile, and get your ass out there to play hostess, before I really give you something to pout about."

"Jesus…" she says under her breath, shaking her head incredulously. "You sound just like my father. *'I'll give you something to cry about…'* That's what he used to say."

I'm unmoved by her comparison. "Well, if this is the way you acted with him then I can't say I blame him."

Her hand flies up to slap me, but I catch her wrist easily before she can get anywhere close. I give it a good hard wrench and her knees buckle from the pain. When I let her go suddenly, she falls to the floor next to my bed with a dull thump.

"If you ever even *think* about doing that again," I hiss, "I'll break your wrist so badly you'll never hold a pencil again, let alone a bow. Do you understand me, Julia?"

She looks up at me from the floor where she's cradling her arm. Tears are now streaming down her cheeks.

"Do you understand me?" I repeat, more slowly this time.

She nods.

"You have five minutes, Julia. If you're not out there, I'm going to tell them you're sick and ask Tom to leave. Trust me, you do *not* want him to leave this apartment when I'm this angry."

She's still staring after me as I standup and exit the bedroom, without so much as a glance backward.

It takes six minutes, but Julia emerges from the bedroom looking fresh-faced and smiling. She holds her right arm close to her body.

"Merry Christmas!" she says brightly.

39

Julia is in the shower, getting ready to go out to dinner when I pick up her phone and start reading through her texts and emails. I've been watching her outgoing and incoming messages very closely for the last week, waiting to see if she'd tell Matthew about what happened Christmas night. But so far there's nothing. She's also been making much more of an effort to stay on my good side since that night, so I reward her with New Year's dinner out. I think it's going to be an uneventful night until the waitress stops by with the bill.

The girl is very busty. In fact, it looks as if she might spill out of her blouse at any moment. What is it with waitresses? They can't seem to keep their hands off of me. This one, with long sandy hair and blue eyes brushes my hand with her finger as she hands me the folio with the check. I smile up at her and she leans down to whisper in my ear. When she's gone, I find Julia staring across the table at me, clearly furious.

"Unbelievable!" she exclaims.

"What?" I ask innocently.

"Her! What nerve to flirt with you with me sitting right here!"

I wave a dismissive hand at her.

"What did she say to you just now?" she demands.

I don't like demands. "Nothing."

"Jeremy..."

You know what? Maybe she should know. “Fine,” I say leaning across the table. “She let me know that her phone number is on the back of the bill.”

“What? Give that to me. I’m going to call the manager over.”

My eyes darken, as does my tone. “You’ll do no such thing,” I say with such finality that she drops the subject. I glance at the girl’s number and tuck it into my pants pocket. Julia watches in silence.

I’ve never been one for the big Times Square scene on New Year’s Eve, but I do enjoy a nice meal out and an expensive bottle of champagne. Especially when I plan on sticking Julia with the bill. The restaurant is bright and festive and loud. So loud, in fact, that I almost miss Cal calling me from the other side of the room.

“Well, look who it is! The horn player who *almost* won the Kreisler!” he says in a voice that’s uncharacteristically booming, not to mention a wee bit slurred. It would appear Mr. Burridge started his celebrations before he got here. There is a girl from the flute section with him. Cal motions for her to follow the hostess to their table, while he stops by to see us at ours.

“How’s that ego feeling, Jeremy? Still stinging a little?”

“Go to hell, Cal,” I say flatly.

“Please don’t do this here…” Julia intervenes. She puts a hand on top of mine but I pull it away.

Even in his drunken stupor Cal notices. “Everything okay, Julia?”

“Yes, thanks, Cal,” she says. “So… it looks as if you and I are the last two to perform next week. Are you ready?”

She’s trying to change the subject but all she’s doing is pissing me off more. I don’t want to engage him—I want him to get the fuck away from me.

"Mostly yes. I'm working on something special for my encore."

"What's that?" she asks as I roll my eyes across from her. She needs to stop encouraging him.

"It's an old Chuck Mangione song called 'Lullaby.' I've made an arrangement of it for horn and piano."

"Oh Cal, that's going to be beautiful!" she exclaims loudly.

Could she sound anymore ridiculous?

"It was a favorite of my mom's and I really wanted something that no one else has used before."

"Yeah, well, isn't that sweet," I say, throwing my linen napkin down on our table and getting to my feet. "Julia, we need to get going. You settle the check, and I'll see if our cab is here."

"Cal, I can't wait to hear you play—congratulations again." Julia beams.

I hold out my hand to help her up. When she doesn't notice I grab her arm, maybe a little too hard. She winces and shoots me a look, but doesn't comment on it. Cal's eyes are moving from me, to her, and back again. He's knows something's not right, but he's too stewed to do anything about it.

"I really appreciate that," he says. Then, as if something has occurred to him, "You know, Julia, you should stop by the after-party I'm throwing at Nunzio's. You could bring a date if you want. Maybe one of those nice guys in the violin section," he says pointedly.

I stare at him with undisguised hatred.

"Fuck you, Cal," I sneer under my breath.

He just smiles and walks away to his own table.

"Jeremy!" Julia hisses when Cal is out of earshot. "You could be a little more gracious, you know? You look like a sore loser."

I'm still clutching her bicep. She must realize how big of a mistake she's just made because she starts to back pedal. And fast.

She reaches up and touches my face gently.

"Don't you see?" she begins with a softer tone. "I know you're the better player. You know it. Just because Cal won, doesn't mean your life and career are over. It doesn't mean I love you any less."

I stare at her in silence for a long moment as she watches me expectantly, hopefully. "Are you really that naïve, or are you just that stupid?" I ask her coldly.

She holds her smile a bit too long, not realizing at first that I'm not kidding. "Jeremy…"

"I'm going," I say, dropping my grip from her arm. "If you aren't out there by the time the cab is, you can ask your old buddy Cal to see you home. I really don't care either way."

And with that I walk away from the table and through the door. After a few minutes she follows me out into the frigid night air. When a car pulls over, I open the door and get in, leaving her to look in at me from the curb.

"Get in or close the fucking door, Julia," I order from the back seat.

She gets in and sits silently by my side. I act as if she isn't there, refusing to even glance her way. When she makes a move to touch my hand on the seat next to me, I yank it away. As we pull up in front of the building I'm out the door in a flash. I don't offer her a hand out of the cab. I simply get out and keep walking.

"Hey!" I hear the cabbie call as Julia gets out and starts to follow me. "You gonna pay?"

When I look back over my shoulder she's digging through her purse for cash. Upstairs, I find Brett watching the Planet of the Apes marathon on TV, what's left of a bottle of wine on the coffee table in front of him. He looks up when I come in.

"You're home early."

"Yeah, well, we ran into Cal Burridge at the restaurant, and I had to leave before I stabbed him in the heart with my steak knife."

"Oh, no. That definitely would not be good. Where's Julia?" he asks, looking behind me.

"She's on her way up. I left her to take care of the cab."

By the time Julia makes her way upstairs, I have changed out of my dinner clothes into sweats and a t-shirt, and I'm pouring myself a glass of the Chardonnay from the bottle my brother has open.

"What took you so long?" I ask, as she comes in.

"Gee, I don't know," she replies, dropping her keys and purse on the counter. "It took me a while to scrape together the cab fare after you stuck me with the restaurant bill. You couldn't have waited for me?"

I lean against the counter and sip my wine, looking at her over the rim of the glass. I can actually see the rage as it washes over her, an angry red that blazes up from below her neckline all the way to her forehead. Brett is trying not to appear too interested in this spat but I can see him watching us out of the corner of his eye. If there's one thing musicians have, it's exceptional peripheral vision. We don't miss a thing.

"How dare you treat me like that when all I've ever done is support you! Don't you ever humiliate me like that again!"

Oh, now she really has gone too far. Faster than she can blink, I've set the glass on the counter and we are standing toe to toe, me towering over her. "You want to rethink that comment?" I ask her calmly.

Her internal struggle is playing out across her face like a movie. I see it all. Fear, pain, confusion. Finally, to my surprise, she settles on courage. "Go to hell," she whispers with venom in her voice.

Oh, baby. You just chose wrong.

By the time Julia realizes I've hit her, she's already on the floor, looking up at me incredulously. Blood trickles through her fingers as she holds her hand to her nose and mouth. Without a second glance, I pick up my wine glass and go into the living room to join Brett on the couch. I watch as he looks her way, makes eye contact and turns back to the television.

"Your favorite part is coming up in a few minutes," he says, gesturing towards the screen.

"Good!" I clink my wine glass with his.

"Happy New Year, bro," I say.

"Back at ya," he says.

Julia is crying quietly on the kitchen floor.

It's close to four in the morning when I roll over and run my hand up and down her outer thigh. She doesn't stir so I reach around and cup her breast in my hand, rolling my thumb around her nipple until it hardens to a tiny peak. Now she murmurs my name as she wakens slowly, reaching her arm back behind her, touching my face. Even in the dark I can see her swollen lip and the angry scab that's forming where it split. I can also just make out where there is still a purple/green bruise on her wrist from Christmas Eve. She's been covering it with long sleeves and sweaters. Good. Something to think about next time she considers crossing me.

"I'm so sorry…" she whispers. "Please don't be angry with me. Please, I won't do that again. I know I deserved it…"

I don't reply, just hook my thumbs into the waistband of her panties and tug them down. She raises her legs in turn so I can pull them off of her. She starts to turn toward me, to face me, but I push her back. Without preamble I thrust hard into her and she sucks in her breath. It's easy to see this isn't unpleasant for her, but it's hardly the extended foreplay she's used to from me. A few more quick thrusts and I've taken care of my business. Julia, on the other hand, looks at me over her shoulder with eyebrows raised.

"Something wrong?" I ask, daring her to complain.

"No," she says quietly as she rolls back over and pulls the sheet tightly around her body.

I throw my legs over onto the floor and pull on the sweats I was wearing earlier in the evening. Next come my t-shirt and sneakers.

I catch her shooting me a furtive glance. "What?" I ask with evident irritation.

"Are you … going out?" she asks softly.

"Yes."

She touches her fingertips to her swollen face unconsciously.

"Do we have a problem?" I ask, forcing her to meet my eyes.

She shakes her head right away. "No. No problem, Jeremy."

I give a quick nod and walk out of the bedroom, grabbing my keys off the dresser and whistling all the way out the front door.

40

I'm using my hand as a visor against the stage lights as I peer out into the empty concert hall from backstage. I just want to be sure that Matthew isn't lurking up in the balcony somewhere, hoping to see Julia's dress rehearsal. She says he's away until tomorrow morning, but you never know what he'll do when it comes to his sweet little 'Orphan Julia.' Just in case, I've asked Brett to sit up there and keep an eye out. I spot him and he gives a nod that he sees me too.

On stage, Maestro Gregory Sutton is addressing the New York Symphony, one of the best orchestras on the planet. Julia is seated out in front of them, cello between her legs, looking a little too comfortable for my liking. I am, however, pleased to see that the swelling in her face has gone down. That was stupid of me to hit her where someone might notice. Next time I'll be more careful.

It's the Sunday going into "Kreisler Week" and tensions are running high. The pianist and violinist had their dress rehearsals yesterday. I was there to see their performances for myself, to know exactly what I'm up against. I don't want any surprises.

Lucy, the pianist, was actually better than I thought she would be. But, considering the fact that pianists have won the last few Kreisler's, no one, including Lucy herself, thinks she has a shot at the gold. I heard her telling someone this is her warm-up for the Tchaikovsky Competition next year.

True to character, the Russian violinist had a hissy fit during his rehearsal, threatening to kick the principal violinist's teeth in if he didn't play softer during the concerto. Someone from the competition stepped in, and the hothead was told he'd be cut if he didn't calm down.

This afternoon, it's Julia and Cal's turn. Julia has already played through the Rachmaninoff Sonata with the symphony's pianist. Now, they're getting ready to run the piece that she'll play with the entire symphony, a cello concerto by Mozart contemporary Luigi Boccherini.

The Maestro turns around on his podium and says something to her that I can't hear. She smiles, nods and sits up straight, getting her bow into position. Sutton conducts the orchestra in a brief introduction and then Julia starts to play. Her bow glides effortlessly over the strings. She makes the intricate scale patterns sound like child's play. Back and forth, back and forth, the bow rocks from one string to the next in quick succession. Then suddenly she's teasing, dragging out the notes one by one while the orchestra rests in silence before taking off again. Now she's harmonizing a melancholy melody with the symphony strings. The whole damn concerto is like this. By the time she gets to her cadenza in the final movement, it seems as if every single member of the orchestra is watching her, rapt.

Shit. This cadenza—a virtuosic solo part within the concerto—is fucking brilliant. She's all over the fingerboard. When did she write this thing? I was so busy focusing on how she was playing the other two pieces that I didn't pay any attention to the work she was doing on this one. Which, apparently, has been substantial. If I had known, I might have been able to do something about it. Well, there's still time, I suppose.

The Maestro has to actually tap his baton on the podium to get the orchestra's attention off of Julia and back on him for the very last measures. When the concerto has ended there is a long moment of silence and then the orchestra starts to applaud. And not just the polite little tap-tap-tap thing they do with their bows on the music stands. These people are actually hooting and cheering and whistling. The Maestro holds out his hand for Julia. She sets the cello on its side and joins him on the podium facing the symphony. The applause grows even louder. I can see the crimson color of her face from here. What a lightweight.

When they finally let her go, Julia practically skips backstage.

"Oh, my gosh! Jeremy, that was amazing! What a rush to play with an orchestra like that!" she says giddily.

I don't say anything, just leaf disinterestedly through a magazine that someone has left on a table back here.

"Well?" she finally asks, impatiently. "How'd I do?"

I put the magazine down and meet her hopeful gaze. I clear my throat. "If you want my honest opinion, I've heard better."

"Excuse me?" she says, cocking her head slightly to one side.

"I've heard it played better by other cellists. But you were perfectly...." I appear to struggle for exactly the right word, "... adequate."

"But all those musicians...their applause…" she starts to protest.

"Julia, do you think you're the only one they do that for? They did the same thing for the pianist and the violinist yesterday. They'll probably do the same thing for Cal now. They're just being polite."

In fact, there was some average applause for the pianist and they actually hissed at the obnoxious violinist, but she doesn't know that.

Julia looks as if I've popped her favorite balloon. I guess, in a way, I have.

"Come on, get packed up. I want to sit down in the audience for Cal's rehearsal."

Her disappointment turns to concern. "Are you sure you want to do that, Jeremy? Why don't we just go home ..."

"I told you what we're doing," I snap at her. "Now put the damn cello away and let's go."

She nods and goes to do as I have instructed. As I watch her, I note that all traces of giddy are gone.

41

When Julia and I slip out into the concert hall, the Symphony is regrouping on stage after a brief break. It's such a different experience, watching the pros. There's none of the horsing around and petty nonsense that you see in a college orchestra—even a group as advanced as the McInnes Conservatory Orchestra has to be wrangled by the conductor. Not here. Then, Maestro Gregory Sutton steps onto the podium and everything stops. All eyes are on him and you could hear a pin drop. These are professionals.

"Cal Burridge will be out in just a moment here," he begins, facing the orchestra. "He and I have already worked out his preferred tempo so please just keep an eye on me. He'll do a cadenza at the end of the final movement. I'm just going to be marking beats for you there until the measure before the orchestra comes back in. You know the drill here, ladies and gentlemen. Light, bright, buoyant. This young man plays Mozart brilliantly, so you're in for a treat."

I realize that my knuckles are turning white as I grasp the armrest. What a joke. It should be me up there. And where the hell is Burridge anyway? As soon as I think it, he sprints on stage, barely balancing his horn and music as he makes his way to his seat out front of the orchestra to the left of the podium.

"Ladies and gentlemen, may I introduce to you the winner of the French horn division of the Kreisler International Music Competition, Mr. Calvin Burridge," the conductor says to his ensemble. Cal approaches the podium and shakes hands with the Maestro before giving a nod and a smile in acknowledgement of the musicians' applause. His face is a little rosy from the attention. The idiot doesn't even know how to act in a professional setting, let alone play in one.

The Maestro waits for Cal to set up his music and blow a few notes through his horn. The oboist plays a quick A for him and he makes a big show of tuning, moving each of the horn's crooks in and out and back in again by fractions of an inch. Fucking prima donna.

"Jeremy, really. Are you sure you want to be here?" Julia whispers next to me. "You look so … unhappy. We don't have to stay if you don't want to."

"You've got that right," I snap at her, then think better of it and soften my tone. "I'm sorry, Jules. Thanks for worrying about me, but I'm fine." I pat her hand, and she smiles at me sweetly. All is forgiven. For now, anyway.

The Maestro leans down and says something to Cal before turning to his orchestra. He picks up the baton from the podium that holds his score. And then his hands are raised, but still, as if they belong to a marionette suspended from wires in the ceiling above. They just hang there for what seems like a very long time before he gives them their downbeat and the Mozart begins.

In the opening of the Mozart's *Horn Concerto No.3*, the orchestra paves the way for the horn by playing the main theme for several measures. The soloist pops in with a note here and there but spends several measures counting. Cal is silently blowing air through his horn to keep it warm and in tune.

As I'm watching him wait for his big entrance, I notice Cal is even redder than before. He's starting to sweat now—and not just a nervous perspiration, it's pouring off of him in buckets. He actually mops his brow with the towel he uses to clean his horn. He coughs.

"Jeremy, I think something's wrong with Cal," Julia says, patting my arm.

"He's probably just nervous."

If I were him, I'd be nervous right about now, too.

He's tugging at the collar of his shirt, unbuttoning the top button. He takes a swig from the water bottle next to him. All the while, Maestro Sutton leads the orchestra, unaware that there is something happening behind him.

"Jeremy, I think something is really wrong. Please go help him!" she implores.

I look around but there really isn't anyone else in the audience. Which is exactly what I was counting on. "Shit," I mutter, getting to my feet and walking down the aisle toward the front of the house.

I know this concerto very well, and Cal's entrance is coming up any second now. Three... two... one... Maestro Sutton throws his downbeat toward Cal without even glancing at him. But Cal doesn't come in. He's leaning forward in his chair as if bracing for a crash landing.

"Cal?" I call out over the orchestra, which has continued without him.

He looks up briefly and I see he has a hand to the base of his neck. He doesn't look good at all. In fact, he's starting to slump toward the floor.

"Maestro!" I yell as loud as I can, trying to be heard over the music. "Maestro, stop!"

The concertmaster notices me waving my arms and gets the conductor's attention. He turns around, leaving the orchestra to slowly peter out, one section at a time as they realize something is terribly wrong.

"Quick! Someone call 9-1-1!" Sutton calls over his shoulder and jumping off the podium just as I vault up onto the stage. We reach Cal at the same time. He's on the floor now, face-up, still clutching his horn.

Now that I'm up close to him I can see his lips are swollen and red hives are quickly dotting his entire face. His breathing is labored and his eyes are wild with panic and fear. I take the horn from his hands while the Maestro reassures him.

"Just stay calm, Cal," he says soothingly. "Help is on the way. You're going to be fine."

"Maestro, I think he keeps an epinephrine pen in his horn case…" I say, getting to my feet and sprinting backstage, his instrument still in my hand.

"Cal, stay with me…" I hear the Maestro say.

I find his case and open it, already knowing what I'm going to find there. Nothing. I take the mouthpiece out of his horn and slip it into my right pocket. From my left, I produce an identical one and pop it back in to replace the other. Then I set the horn on the table by his case. When I turn to run back out on stage, Julia is standing there watching me.

Crap. How long has she been there and what did she see? Nothing. She looks too scared to process anything. I run past her, giving her a quick pat on the shoulder as I do. Never miss an opportunity to fuck with someone.

"Hang in there," Sutton is saying as I return. "Come on. Let's breathe together. In… Out… In… Out..."

"It's not there," I say, the faux alarm evident in my voice. I'm leaning down, peering at him from over the Maestro's shoulder. Cal is staring up at me and his enlarged lips are turning a distinct shade of blue. Even in this moment I can see that he knows exactly what has happened. I wink at him.

"In…come on, Cal, help is on the way! Out… In… Out…"

"Should we do CPR?" I ask.

"No, it's not his heart… In, Cal. Breathe in, Cal…."

And then everything becomes perfectly still and quiet, there is no *IN*. His eyes have glazed over, open to the ceiling and unseeing. Cal Burridge is dead.

"No," I say softly at first, just as I have practiced in my mind. Then I ratchet up a notch for effect. "No! No, no, *no!*" I start thumping on his chest even though it is obviously too late. Someone tries to pull me away but I shrug them off. It isn't until the paramedics come bursting in that I stand up and back away.

Julia is standing by, watching with a hand clapped over her mouth. She's shaking her head.

"Jeremy...what...why…" she can't get the words out.

But I can. "He's dead, Julia," I say, trying to muster my most reverent tone.

She throws herself into my arms. "He can't be! What happened?"

"I think some kind of an allergic reaction."

She's looking up at me in disbelief, green eyes glimmering with tears that spill down past her lashes and make tracks down her freckled cheeks.

I pull her closer to me, against my chest and pat her back comfortingly. I rest my chin on the top of her head so that no one will see me as I smile into her hair.

42

It's standing room only in the McInnes lecture hall being used for today's press conference. As I take my place in a reserved seat down at the front, the number of people crammed in here surprises me. It's certainly never this full for a music history lecture. Looking around, I spot Kreisler competitors, McInnes students and faculty. But, interestingly enough, the largest contingent appears to be made up of the print and broadcast outlets. I was expecting some media attention, but no more than an arts reporter or two.

The sad reality is that the arts get very little attention in the mainstream media. To some people, classical music is a dull, stuffy affair for rich, elitist snobs. So to see so much interest in what would normally be a single paragraph seems odd to me. Still, I suppose the untimely death of a "brilliant young musician, poised to take the arts world by storm" probably makes for good hair salon and doctor's office reading. Maybe even a blurb in the section of People Magazine reserved for the lowly, non-Hollywood mortals.

Clearly, Lester Morgan is not expecting the blinding barrage of flashbulbs that explode in his face when he enters the room. He looks exhausted and shell-shocked by the events of the last twenty-four hours. The reporters are shouting questions at him before he can even get the microphone adjusted to his height.

"Lester! Was Calvin Burridge murdered?"

"Why was Cal Burridge killed?"

"Have there been threats against any of the other competitors?"

I can't believe what I'm hearing. Since when did this become a murder? Okay, I know exactly when this became a murder—but when did it become a murder to *them*? Obviously I'm not the only one stunned by this revelation. All around me people are turning and whispering to one another. Add that to the press' outbursts and the room is suddenly a whole lot louder.

Lester closes his eyes for a moment and stands perfectly still. He's silent as he waits. And waits. It takes a full two minutes for the reporters to realize that the man is not going to speak until they shut-up. So they do. Only when the room has totally quieted does he take a deep breath and nod to no one in particular.

"Good afternoon," he says very quietly, very somberly. "I'm Lester Morgan, Director of the Kreisler International Music Competition."

"Mr. Morgan, was Calvin Burridge murdered?" One reporter repeats her question from the back of the room, and the buzz starts up again.

Lester stares at the offending woman with a harsh gaze and waits until, once again, he can speak uninterrupted.

"First let me say that we are shocked and saddened by the untimely death of such a musical talent. Calvin Burridge was a well-liked and respected member of the musical community with great prospects for a successful future. He was this year's Kreisler Medalist in the French Horn category."

The last sentence comes out a little choked and Lester has to pause for a moment.

"On behalf of the competition and its organizers, I would like to extend my deepest sympathies to the family of Mr. Burridge. I would also ask that you respect their privacy at this difficult time. What I'm here to address is the competition. After a lengthy meeting, the Kreisler Committee has determined that while Calvin's award will stand, the concert will go on with the runner-up in the horn division, Jeremy Corrigan."

At this point Lester gestures to me and I stand up and face the crowd behind me. My face is a study—quite literally—in respectful solemnity as I nod an acknowledgement. A few flashes go off and several journalists look ready to ask me questions but one look from Lester squashes that impulse. I sit down again and he continues.

"Jeremy has graciously agreed to perform in the horn slot tonight, as previously scheduled. And I note the fact that he's willing to do this without a dress rehearsal. We are very grateful for his flexibility and willingness to ensure the Kreisler International Music Competition resumes without delay. Regardless of the gold medal winner at the end of the competition, Calvin Burridge will be memorialized in every program at every performance. He is and shall be permanently recognized as this year's winner in his category."

Even Lester's powerful glare cannot keep the press at bay any longer. He's assaulted by questions coming from every corner of the room now. He holds up his hands as he tries to be heard over the din.

"While I'm happy to answer any inquiries you have regarding the competition itself," he says as loudly as he can without shouting, "I'm going to ask NYPD Detective Roberto Vasquez to take your questions regarding the events of last evening."

A stocky Hispanic man takes Lester's place in front of the microphone.

"Good morning," he says, unable to get anything else out before the questions are flying at him.

"Detective Vasquez, what makes you think this is more than just an accident?" asks a reporter from the local NBC affiliate.

Vasquez doesn't bat an eyelash. "We don't know that this is more than an accident. But the fact is that the timing, location, and circumstances surrounding Mr. Burridge's death are a little out of the ordinary. Just to cover all the bases, our department would like to conduct a brief investigation."

This guy is good.

"Will there be an autopsy?" a woman calls out from the third row.

Good question.

"It's being conducted as we speak. The Medical Examiner should have a report for us in a few days."

"What do you expect to find?" the woman follows up.

"I can't speculate. What I can say for now is that it would appear Mr. Burridge had some kind of acute anaphylaxis."

"Are you saying that someone may have poisoned him?" another reporter asks, and there is a sudden outburst from the entire press corps.

They're just yelling out questions now.

"Do you know when he ingested the substance that triggered the attack?"

Vasquez holds up his hand. "Please, one at a time!" he's saying over the din. "I'm not going to speak unless you all calm down."

That gets the point across. The reporters settle down and then one voice speaks out loud and clear.

"Detective Vasquez, can you comment on the rumor that someone reported Cal Burridge's death to the police as a homicide? And was there enough credibility there to cause you to open this investigation?"

What. The. Fuck?

My eyes swing to the back of the room with everyone else's. There's a guy, probably in his twenties, standing with a microphone and portable recorder in his hands, waiting for the officer to answer his question. Now we all swing back to Vasquez. It's like watching a freaking tennis match.

"I'm sorry, who are you?" Vasquez asks, squinting to get a better look at the reporter. There is something in the way he speaks those five words that conveys suspicion. Clearly the young man has hit on something, and clearly the detective wants to know how.

I'm holding my breath. I never hold my breath.

"I'm Aaron Adler, a reporter for National Public Radio," he says, standing a little taller against the scrutiny of his colleagues.

Too late, Vasquez realizes he has given the press something to sink their teeth into. He didn't deny it soon enough. In fact, he didn't deny it at all.

"Look folks," Vasquez continues as if the NPR guy never spoke. "I, personally, do not believe there was any foul play here. I'm just saying that we cannot immediately determine the events leading up to this young man's death. Once we can do that, we'll have a full report for you. That's all I can say until that time."

Vasquez steps away from the podium, and Lester returns to the microphone. "Thank you for your time, ladies and gentlemen," he says dismissively. The reporters are still calling after him as he and Vasquez leave the room together.

"Hey, man, good job in there!"

The NPR reporter looks even younger up close. He gives me a brief smile as I sidle up to him in the hallway. "Thanks."

"Seemed to me you got under his skin."

He shrugs.

"I wasn't trying to. I just wanted to see his reaction to the question."

"Wow," I say, sounding impressed, but feeling relieved. "So it was just a ploy to see if he'd trip up and confirm your theory?"

He's impassive.

"You're the other horn player, aren't you?" he asks, suddenly recognizing me.

"Yeah, I'm Jeremy Corrigan. Cal and I were pretty tight," I lie in my most sincere tone. "We've been playing together for years."

"I'm sorry. I hear he was a great guy."

Sure as hell didn't hear it from me.

"He was. I'm really struggling with taking his place on stage tonight. There's a part of me that wants to back out, but I know Cal would want me to represent him up there."

He nods his understanding but doesn't say a word.

"Well, I'd better get going ..." he says, throwing a messenger bag over his shoulder.

"Did someone ..." I start my sentence and let it hang there.

"What?" he looks up with interest.

"I'm sorry. It's just that I ... Well, if someone really did hurt Cal on purpose, I want to do everything I can to help find the bastard. *Did* someone suggest it was intentional?"

I'm giving him my most impassioned tone as I lean in closer. This is like our little secret. To that point, he looks around and makes certain no one is within earshot.

"It wasn't just one person who suggested it," he says quietly.

Before I can respond he turns and walks away, leaving me looking after him dumbly.

And that's when I spot her.

43

Louise Kutter doesn't notice me as she walks out of the press conference, through the clusters of people chattering animatedly in the corridor. I start to follow her at a distance, as she makes her way to the lobby of the building, past security and out onto the street. From there it is easy to fall in behind her without fear of being seen.

Clip clop. Clip clop. Clip clop. She's wearing tall, black boots with ridiculously high heels, which smack loudly on the pavement as she walks. A matching black leather duster just skims the tops of them and her long, dark hair is pulled back into a severe ponytail. All she needs is a riding crop and she could pass for a dominatrix in one of those sex clubs downtown.

I'm not surprised she decided to attend the meeting. After all, Cal was her pick, right? He was the one she fought the rest of the committee for. Oh, Louise, Louise, you really should be more careful about which horse you back in a race, or you might just lose everything. I glance at my watch. Ten-thirty. With my big concert coming up tonight, I don't want to spend all day following this chick around Manhattan. But I suppose I can spare just a little time for sweet Louise. Clip clop. Clip clop. Clip clop.

She turns south on Broadway towards the subway station. I can't let her get too far ahead now, or she might hit it just right and hop on a train before I have a chance to…to what? Who the hell knows, I'm winging it. I just know that something has to be done about this bitch before she can do me any more harm than she already has.

Louise clip-clops her way to the very end of the platform where she leans forward and peers down the tunnel, looking for some sign that the arrival of a train is imminent. I stick to the back wall, moving slowly, looking down at the ground but still watching her out of the corner of my eye. Around us, the platform is busy, but not insane. The majority of the commuters have already made their way to offices all over the city.

There are a few nannies of various ethnicities with ironclad grips on their small charges. A group of about ten white-blonde tourists are clustered in one area, excitedly snapping pictures of one another and trying to decipher subway maps. I think they are Swedish. Or Danish. One of those cold countries filled with tall blonde people. And then there is Louise Kutter—one of the most prominent musicians in the country—as renown for her bitchiness as she is for her playing. Someone really should teach her a lesson. Today I'm thinking that someone might be me.

When you first see the lights of the subway down the tunnel you can't really tell if it's coming on the local or the express track. In fact it's not until it's almost upon you that you are really able to judge if this one is going to stop at your station or whiz right past you in the center track. This morning my money is on the local.

I'm only a few feet behind her now and she has no idea I'm even there. It would be so easy to just reach out my hand and brush my fingers against the smooth grain of that Italian leather coat. The metallic claps, creaks and groans are growing exponentially louder now as the twelve cars barrel toward us. Again, Louise leans out to look. Just can't help herself, can she? The brakes are squealing so loudly now that no one hears her when she screams.

Louise is looking up at me in a stunned daze of fear and confusion.

"What…? What happened?"

"Miss Kutter, are you okay?" I have my most concerned face on as I hover over her.

"I—I don't know. What happened?"

"Do you recognize me? I'm Jeremy Corrigan, one of the Kreisler competitors."

She starts to shake her head but then something clicks in her mind. Her eyebrows knit together as she strains to recollect me through the shock. "Yes," she says slowly. "Yes, of course. Jeremy…"

"Miss Kutter, you took quite a tumble. But I don't think you hit your head. Your foot, though, I think that might be broken."

"Yes," she repeats, glancing down the length of her body to where her left boot is a little too far to the left. I'm amazed she can't feel the pain yet.

Adrenaline, man, best narcotic on the planet.

"Lady, this kid saved your life!" a transit cop is saying over my shoulder. "If he hadn't been there to catch you, you would've gone right over the edge of the platform and onto the track."

Louise looks from the cop back to me. "Is that true, Jeremy?"

I shrug and shake my head dismissively.

"Nah. It was nothing. Instinct. I was just so stunned to see that it was you. You really need to be more careful if you're going to wear narrow heels like that. They can get caught on just about anything."

Like my foot.

She's trying to sit up now.

"Whoa! Lady, you gotta stay put. The ambulance is on its way," the cop says.

I can see the confusion in her face lifting a little and I'm fairly certain that the pain is about to hit her like...well, like a train, for lack of a better simile. I'm not wrong.

Louise starts to moan, quietly at first. "Oh...oh! I feel it now…"

I squat down beside her and take her hand in mine, while the cop clears the nosy onlookers around us. "Okay, Louise. It's going to be okay. They're going to take you to the hospital and get you all patched up."

Even as I say this I can hear the squall of the ambulance siren nearby. She grips my hand tightly, tears starting to flow from her eyes. "Oh, God, it hurts so much…" she says through clenched teeth.

"It's okay, just squeeze my hand as hard as you need to."

She forces herself to focus on me, to really see me. "You saved my life?" she asks.

"I did."

"I don't…I don't know how I can…"

"Enough of that now. I just happened to be in the right place at the right time."

I can see the EMT's coming down the stairs, backboard in hand.

"They're here, Louise. They'll give you something for the pain in just a second."

"Jeremy…"

"Yes?"

"Thank you." I smile down at her. She's struggling to say something else. "I'm sorry," she whispers up at me finally. "I'm really so sorry..."

"I know," I say in a flat tone that belies the concern on my face. "Don't do it again, Louise. There might not be someone there to catch you next time."

By the time she can process what I've said, she's surrounded by paramedics and I'm back out on the sidewalk, zipping up my jacket against the frigid morning air.

44

"Wow, you look amazing," Julia whispers reverently when I open the door to my dressing room.

She's right. I'm wearing the new tux I bought last week in the city.

"Jeremy, it's a full house," she reports excitedly, bouncing up and down on her toes. "I mean the concert hall is packed to the rafters. They don't even have seats for me and Brett so we're going to watch from backstage."

"Excellent!"

"Have you warmed up?" she asks, taking a seat on the couch next to my horn.

"Yup, good to go. Did you spot the judges panel?"

She shakes her head. "No, they've got them set up in the broadcast booth. No telling who's back there."

I can tell you who's not there. Louise Kutter.

"Can I get anything for you? Water? Something to eat?"

"No, I'm fine."

"Well, I'd say I'd cook something special for you later … but we both know how that would turn out," she says with a sly smile.

I can't help it, I have to smile back. She really is an appallingly bad cook.

"Yeah … thanks, but no thanks."

A quick rap on the door and my brother sticks his head in. "Hey, man! You should see the crowd out there! More than the first two nights combined! Of course … they could just be a bunch of morbid Lookie-loos wanting to see where the other horn player dropped dead…"

"Brett!" Julia squeaks loudly. "That is not funny!"

He gives me a sheepish shrug. "You're right," he says in what I recognize to be his most placating tone. "I'm sorry Julia. That was in very bad taste."

She gives him a 'humph' of disapproval, and shakes her head.

"Really, I'm sorry!" he holds up his hands in surrender. "I know he was a good guy. Sometimes, it's just easier to laugh about stuff like this."

Oh. Good save, bro. I'll have to remember to use that one myself.

"So what did you finally settle on for an encore?" Julia asks, offering her forgiveness by way of changing the subject.

"Oh, man, you've got to do '*The Flight of the Bumblebee*.' You really haul ass on that thing," Brett says with the enthusiasm of someone who's already a few beers into a six-pack.

"Actually, I changed my mind," I inform them as I run a comb through my hair one last time. Just a few more minutes to go.

"Oh?" asks Julia.

"Yeah. I'm doing that Chuck Mangione *Lullaby*."

I can see her puzzled expression in the mirror. "Cal's encore?" she asks.

"Well, it's not like he owned it or anything..."

"When did you have a chance to learn it?"

"I don't know. I was interested in it after he mentioned it on New Year's Eve."

"Like last week? I haven't heard you practice it once…"

Another knock at the door cuts her off before I have a chance to do it. "Jeremy, time to head backstage," the stage manager calls.

"That's me, then," I say, picking up my horn and placing it under my arm.

"Where's your music?" Brett asks.

"No music," I say proudly.

"You memorized everything?" he asks incredulously.

"Yup."

I hold out my hand for Julia to take, more as a distraction than anything else. I don't want her thinking too hard about this encore thing and it works. Her confused expression melts away and she grabs hold as the three of us head toward the stage, and my destiny. They weren't kidding. The audience is absolutely overflowing with people. I'm standing in the stage left wings, peering out from behind the curtains as the orchestra tunes.

"Good luck out there," Maestro Sutton says, putting a hand on my shoulder as he walks out past me to take his place at the podium. There is a healthy round of applause for him, and once he's settled in front of the Symphony an expectant hush falls over the audience. I take one last swig of water and hand it to the stage manager. I straighten my tie, take a deep breath and stroll out on stage with the confidence and charisma of a politician on Election Day. The audience applauds loudly as I walk to the podium to shake hands with the Maestro and the Concert Master. But then I do something a little unexpected.

I walk to the very front edge of the stage and face the audience. I don't have a microphone but the acoustics are great in here and I think I'll be heard well enough. I'm sure the Maestro is wondering what the hell I'm doing. He was just about ready to give the downbeat.

"Good evening," I say in my loudest, clearest voice. "I would like to dedicate this recital to Calvin Burridge. A true friend, a brilliant musician and a good man. He will be missed by all those whose lives he touched. It should be Cal standing on this stage tonight, but I'm humbled and honored to stand here in his stead."

I give the slightest nod to signal I have finished and the entire audience erupts into deafening applause. It's even more than I expected. I walk back to where a chair has been set out for me and I push it to the side, choosing to give this recital standing. The audience is still clamoring when the Maestro catches my eye and gives me a raised eyebrow. I'm not sure if it's about the impromptu speech or the impromptu decision to stand. I smile and give him a little shrug. To my surprise, he returns both and raises his baton to begin.

And then, there is the magic. Even I'm not prepared for how good I am on this particular night. Without the burden of nerves or fear or guilt, I'm free to be brilliant.

After the single orchestral chord that opens the Strauss Horn Concerto No.1, it's all me. My tone is triumphant and brilliant as I land the opening solo fanfare the way a skater lands a triple axel. Like me, it is absolutely fearless. When the orchestra rejoins, we are off on a musical journey that moves from the sweet and languid to the bold and fiery. The third and final section of the concerto builds from almost nothing into a blazing display of bravura. And just when you think it can't grow any more intense—it does, as I mount one last finger-blistering climb to the high C.

They are on their feet and calling "bravo" before I can even take the horn from my lips. I allow myself the luxury of taking a moment to let it all soak in. After a deep bow, I straighten up and look out across the floor and balcony seats at the thousands of people standing for me. They are clapping for me. It just confirms what I have known all along, that this was never meant to be Cal's night. It is mine. The single greatest moment in my life.

Finally, it's all falling into place.

PART Three: Julia

45

I'm standing in a sea of pink flowers. Dr. Sam and Matthew both know I love any and all blooms of the pink variety, so they have ensured there are plenty of them for me to enjoy in my dressing room. There are also a good number of newspapers. Brett and Jeremy and I have been collecting them from newsstands all over town, all day. *The Times, The Post, The Arts Review*, even *Newsday* and *The Connecticut Courier* are proclaiming Jeremy's brilliance in the face of tragedy. They say he has single-handedly rescued the Kreisler Competition from its nosedive into a sea of lurid headlines and reminded the world of the healing powers of music. I couldn't be more proud of him.

"Jeremy, would you please get my zipper for me?" I ask, after getting tired of wrestling with it.

I'd hoped that Matthew would at least stop by to wish me luck in person, but there's been no sign of him all evening. Maybe he's decided not to come. Maybe…

I stop myself. I can't worry about that right now, my mind needs to be on my music, my performance.

Jeremy tugs the zipper of my black velvet dress the last few inches. It's nothing fancy, but I love it. The way it sits just off my shoulders, the way it hugs my waist tightly before it flares out into a soft, flowing skirt. It makes me feel pretty, and so does the man standing behind me in the mirror. He kisses one of my bare shoulders and I feel the electricity throughout my entire body.

Things have been tense between us for the last few weeks, but I know that's only because of the pressures of the competition. Once that's over, I'm sure he'll go back to being his sweet, loving self. Until then, I do my best to gauge his mood and make him happy. I'm good at that.

"I have something for you," he says, pulling a tiny satin pouch from his pocket.

"Really?" I ask with sudden excitement. Of course he'd come up with some grand romantic gesture.

"What is it?"

"Oh, just a little something I really thought you should have for tonight."

"What, what, what?" I'm bouncing up and down on my toes.

"Calm down!" He laughs. "Now, close your eyes and don't open them until I tell you to."

I do as he asks.

"Oh, Jeremy, I'm so excited! I mean, after last night, there's no doubt in my mind that you're going to take the gold, but I feel so lucky just to be here. And to have you with me…"

I feel him fasten something around my neck. Jewelry! How extravagant! How sweet.

"Okay, open your eyes!"

I do, and suddenly I'm frozen, ice cold to my core. My hand touches the emerald that sparkles against the black velvet.

"But this is the necklace. The necklace from Montauk," I say slowly.

"I know!" he agrees. "It looked so beautiful on you, I knew I had to go back and get it."

What? No, he wouldn't. Would he?

"You went back there? To … to that shop?"

He nods proudly.

"And was she there?"

"Who? Your mother?"

I wince at his use of the word. Did he really think that this would make me happy?

"Jeremy …"

There's a rap on the door before I can finish the thought.

"Julia, you're on in five!" a voice calls from outside.

I take a deep breath and my hand falls from the pendent. I know his intentions were good and it's not worth making a big deal out of this, so I smile and give him one more, quick embrace.

"Thank you for thinking of me," I whisper as I hold onto him tightly. "I love you so much, Jeremy." He leans down and his lips find mine for a long deep kiss. Finally, I pull away with a giggle. "Hey, can we pick this up later? I have someplace I need to be right now." I can't help but notice his eyes are more brown than green today as he looks back down at me, and they are crinkling around the edges in that way which makes my heart beat just a little bit faster.

"I just...there's something I really need to say before you go out there, Jules," he says.

"Jeremy, I don't have time …" I start to protest, but then he's down on one knee.

Oh. My. God. Is he really going to ask me to marry him right here? Right now? This is insane!

"Jeremy?"

He takes my hand in his and holds it tightly. "Jules, we haven't known each other very long," he starts, "but sometimes you just know, right?"

He seems to be waiting for a response, so I nod, trying to keep myself from screaming *'Yes!'* before he can even ask the question.

"These last months have been some of the best of my life," he is saying. "I can't tell you how much satisfaction it has given me to see you transform from a timid little mouse ..."

Mouse? He's going to bring up the Mouse thing now?

"...to a pathetic, lovesick, ignorant whore."

What? Wait a minute. Somehow, I'm not processing what he's saying. I'm hearing the words, but they don't match the loving adoration that's on his face. This must be a joke. A really, really bad joke.

"Jeremy, that's not very funny..."

But he continues as if I haven't spoken.

"I was the one who found your slut mother, Jules. I was the one who brought you together. And you did not disappoint. Oh, God, how I wish I'd had a camera to record your pitiful little face when you recognized her!"

My hand has grown clammy in his. I try to pull it away, but he holds it tight, still looking up at me, lovingly, while the hateful words pour out of his mouth. I'm starting to feel sick as he continues on in earnest.

"I'd hoped to get your father in on the act too, but that wasn't possible ..."

He found my father? This is no joke. This is... I should stop him, but my mouth is so dry that I can't even part my lips.

"As it turns out, the fucking coward killed himself right after seeing you graduate from high school! I know this because I saw his suicide note in the police files and he describes it in great detail. How much you look like your mother, how he didn't deserve a daughter like you, how ..."

"Stop it!"

When I finally find my voice, these two words come out with a ferocity that I didn't even know I was capable of. Jeremy stops talking, but he doesn't stop smiling.

"What are you saying?" I ask, not even realizing that there are mascara-stained tears streaming down my face. "What are you doing?"

"Oh, Jules, don't you know? I'm doing what I've been doing since the night I ran into you at the diner, 'accidentally' on purpose. I'm fucking with you, you stupid cow!"

He's laughing now. Laughing at my face, which is now twisted into a pallid mask of horror and incredulity. He points at me.

"Oh, oh, God!" he howls, laughing so hard that he can barely breathe. "You should see your expression! If you only knew how many times I've wanted to tell you how plain and boring you are. And how stupid! So, so stupid! You didn't even realize what a fool you've made of yourself all these weeks. Everyone has been laughing at you behind your back. Apparently, you're the only one who's deluded enough to think I could ever love someone as dim and dull as you are."

I cannot tear my eyes away from Jeremy as he gets to his feet, still holding my hand. He manages to catch his breath and stop laughing, leaving just that hint of a smile curling at the corners of his mouth up.

"Julia! We need you now," comes the stage manager's voice from outside of the closed door.

"She'll be there in just a second," Jeremy calls out for me. Then, he leans down, so that his lips are right next to my ear, as if he is going to tell me the deepest of all his secrets. And he does.

"Now, when you go out there on stage, Jules, you think about me, and how I never loved you. I never even *liked* you. And you remember that the only reason you're even standing on that stage is because everyone feels sorry for you. You're pathetic, and you're nothing but a stupid cunt," he whispers. Then, he kisses my cheek sweetly, and walks out of the dressing room and into the hall, leaving me staring after him.

"Julia?" The stage manager sticks his head in the door. "You have got to come with me *now*," he says with some urgency.

One moment, I'm looking at him and nodding wordlessly, the next, I'm down on my knees, vomiting in the trashcan.

46

Veteran thrill-seekers know that riding a rollercoaster isn't all about the euphoria of the fall. There is this moment when, after a deliciously slow, agonizing ascent, you hover—as if on the very cusp of the earth. For this brief instant, all of the scenery and the noise and distractions of life fade away, giving you an unobstructed view all the way to the horizon. In that one brief, magical moment, everything crystallizes, and you can see what it is you've been missing all along. And then, just as you begin to grasp what it is you are seeing, the world drops out from under your feet, and you find yourself hurtling through time and space. I have just had my moment of crystal clarity. Now comes the inevitable, sickening feeling of the free-fall.

I'm in a daze as I take first one shaky step out of the wings, and then another and another, each hollow step echoing across the empty stage. The orchestra doesn't join me until later in the program, so I'm alone up there. Somehow, I manage to get to my chair without stumbling. On autopilot, I situate myself and slip the cello between my knees. But when I pick up the bow, my right hand is shaking so hard that there's no way I can draw it across the strings. I don't know what to do. So I do nothing.

Movement from the audience catches my attention and my eyes are drawn to Jeremy, the handsome, sexy, love of my life. He's waving at me, a smug little smile on his face. Next to him sits the woman who gave birth to me. I can only gape at the two of them, his words ringing in my ears. I'm aware of some awkward shuffling and murmuring in the audience, but I simply cannot take my eyes off of the two people sitting directly in front of me. How could he do this to me? How could he be so vicious? And why now, of all times? I know the answer, of course, but I refuse to believe it.

I can't do this. There's no way I can play. If I don't get off of this stage, I'm going to melt into a pathetic puddle. Okay. I just need to get on my feet and walk the ten steps back off stage. Then I can run. I don't know where, but it will be far away. Somewhere where I can simply let the darkness envelop me while I try to forget this nightmare.

Just as I grab the neck of the cello so I can move it, I hear clapping. A single set of hands from somewhere out in the vastness of the house. I manage to tear my eyes from Jeremy and there, just a few rows back and to the left, is Matthew. He's clapping as hard as he can. People around him start to murmur, and a few join him in standing and applauding. He doesn't take his eyes from mine as row after row of people get to their feet and applaud, for a reason they don't quite understand.

Matthew gives me a smile and a nod, both of which tell me everything that's in his heart. He's silently telling me that it's going to be okay. That, whatever it is that has sent me into this spiraling descent, he's going to be by my side and I'm going to be okay. And, just like that, the spell is broken. I don't have a tissue, so I use the back of my hand to swipe at the tears that have started to spill from my eyes. I nod back at him, get to my unsteady feet and take a small bow in acknowledgement of the audience. Then I hold out my shaking hand in a gesture for them to be seated. I settle back into my own chair, keeping my eyes locked on Matthew's. I don't dare move my glance because I know that if catch even a fleeting glimpse of Jeremy, it will all be over. I take a long, deep breath, pick up my bow from the music stand and start to play without preamble.

The Bach *Suite*, usually so light and buoyant, now has a hint of melancholy around the edges as I play it. Under my fingers, it has turned it into something wistful and nostalgic. I hold the notes a little longer—dig into them a little deeper. Rather than my usual crisp run up the fingerboard, I allow my fingers to linger and rock a little more. This is an entirely different Bach to my ears, and to my heart.

And still, my gaze does not leave Matthew's. In these minutes I can feel him telegraphing his love to me—and his adoration. Without a single word, he is telling me he would walk through fire for me. He would give anything, be anything, do anything to be with me for the rest of his life. I can see all of it in his eyes. And he knows it. Because we are the only people who can read one another's souls. He gives me the strength I need to face the piece that brought Jeremy into my world.

When my accompanist begins the slow movement of the Rachmaninoff Sonata, I'm not sure until the very last second that I'll be able to draw my bow across the strings and act out, in music, the tale of the lovers. But, when the horsehair touches the gut, something unexpected happens. Every bit of confusion, of hurt and anger seems to wick from my heart, down my arm and to my cello. Like the Bach, this too is an entirely different composition—hauntingly beautiful in its bleakness.

Finally, with the worst of it behind me, the bright and buoyant Boccherini *Cello Concerto* is a relief to me, though my heart isn't in it. It is meant to be lighthearted, and while I'm nailing every note, every phrase, there's something slightly off about the piece. I know it's enough to possibly put me out of contention for the gold, but that's the least of my concerns right now.

If the audience suspects something is amiss, they don't show it. The standing ovation comes in one swift wave across the concert hall. I catch a glimpse of Matthew, making his way out of his row and up the aisle, undoubtedly coming to meet me backstage. From where I'm standing, I also have a direct line of sight to Jeremy's seat. At least, what used to be Jeremy's seat. It's empty now. Kelly is there though, and she's crying—ppenly weeping as she stands and claps passionately. I turn my head so I don't have to see her. I'm not sure how long I stand there like that, staring blankly out into the blur of faces, but I jump when I feel the Maestro's hand on my shoulder.

"Julia," he whispers, "we should do your encore now."

I nod and sit once more, and the audience joins me, a hush falling over them.

I don't hear the harp right away—it seems to come from out of nowhere. And then slowly, oh so slowly, I pull a gossamer thread of sound from my cello. It is *The Swan* by Saint-Saens. I don't need to read the music for this because I know it by heart. So I turn my eyes upward, as if looking to heaven. In my right hand, the bow barely skims the strings. All the while, the fingers of my left hand slide easily up and down the fingerboard to find their pitch. They rock back and forth in place to create the slightest quivering vibrato in each note.

I shift and wrap myself around my cello, embracing it, clinging to it as if it is the only thing keeping me afloat. Actually, at this very moment, that's exactly what it's doing. I turn my eyes to its top scroll as it rests on my shoulder, staring longingly at it as if it's my lover. Actually, at this very moment, that's exactly what it is. When the last note comes, I draw it out, stretching and stretching and stretching, until it simply isn't there anymore. Until I'm listening to its shadow.

When it is done, I drop my head to my chest and start to cry. I can't hold back for even another second. The sound of my sobs are drowned out by the roar of applause that has filled the concert hall, but I heave, up and down, my bow hanging down from the arm that has dropped to my side. I want to stay like this until Matthew comes to get me. But then, I remember that day not so very long ago, when he chided me for thinking I was made of glass. I'm not. So I wipe the tears, get to my feet and take one last bow. I acknowledge the Maestro and the orchestra, and hold up my bow with a wave to the audience.

I see Matthew standing, just off of stage left, his arms open and waiting for me.

I walk into them and I collapse.

47

It's a very specific kind of sleep that comes within the walls of a hospital—a shallow sleep filled with low voices, punctuated by foreign hums and beeps. The lighting is never quite right. It's too light for night, too dark for day. And there always seems to be someone shuffling in and out of your sphere of consciousness, leaving you wondering what is a dream and what isn't. It's a miracle anyone gets better in a hospital.

When I open my eyes again, Matthew is exactly where he was two hours ago, sitting on a hard plastic chair, hunched over the side of my bed and holding my hand.

"Hi," I murmur sleepily, squinting my eyes until they can adjust to the florescent lighting above me.

"Hi," he says, leaning forward. "How're you feeling?"

"I don't know."

"What do you mean?"

"I mean, I don't know, Matthew," I say with the slightest hint of irritation. "I feel a lot of things right now. It's going to take some time for me to sort through them all."

He nods. "I understand that. But how are you feeling physically?"

"Tired."

"You look it," he agrees.

"Do I?" I ask, suddenly curious. "Take a picture of me."

"What?"

"With your phone. Take a picture. I don't have a mirror and I want to see what you're seeing," I insist.

He isn't happy about it, but he does it anyway, and passes me the phone. I take a sharp breath in. I'm not sure I'd have recognized myself had I not known who I was looking at. My God, I'm so pale that my freckles look like leopard spots across the bridge of my nose. And the circles under my eyes make it appear as if someone has punched me. Actually, someone has punched me recently, and I notice the makeup that I've been using to camouflage that has worn off. Luckily, Matthew hasn't made that connection yet. I pass the phone back to him.

"Matthew?"

"Yes, Julia?"

"I want to come home. Can I come home?" I ask quietly.

He wraps his big, strong hand around my small, cold one, rubbing it gently to warm it. "You never have to ask Julia. I don't care what's going on between us. It's your home for as long as you want it to be. As long as I'm alive, you will have a place with me. No matter what."

I give him a wan smile. "I was hoping you'd say that."

There's been an IV. line set up in my arm all night, rehydrating my spent body. I'm scheduled to have an iron infusion in a couple of hours. From midnight till about three in the morning I was shuttled from floor to floor, for MRI's, Cat Scans and God only knows what else. They must have taken a quart of blood throughout the course of the night. It's nearly seven in the morning when the doctor finally stops by to see me.

"Well? What is it?" Matthew asks as soon as he steps into the room. "What's wrong?"

A balding man in his late fifties, Dr. Franklin brings an air of calm into the room with him. He looks from me to Matthew and back again.

"Miss James, perhaps your … friend should step outside for a few moments while you and I speak," he suggests.

I shake my head. "No. Thank you for offering, Doctor, but I'd like Matthew to be here for whatever you have to tell me."

He clears his throat and flips through a few pages on his clipboard chart before speaking again.

"Okay, well, first of all, you're very dehydrated. The IV fluids should help with that. And, as you know, you're severely anemic right now. I believe that your rigorous rehearsal and performance schedule, along with the tremendous stress, all contributed to your collapse last night."

"Well that's good news," Matthew says, the relief evident in his voice and on his face. "I was so afraid it was going to be worse …"

"But those aren't the only issues," the doctor cuts him off. "Miss James—Julia—did you know you have a hairline fracture on your right wrist?"

I suddenly feel very uncomfortable. Maybe I should have had Matthew step out for this part. But it's too late for that now, so I press on and hope for the best. "I—uh, I thought I might," I say quietly.

Matthew's gaze swings to me, his brows knit together.

"Weren't you in pain when you were playing?" the doctor asks.

Yes, actually.

"A little, I guess. But nothing unbearable," I lie.

"And your face …"

Oh, God. No. Please don't say it. Matthew is going to lose his mind if the doctor says it.

"There has been some trauma consistent with … well, consistent with a blow."

Dr. Franklin sits on the edge of the hospital bed and takes his glasses off. He peers at me intensely. "Julia, has someone been hurting you?"

Matthew is on his feet in a split second, which maybe isn't his smartest move given that the doctor clearly thinks he might be the one hurting me.

"Sit down!" Dr. Franklin barks so firmly that Matthew sits without further comment.

Now they're both staring at me expectantly, waiting for some kind of answer.

"Matthew," I start out slowly, softly, "I need you to promise me you're not going to go running out of here and do something stupid."

"Julia, did Jeremy hurt you?" he asks in a tone that even I don't recognize.

"I'm not saying another word until you swear to me that you won't …."

The doctor looks back at me over his shoulder. "Your friend isn't going to do anything foolish because he'd never want to do anything to upset you. Isn't that right?" he asks Matthew pointedly.

He gets the message, closing his eyes for a second and taking a deep breath to calm himself. "Okay. I promise, Julia," he agrees through clenched teeth.

Satisfied, I turn my attention back to the doctor.

"Doctor, I'm just getting out of a bad relationship," I say quietly. "All I can tell you is that it's over, and I'm not at risk anymore."

Matthew is beside himself, shaking his head as he fumes silently.

"All right, well, I'm going to suggest you press charges …"

"Damn straight she'll press charges!"

"I'll consider that doctor, I will," I promise, ignoring Matthew's outburst.

"Good," Dr. Franklin says as he stands up. "We'll get a soft cast on the wrist and you'll need to take a break from playing for a couple weeks."

I nod my assent. "Fine. Fine. When can I go home?"

The doctor clears his throat again. "Well, I think we can discharge you just as soon as my colleague, Dr. White, stops by for a consult. I've asked her to do a quick exam."

"For what? What else is wrong?" I ask, reaching for Matthew's hand. He's beside me in an instant and we both stare at the doctor, wondering if he has saved the worst for last.

"Julia, Dr. White is an Obstetrician. You're pregnant."

He has.

48

The cavernous concert hall is empty, and it's freezing. I shrink a little further into my sweater and try to concentrate on the Schubert that Matthew and the other members of the Walton Quartet are rehearsing on the stage, but I can't. I hear Jeremy's voice in my head. I pick apart every despicable thing he said to me and try to find some kind of reasonable explanation for his behavior. But there is none. It's all I can think about, because if I let my mind wander any further, I'll have to think about that other thing. And, of course, that's exactly why Matthew insisted he needed me to attend this rehearsal—under the guise of "helping them with the acoustics."

"How's it sounding out there?" Joe Dancy calls out to me from the stage. He's the first violinist for the group and he's playing into this charade by asking me the same question every fifteen minutes or so. I don't feel like shouting anymore, so I give him the thumbs up, and they continue on.

I'm numb. My waking hours are spent in a trance, moving from one room to the next, one task to the next. It's as if my very bones are restless. I'm not comfortable sitting or standing, reading or watching television. With my arm in a cast, I can't even use the cello to channel some of this sadness and fear. I'd hoped that being here, listening to the music might make me feel a little better, but even the notes of soulful Schubert aren't able to penetrate the fog that's settled in around me.

Dammit! I am *not* crazy! He loves me, I know he does. No one could be so loving and attentive and caring and tender without actually feeling *something*. That's not possible…is it? No. Of course not, nobody is that good of an actor.

"Ugh," I grunt to myself and I rub my eyes, as if this will dispel his image from my mind. It doesn't. In fact, the only time I find any peace at all is when I'm asleep.

I take a tissue from the wad of them in my bag and wipe the tears that have slipped down my cheeks. No. I'm wrong. How could I have been so stupid? Why couldn't I see him for who he was? These are the questions that plague me all day long. Jeremy Corrigan is handsome, sexy and charming. I wanted so much to believe that someone like him could love me. And now look at me. I'm a fool, and everyone knows it. I shudder to think what people have been saying about me behind my back. He said they've been laughing at me all these weeks. They were probably taking bets on when he would kick me to the curb.

"Julia?"

I look up and see Joe on the edge of the stage, peering out at me. Has he been talking to me?

"Uh, yeah, Joe. Sorry, what did you say?" I call back to him, pulling myself out of my own head, grateful that he can't see me well enough to notice the tears

"I was just asking if you think we'd be better off a little further upstage for this piece?"

Seriously? Now they're just making shit up to keep me busy.

"Nope. Sounds good from here," I holler back at him, and he nods.

I pretend to be attentive while they chatter and make notes. Matthew looks out at me and smiles periodically. But once they're playing again, I slump back down into my seat.

DING!

I am startled by the noise coming from the phone in my bag. Who the hell would be texting me now? The only person who texts me is busy playing his viola at the moment. Unless of course... No, no way. It can't be. I know how insane even the thought is, but I can't help myself, I start to rummage in my bag until I find my phone at the bottom and pull it out.

Jeremy's photo is staring back at me from the animated bubble that frames his text message. I run my thumb over the image, as if to touch him.

Come out front.

I feel my breath catch in my throat and my eyes jump to Matthew, who's too busy playing to notice what I'm doing. Should I go? Does he want to apologize? Maybe he's regretting the way he acted and what he said. Well, I won't know unless I meet him. I move quickly and quietly up the carpeted aisle of the hall and out through the lobby, eerily still and abandoned.

I push through one of the heavy glass doors and stumble out onto the sidewalk, just catching myself before I eat the pavement. I straighten myself up, and look around, hoping he hasn't witnessed my clumsiness. But Jeremy is nowhere to be found.

Huh.

I look down at the phone again, thinking maybe I have misread the location. Nope. This is the only spot that could be considered out front. My heart sinks. He's just messing with me, obviously. I turn around to go back inside, but just as my hand touches the door handle, I feel a tap on my shoulder. Oh, thank God. When I spin back, there is a small, tentative smile on my lips. A hopeful smile. But, it's not Jeremy who's the recipient of my expression.

"Hello, Julia," my mother says.

I'm speechless as the smile fades from my face.

"What…what are you doing here?" I ask, stunned to see her.

"I wanted to see you. I tried to see you at the hospital, but they wouldn't let me. I—I was so worried when I went to find you backstage and they told me you'd collapsed. Are you all right? You look so pale…"

It's amazing what a little anger can do to shock your system right back into a normal rhythm.

"I'm sorry, but do you have any idea how ridiculous you sound?" I ask, taking a step closer to her. "You were 'so worried' about me? What the hell were you doing when daddy was breaking my ribs and throwing scalding coffee on me? Or for the ten years after that when I was in an orphanage? But you're 'worried about me' now." My tone is equal parts incredulity and venom.

If she's fazed by the outburst, she doesn't show it. "I know there's a lot of ground for us to cover. And we will. But for now, I just want to know that you're okay now. My God, Julia, you play the cello like…like an angel! I have never heard anything so beautiful in all my life! I'll be forever grateful to that young man for bringing you back to me," she says with a sniff. She's blinking back tears now.

I can only stare at her in wide-eyed astonishment. It takes a full ten seconds for me to find the words.

"You're unbelievable," I mutter. "As I recall it, I didn't leave *your* life, you left *mine*. And who, exactly, do I have to thank for reintroducing us?"

"Don't you know? I thought for sure he'd have told you. Your boyfriend, Jeremy. He tracked me down after our…meeting…in Montauk. He sent me the ticket for your recital. He told if I came to the city, he'd tell me where to find you. So, I came and I called. He said you'd be here."

Of course. Jeremy was never here—he was just texting to get me to come out and meet her. Or, more likely, he's here, somewhere, taking some perverse pleasure in watching our family reunion out here on the street. I look around me, expecting to see him dart around the corner or into a doorway.

"Julia?" she says, looking at me with my own eyes, though, hers are filled with concern and mine are filled with rage.

"Go."

"What?" She actually sounds surprised.

"Leave," I say firmly. But she doesn't budge.

"Now Julia, I know you're upset…"

I think I'm going to scream at her, maybe even hit her. But when I open my mouth, the only thing that comes out is a sob. And another and another. It is all there then, welling up in me, clawing at me, drowning me. Jeremy. The baby. The Kreislers. The love. The abuse. The fear. Kelly makes a move to embrace me, but I step back quickly, shaking my head and still sobbing.

"No!" I shriek. "No, don't touch me!"

"Julia? Julia!" Matthew's voice is behind me. "What's going on out here?" he asks, looking from me to her and back to me again. He's never met this woman, but there's no mistaking who she is. "What the hell are you doing here?" he demands.

She isn't as calm and self-assured with Matthew as she was with me. "I'm sorry, who are you? And what business is this of yours?"

"I'm the only family she has on the face of this earth, lady, and there's no way I'm going to let you hurt her again. I suggest you get yourself back to Penn Station and onto a train, before I escort you all the way home myself."

"I don't think you have any right to..."

"Stop it!" I sob, cutting her off. "God, just go! Please, go!"

Matthew glares at her, daring her to say something. With a thoughtful nod, she slings her purse over her shoulder and starts to walk away. But then, she stops.

"This isn't over, Julia," she says resolutely. "I'm not giving up on us." She turns and walks down the street and into a crowd on the corner.

Matthew pulls me into his arms and I bury my face in his chest and cry until there are no more tears. He strokes my hair and murmurs soothing words into my ear.

"What the hell happened?" he asks when I've finally quieted.

"I got a text from Jeremy to come outside," I sniff, "and there she was, waiting for me."

"Jeremy texted you? Just now?"

I nod, and something seems to occur to him.

"Julia, did you text him first, or let him know you'd be here this afternoon? You can tell me, I won't be angry..." I shake my head adamantly. "Then how did he know you'd be here? Who could have told him?"

Suddenly, I'm sitting in the diner with Cal, talking about My Orbit. Learning about how I'd been unknowingly telling the world my whereabouts and recalling that I never did get around to asking him to delete the app from my phone. I'm nearly knocked off my feet by the revelation.

"You did," I whisper.

"I did what?" he asks, confused.

"You told him where I was. You've been telling him where I am for months."

"Julia, are you insane? How could you think I'd…" And then it hits him, too. He slaps a hand over his own mouth and closes his eyes. "God damn it! It never occurred to me that anyone other than me would be keeping an eye on you with that stupid app. Jesus. Julia, I'm so sorry. I led that son of a bitch right to you."

I pull him to me again and squeeze him hard. I don't say anything, because I know this man well enough to know there is nothing I can say. He won't be forgiving himself anytime soon.

49

Matthew thinks that I'm going to fight him, that there is no way I'll get out of my bed, get my act together and attend the Kreisler medal ceremony tonight. But he's wrong about that, as he sees for himself when he comes into my room to wake me from my long afternoon of napping and crying.

"Julia?" I can just hear him in my room from where I stand under the shower. He raps on the door softly and then his voice is closer. "Julia? You okay in there?"

"Matthew? Come in," I call out over the running water.

"How're you doing?" he asks.

I stick my sopping red head out from behind the shower and find him leaning against the vanity.

"A little better," I say as soapy water drips from my hair down my face. "The iron infusion helped a lot. I didn't realize how awful I was feeling until I started to feel better."

He nods and looks as if there's something he wants to say but isn't quite sure how to say it. At this point, it could be any number of the ridiculous occurrences of the last several days. The baby, my mother…

"Can we talk about what happened with Jeremy?" he asks.

And he chooses what's behind door number three: The abusive love of my life. I hold up a finger and pop my head back into the shower for a quick rinse. When I'm done, I thrust one of my arms out from behind the curtain, hand outstretched.

"Towel, please."

He hands it to me and, after a minute, I step out, sopping and swathed in Egyptian cotton. He follows me as I pad out of the bathroom, through the closet and into my bedroom. When I flip on the light, he can see that I have already got a dress hanging on the back of my door. I pick up a smaller towel from the dresser and use it to wrap my hair up into a turban. Matthew sits on the edge of my bed, waiting patiently as I rifle through my dresser drawers for panties, bra and tights. I hold onto the tights a little too long, having a brief, wistful flashback. I shake my head as if to dispel it and sit besides Matthew on the bed.

"I loved him. I—I still love him. And now I'm having his baby." I'm grateful when he senses, correctly, that I'm not looking for any commentary here, and he waits in silence for me to finish my thought. "He...he says he never loved me. Never could love someone like me." I look down at my hands in my lap, unable to look at him when I tell him the disgusting lengths that Jeremy went to in order to hurt me—to destroy me. "He told me that my father committed suicide. I don't know if it's true or not. And my mother, I think he found her and orchestrated that whole catastrophe out in Montauk."

"And..." he says tentatively, obviously not sure how far to go, "he hurt you?"

I clear my throat. It won't help anyone if he gets upset, so I need to downplay this as much as possible. "He got a little rough with me, but I was asking for it, really."

"Julia! Do you hear yourself?"

"No—listen to me, Matthew," I say, holding up a hand in protest. "It was me. I tried to slap him at Christmas, and he grabbed my wrist to stop me. He was protecting himself."

"Oh, please!" he snorts indignantly. "Protecting himself from all five feet of you? You cannot be serious. Besides, that's not all he did, is it?"

"No," I say quietly. He waits for the rest of it. "He was very angry on New Year's Eve and I made it worse. I should have just stayed out of his way and kept my mouth shut."

Matthew is shaking his head vehemently now. "What did he do?" he asks slowly, deliberately, belying the rage that I know is consuming him at this moment.

"He hit me. It was just… I only had a bloody nose and mouth."

"*Just?* Is that all? Well, thank God for that. I thought he did something serious." His tone is dripping with sarcasm. "And Brett? Did he know any of this was going on?"

I nod slowly. "He was there," I murmur.

"What?" he asks, incredulously. "Are you telling me that he was there and he didn't do anything? He didn't help you?"

I can't even meet his eyes as I shake my head. I'm mortified by my own naivety. Oh, hell, let's just call it what it is: my own stupidity. Gullibility. How could I have let myself believe that a man like that could ever… My thoughts are interrupted when I feel Matthew's arms around me, pulling me into him. I rest my head on his chest and start to cry.

"Julia?" he asks over her head.

"Yes?" my answer is muffled in his shirt.

"Did he... Did he force himself on you?"

I sit up suddenly, sniffling and wiping the tears from my face. "No, Matthew. Never. It wasn't like that. We were… I'm sorry, I know you don't want to hear this, but we were really good together like that. Those were some of the best moments. I felt like I was really seeing who he was then. The tender side…"

He holds up a hand and I stop. I'm right, he doesn't want to hear this.

"I'm having his child," I say.

"I know."

"Are you going to tell him?"

"I don't know. I don't even know how I feel about him right now. I'm so angry and hurt. But it's not like you can just snap your fingers and fall out of love with someone. You know what I mean?"

The moment I utter the words I wish I could stuff them right back in my mouth. I can't believe I have just said that to him, of all people. Of course he knows. He's only been telling me for years.

"Anyway," I start again, "if what he said to me is true, if he was really just using me, then how can I possibly tell him? I'm afraid…" I let the sentence trail off.

But I know he understands what I'm saying. The horrifying truth is that I don't have the luxury of feeling sorry for myself, because I no longer have the luxury of closing my eyes to the realities of Jeremy Corrigan. There is no telling what he would do if he found out I was carrying his baby. Or what he would do to me.

No. The time for fairytales and happily-ever-after has passed.

50

"Just the finalists, Miss," the backstage security guy is saying to me in a thick Brooklyn accent.

"I'm not leaving her," Matthew replies stubbornly.

"Then she's not going back there," he responds.

We are at an impasse. There is no way I'm going back stage to face Jeremy Corrigan on my own. I put a hand on Matthew's arm and lean close to his ear.

"Give him money," I whisper.

"What?"

"Give him cash," I insist. "That's what Jeremy does with these guys and it works every time."

Matthew pulls back and looks at me skeptically. "Would twenty do it?" he asks the large man guarding the entrance.

The guy looks upward toward the ceiling when he replies. "Forty'd be better," he says almost to himself.

"Fine," Matthew says with exasperation as he pulls two twenties from his wallet and slaps them down on the counter in front of him.

"Good luck," the man says to me as he waves us through.

We walk together down the long, dim, chilly hall, the click-clack of my heels the only sound between us. I'm not quite sure how I'm even standing right now. The competition, Jeremy, the baby, my mother—I should be a basket case. Maybe I'm in shock. Maybe I'm in denial. Probably both.

When we get back stage, the other finalists are there. All of them.

"Come on, let's sit over here," Matthew says, gesturing to some chairs all the way in the back of the wings.

"No. I have to see him," I say firmly.

"Julia…." I give him a look that makes him stop mid-sentence. "Fine, then I'm going with you," he says with equal firmness. I don't argue.

When Jeremy turns around, he looks down at me first and then up at Matthew. "Well, well. Didn't take long for you to scoop up my sloppy seconds, did it, Matthew?" He's smirking.

I can actually feel Matthew next to me, holding his breath and balling his fists.

"Jeremy," I start tentatively, "I…is it true? Did you mean everything you said that night, or were you just trying to upset me?"

He gives me a pitying smile.

"Oh, poor little gullible Jules. Both. I meant every word *and* I said all that to upset you. Though, apparently, I misjudged your resiliency."

I can only nod up at him sadly. I needed to hear this, but it hurts like hell. "Well, I wasn't lying when I said I love you."

"I know," he says simply.

"Jeremy…" I start again and then pause. I want to tell him about the baby. Maybe that will jolt him out of whatever mood this is that he's in. Maybe it will soften his heart and make him realize that he really does love me. Maybe…

He cocks an eyebrow and makes a circling gesture with his hand, signaling that I should get on with it and get out of his way.

"Good luck, Jeremy," I say at last.

"I've told you before, Jules, nothing to do with luck."

With that he gives me a patronizing pat on the shoulder and sets his sights on someone behind us. “Hey, Mila! Wait up…” he says, flagging down a very surprised Mila Strassman as she walks past us.

When I turn to face Matthew again, I’m blinking back un-spilled tears. “Well, that’s that then,” I say softly.

“That’s that,” he agrees.

Mila keeps looking past Jeremy to me. I can’t hear what he’s saying to her, but I’m sure it’s something charming.

“Let’s go sit,” Matthew says, taking the hand that isn’t in a cast.

We sit in chairs across from one another. I notice a newspaper on the table between us and I pick it up. Cal Burridge’s face is staring back at me from the front page of the Courier Journal. The headline reads *‘The Day the Music Died.’* I can’t help myself, I pick up the article and start to read. It’s everything we know up until this point. Cal’s meteoric rise and sudden, tragic death. The reports that he had a severe, life-threatening nut allergy and speculation as to how someone who was so careful could come into contact with a fatal dose.

Well, the Medical Examiner’s report is due to be released tomorrow so we should have more information then. As I read further, there is a smaller sub-article inset at the bottom of the page. Jeremy is pictured there. He’s described as a close, personal friend of Cal’s who is devastated by the loss and honored to carry on in his memory. They call it *‘a beacon of hope in a sea of despair.’*

I flip the paper over and set it facedown on the table so Matthew won’t notice the cover. It would likely send him into a rage.

“All right, everyone!” the stage manager calls out. “We’ll be starting in just a few minutes. Mr. Morgan will be here in just a moment. After he makes a brief presentation, he’s going to introduce each of the winners. Please walk out on stage when your name is called. There are to be no comments from anyone after the medal order has been announced," she says, with a pointed look toward the violinist, Mikhail.

Matthew leans close to me and whispers in my ear. "I heard that when he got second place in a competition last year, he cursed the judges in Russian and stomped off the stage, refusing to accept the award."

He nods and raises his eyebrows to confirm he's telling me the truth. He's trying to take my mind off of Jeremy. I give Matthew a small smile, and pretend he's succeeding.

"Sorry, Brittany!" Lester Morgan says to the stage manager as he comes rushing through a side door. "How's the house tonight?"

She rolls her eyes and shakes her head. "We better hope the fire marshal doesn't come by," she says.

He gives her a small laugh and looks around at the four finalists and the handful of stragglers like me. "Well, this is it, ladies and gentleman. Good luck to all of you," he says.

We mumble back an unorganized semblance of '*thank you*' and he steps out onto the stage. I'm amazed by the dazzling starburst of flash bulbs that greet him when he takes his place at the microphone. Press from newspaper, radio, television and internet news outlets are practically swarming the stage. Lester holds up a hand.

"I'm so conflicted," Lester starts out as the noise dies down. "This is a night of celebration. But it is also a night of mourning. With the loss of Calvin David Burridge, the Kreisler International Music Competition has been changed forever." There is a low murmur from the crowd. "I would like to announce that starting with the next competition, four years from now, we will offer a special award."

Suddenly a motorized screen lowers from the ceiling behind Lester. An image flashes up there. It is a rose-gold colored disc with a French horn embossed on it. It's beautiful.

"Ladies and gentleman, I give you the Calvin D. Burridge Special Judges' Prize. To be awarded at the discretion of the judges in honor of a musician who has displayed not only talent, but also a notable demeanor of professionalism, respect and honor. All traits embodied by Cal."

The applause is almost deafening and the flash bulbs burst anew. Good for you Cal. You got your medal in the end. I'm just sorry you had to get it this way.

"Alright, without further ado, may I present to you the four performers that we consider to be among the best in the world at this very moment," Lester says, rubbing his hands together excitedly.

"Please welcome pianist Lucy Kim…violinist Mikhail Fedoseyev…horn player Jeremy Corrigan…and cellist Julia James."

Matthew gives my hand a quick squeeze, plants a kiss on my cheek and steps back so he can watch.

There is thunderous applause, punctuated by ear-splitting whistles and calls of *'bravo!'* throughout the immense auditorium as the four of us make our way on stage. The flashbulbs burst anew and I'm seeing spots in front of me.

"Ladies and gentlemen, I think we've all waited long enough to hear the name of our winner so let's get down to it, shall we?"

A chorus of agreement from the audience.

A pretty young girl, who I recognize as one of the pages from the competition, comes on stage with a tray that holds three blue velvet boxes. Only three medals—someone on this stage is going home empty handed tonight. Lester isn't kidding about getting down to it. He takes one of his infamous little envelopes out of his pocket and slips out a card from inside.

"Taking fourth place and an Honorable Mention… Mikhail Fedoseyev of Moscow!"

He extends a hand to the violinist who ignores it and stalks offstage in a huff. Lester shrugs comically and the audience laughs. He pulls out a second envelope.

"The Bronze Medalist for this year is…Miss Lucy Kim of China!"

Lucy pretends to be shocked that she has not been chosen. She starts to walk past Lester's outstretched hand like Mikhail did, but then she doubles back to the stunned man with an impish smile. He wags a finger at her prank, and chuckles as the page hands him one of the boxes from her tray. He opens it and pulls out the bronze medal on its long blue ribbon and hangs it around Lucy's neck. She turns and bows to an audience that is already giving her a standing ovation.

When Lucy takes her place behind Lester, it is only Jeremy and I on the stage, standing side by side in front of all these people. God, I feel so tired. I just want this to be over. Please, just let this be over so I can go home.

"Well," Lester says, pulling out another envelope. "The thing here is that once I tell you who the Silver Medalist is, you're going to know immediately who the winner is. So, with all due respect to our second place musician, I'm just going to say that the Gold Medal, Grand Prize Winner of the ninth Kreisler International Music Competition is…"

There is a collective inhalation from the audience. We are all waiting as Lester leans in close to the microphone and looks from me to Jeremy and back again.

"… Jeremy Corrigan, French horn!"

My heart sinks…and skips a beat at the same time. Oh, my God. Is it possible I'm disappointed for me and happy for him at the same time? I step back out of the way, out of the spotlight, so Lester can put the gold medal around Jeremy's neck.

Jeremy is brilliant in his affectation of surprise, humility and joy. I wonder, if I keep moving to the side of the stage, little by little, can I just disappear and go home without anyone noticing? I try it and scoot a foot. Then another. But my theory is blown to sad little pieces when I notice Jeremy noticing me. I see it then. He has no intention of letting me slink off the stage.

Jeremy holds up his hand to quiet the massive crowd, walks to the page and takes the last blue box. He opens it and pulls out the silver medal for all to see. Then he gestures to me and the clapping, catcalls and bravos start all over again. I'm frozen to my spot on the stage, helpless to move as he closes the distance between us until, finally, he's standing in front of me, looking down. He hangs the silver medal around my neck and bends down to kiss me on the cheek, and to whisper in my ear.

"You are nothing, Jules. Nothing."

Before I can respond, he grabs my good wrist and hauls it up over my head, as if he's declaring me the winner of a boxing match.

Funny, I don't feel like the winner. In fact, I feel as if I've just been sucker punched.

51

If you stand on the deck of the Bridgeport Ferry as it heads into the Port Jefferson harbor, you can get a glimpse of the houses tucked away on the bluffs overlooking the port. There's an intricate network of private roads that takes you to those houses—if you know where you're going. But for most people, that glimpse, as the ferry glides by is as close as they ever get to them.

Tuckahoe is a small, unmarked drive that is easily missed and Matthew has to direct the cabbie up and back through the single lane, tree-lined avenue to where it ends in a cul-de-sac. There is a driveway there with a carved, wooden *'Private Property'* sign hanging from a post.

This is Matthew's home, the place where he was living when his parents died. I suspect that this is the last place where he was truly happy. When his parents were killed in a boating accident, he wasn't even ten years old. And, ironically, for as much money and property as his parents had, neither one of them was in possession of a single living relative. Not a cousin or an aunt or a great-grandmother. So he ended up spending the remaining years of his childhood, like me, in the custody of New York State.

"You wouldn't know that no one has lived here for more than a decade," I mumble as we look at the front of the immaculate property.

"Come on," Matthew says, indicating I should follow him around the side of the house.

I've been here a few times before and I know what's coming. Still, I'm never quite prepared for it. We walk along the flagstone path that leads around to the back of the house. There, laid out before us, is the massive lawn. We walk in silence to the far edge of the property, where there is a glorious view of the Port Jefferson harbor. A set of steep wooden steps, built into the bluff, runs down to the beach several hundred feet below.

"I thought everybody lived like this," he says softly from next to me.

I grab his hand and we turn our backs on the frigid blue water below, making our way to the back of the house. We pass the pool, empty and covered. Three Adirondack chairs are set out for maximum view of the sunset, although, they too, have seen better days after seasons of neglect. This place is eerie, like a graveyard for a life long dead.

He fishes the keys out of his pocket and lets us in the back door, where we are immediately met by the smell of dust and stillness.

"When were you last here?" I ask. "A year maybe?"

He shakes his head. "More like two."

Our footsteps echo loudly on the hardwood floor, as if the house is hollow. We make the rounds, opening closed doors to his father's study and his mother's sewing room. The den is lined with huge oak bookcases, which now stand empty, collecting dust.

"Come on, let's go into the kitchen and get ready for Tony. He'll be here soon," I say, trying to coax him out of the distant place where his mind has gone.

Things are less musty in the huge kitchen, where the management company has laid out a spread of baked goods and a carafe of coffee. I fix him a cup and hand it to him. He sips distractedly.

"You know, maybe this was a bad idea," I begin tentatively. "Couldn't we have arranged to meet him in the city?"

He shakes his head as he sips. "Uh-uh," he says once he's swallowed. "He's got an assignment out here somewhere. This was the easiest way to see him as quickly as possible."

Tony Ruggiero is *That Guy*—you know the one—the guy who 'knows a guy.' The guy who can get you anything, no matter how exotic, far-flung or illegal it is. The guy who can dig up the dirt. The guy who can get the job done. You don't ever ask a guy like Tony how he does it, because you're better off not knowing. He and Matthew's father worked together years ago and he's kept an eye on Matthew ever since. It's Jeremy who he's been keeping an eye on for the last couple of weeks, though. When Tony comes in, it doesn't take him more than a minute to find his way to the breakfast bar.

"Sorry," he says through a full mouth, "I'm starving. I came right from a stakeout. Been sitting in a car half the night."

"No, please," I smile, and hand him a napkin.

"What's the firm got you working on these days?" Matthew asks.

"This one's good. Industrial espionage. The client is convinced one of his employees is a mole for the competition. He's right. What he doesn't know, is that it's the secretary he's been banging for six months," he says with a snort of laughter that sends crumbs flying everywhere. "Sorry," he mumbles with embarrassment.

I smile. Tony is a character for sure. He can find out anything about anyone, anywhere. And now he's here to tell us what he's learned about Jeremy.

"So how you doing, Red?" he asks me. "I saw in the paper that you got second place in that big competition."

"I did. But I've been better, Tony," I admit.

"Jeremy did a real number on her," Matthew pipes up. "That's why I called you. I should've done it earlier."

"Yeah," he nods. "You really should have, Matt. This guy's one serious piece a work. He's got sealed records from before he was even a teenager. Some petty theft, breaking and entering. There was an assault charge involving a teacher..."

"Wait, what? A teacher assaulted him?" I ask, stunned by the notion.

"No. The other way around. He assaulted a teacher. Apparently he gave the judge quite a sob story and got community service. The teacher got a fractured skull and early retirement."

I'm speechless. How could I have not known this side of him?

"That's nothing," Tony is saying to Matthew. "By the time he was sixteen he'd taken up blackmail, embezzlement and grand theft auto."

"No. No, no, no. I don't believe it. How could he possibly do all of those things and not be in jail? I think you've got it wrong, Tony," I protest.

They're both looking at me a little sadly. As if I'm in denial and the big bad truth is going to whop me in the head at any moment now.

Tony sighs. "He's a smart motherfucker, Red. He knows how to cover his tracks. He also knows how to twist, spin and manipulate the facts to suit his purpose. I've never seen anything like it. And I've gotta tell you, I think Matthew here is right. I think he killed the other horn player. What's his name?"

"Cal," I say softly.

"Right, Cal. Jeremy had proximity to him. He also had access to the kid's stuff, to his instrument. He was the first one to 'help' him on the scene. He was supposed to get the guy's epinephrine pen, the one that was always in the horn case, only that night it wasn't. At least that's what Jeremy said."

"You think he took it without Cal noticing?" Matthew asks.

Tony shrugs. "Either that or he pocketed it instead of bringing it back out onto the stage."

"Okay, so how would he have caused the allergic reaction then?"

"Well, according to the coroner's report the autopsy showed a swollen throat, mucus in the lungs and other signs consistent with anaphylaxis. We know from Cal's medical records that only one thing had that kind of an effect on him."

"Nuts," Matthew says.

"Nuts. But there weren't any in his stomach at the time of his death. Still, his allergy was so severe that even contact with nuts, nut oils or nut butters could trigger symptoms."

"So, Jeremy put it somewhere on Cal. Or maybe even Cal's horn," Matthew deduces.

"They're saying the point of origin was his mouth."

"His mouthpiece," I whisper.

"What?" they say in unison, turning to stare at me.

I close my eyes for a few seconds, take a deep breath and just say it. Say what's been on my mind for days now. "I, uh…I think I saw Jeremy pocket Cal's mouthpiece."

"Holy shit, Julia!" Matthew says as he hops off of his stool and comes to stand face to face with me. He puts his hands on my forearms. "Are you sure?"

"I wasn't at first, but the more I think about, the more I'm certain of it. It was when he went backstage to look for the epinephrine. He took Cal's horn with him. I think I saw him take the mouthpiece off Cal's horn and replace it with one he had in his pocket. Is that crazy?"

A huge smile spreads across his face. "No!" Matthew is shaking his head excitedly. "No, you're not crazy. He must have put something like peanut oil on Cal's mouthpiece and then swapped it out with an identical one, a clean one, when no one was watching."

"I was watching," I mumble, looking down at my lap. I can't be happy. Not about this. I loved this man. I'm not entirely sure that I don't still love him

"Are you okay?" he asks.

"Am I supposed to be? I'm carrying the child of a killer. I was just this lovesick idiot who couldn't see that he was playing me. I should have listened to you and Cal. You both warned me. You must think I'm such a fool," I sniff, the tears building behind my eyes.

He pulls me forward so that I'm enveloped in his arms, my head resting on his chest. "Oh, Julia, I never thought that for a second. Jeremy Corrigan is a brilliant manipulator. Of course you were out of your league with him. You can't even conceive of the kinds of things he does to other people."

I extricate myself from him and sit up, wiping my wet face with a napkin. "So, now you really think he did it?" I ask them.

"Sounds like it to me," Tony says.

"We've got to go to the police," Matthew says resolutely. "Like now."

"With what?" Tony asks as he pours more coffee. "There isn't anything, Matthew."

"Of course there is. We just figured it out. Julia saw it."

He takes a sip and shakes his head. "No, all we did was come up with a theory. Without a smoking...mouthpiece...we can't prove it. They're going to say Julia is the 'woman scorned.' Besides, the Coroner is calling it an accidental death. That's all the police need to close up their investigation."

"But they can't!" Matthew says indignantly. "We have to find the proof, we have to figure out the best way to take him down."

"Take him down?" Tony snorts. "Matthew, I'm not trying to give you ammunition, I'm trying to warn you. This guy is the real fuckin' deal. He's a card-carrying, dyed-in-the-wool sociopath. You know me—I'm not one to walk away from a fight. But man, my advice to you here is to just let it go. If you push this guy too far and you don't get him put away, you and Julia are in some serious danger."

"Please, Tony. You're giving the son of a bitch too much credit."

With startling clarity, I realize Matthew's wrong. Jeremy is more than equipped to do what we're thinking. I keep my thoughts to myself.

"Listen to me, Matthew," Tony cautions as he waves his hands around in broad gestures for emphasis. "What you're talking about here is opening up Pandora's box, pulling out a can of worms and kicking it into a hornet's nest. Trust me on this, you just stay the fuck out of his way and his own hubris will trip him up eventually."

"I can't do that, Tony. We have to go to the police," Matthew insists.

"Haven't you done that already?"

What? I give Matthew a long hard look and Tony continues.

"I mean, you called in an anonymous tip to the police, right?"

To my sheer amazement, Matthew nods.

"Well, my friend, as it turns out, you weren't the only one."

Now it's Matthew's turn to look amazed. "There were others?"

"A couple. One of them was someone at the Kreisler Competition, a judge named Louise Kutter. I tried to convince her to talk about it, but she's too afraid of Jeremy. And that's for your ears only. Understood?"

"Yeah, of course, he agrees. "And the third?"

Tony Ruggiero puts down his coffee cup and pulls a small folded piece of paper from his pocket. "I think you two need to take a little trip to Philly. There's someone there you really should speak with in person," he says, handing Matthew the paper. "And I don't think you should wait. She could change her mind at any minute."

"Alright," Matthew says with a firm nod. "We'll be on the first flight out in the morning."

52

The thing I remember most about Laurie Daughtry, was the way her long blond hair would swing from side to side as she played her flute. The thing that I liked most about Laurie Daughtry, was that way she always had a smile for me. I was an incredibly shy freshman, out of the care of the foster system for the first time in over a decade. She was a sophomore with an easy, outgoing personality and a great sense of humor. Everybody loved Laurie. And what a talent! It was plain to us all that she was headed for big things.

The woman that I spot now, in this park outside of Philadelphia, has short dark hair in a severe blunt cut. She's painfully thin, her skin pale and pasty. Despite the overcast sky, most of her face is hidden behind huge sunglasses. At Tony's suggestion, I have come alone to this meeting leaving Matthew waiting in a coffee shop a few blocks away.

"Hi, Julia," she says with a weak smile when I approach her.

"Hey, Laurie. It's good to see you," I say, joining her on the bench where she's sitting. "Thanks for agreeing to meet me."

"I wasn't going to. But your friend, Tony…well, he's very persuasive."

"Yeah, he thought it was important that we speak."

She nods and then turns away to face forward, looking off in the distance. I can see that behind the big, dark lenses, there are big, dark circles under her eyes. Is that how I look right now? Pale and haunted? Just another victim of Jeremy Corrigan?

"What happened to you?" I ask her quietly. "One day, you were on the fast track at McInnes and the next day, you disappeared."

She shifts a little uncomfortably and clears her throat. "I dated Jeremy for a while. You probably know that much, right?"

"Vaguely…" I lie to her.

Who wouldn't remember those two beautiful people walking through the hallways holding hands and sneaking kisses back stage? They were hard to miss.

"Yeah, well, it was really nice at first. He was so… attentive. He showered me with gifts and expensive dinners. One night, he surprised me with a carriage ride around Central Park. He was all about the grand, romantic gestures."

She pauses here and moves her gaze slightly, looking further into the distance. I wait, watching her take a tentative breath before she speaks again.

"Then things got weird. He started to make mean little comments, always taking jabs at me. How I looked, how I played. He wanted to know where I was every second of every day, but refused to give me any details about where he had been all night. Pretty soon, he was flirting openly with other girls and bragging about having sex with them."

My stomach is churning with every detail that spills from her lips. I think of his little digs and mysterious nights out. I picture the waitress in the restaurant on New Year's Eve. Dear God, it could so easily be me telling this story.

"That's when I was done," Laurie is saying now. "I just stopped. There wasn't a big break-up or anything. I just… stopped answering his calls. I got in and out of rehearsals as quickly as I could, and surrounded myself with other people, knowing that he wouldn't try to confront me unless I was alone."

I remember when this happened. There was a lot of buzz around the orchestra that Laurie had dumped Jeremy. And, knowing him the way I do now, I'm quite sure that gossip would have made him furious.

"One day he managed to catch me alone on the sidewalk. He was actually very nice, very apologetic. He said he knew he'd been a jerk and promised to leave me alone if that was what I wanted. Of course, I felt like an idiot, like I had overreacted. He asked if I'd like him to bring my things from his apartment. Somewhere in my mind, I thought I would be better off coming to him. I felt better with the thought that Brett would be there. So, we decided on a meeting at his place in Brooklyn the next night."

She pauses now, just stops and gazes at the nannies pushing strollers carrying their bundled charges. It's a parade of tiny little hats with tiny little pompons and mittens. Laurie looks at them wistfully before she continues.

"Anyway," she says after a few moments, "I went to his place on a Friday night. Brett was there, too. Jeremy offered me a glass of wine. I said 'no thanks' and did a quick scan of the room for my things. I didn't see a box or a bag anywhere. That made me a little nervous, so I told him I was in a bit of a hurry. He asked me who I was off to fuck now. When I told him to go to hell, he slapped me. Hard. I was so stunned, I just stood there holding my face. He was going on and on about how no bitch was going to make him look bad. The next thing I knew, he had me by the hair and was dragging me to his bedroom."

I can't help myself, I gasp out loud. This is so much worse than I'd imagined.

"Surely Brett must have done something…" I say, hoping to hear that he had. But I know better.

She gives me a rueful smile.

"Julia, I begged him to help me. Do you know what he said? 'Sorry, Laurie, this is where I get off.' Then, he picked up his keys and left me alone with that animal. Just walked right out the door knowing full well what was about to happen."

Before I can think about whether or not it's appropriate, I have asked the question. "Laurie…what *did* happen?"

She takes a deep breath and blows it out through pursed lips, steeling herself for the rest of her story. "He started to rip my clothes off. Literally ripped them from my body. When I fought him, he punched me in the face so hard he broke my jaw. The pain was unbearable, and it was all I could focus on, even as he was pushing me onto the bed."

Her voice chokes here and she looks away from me again, but not before I see the tears starting to stream from behind the glasses. I wait in silence, until she's ready to speak again.

"He raped me, Julia. Raped me, and beat the shit out of me for over two hours. The worst of it was that the whole time he talked about my three sisters. He recited their names and ages, the schools they attended and what each one looked like. He told me that if I breathed a word of it to anyone, he would hurt them, too. I saw it in his eyes, Julia, he meant it."

"My God…" I murmur from behind the hand that covers my mouth.

"When he was through with me, he helped me into the shower and bathed me. It was all very…tender. I could barely stand at that point. He brushed my hair gently and found some clean clothes I'd left there. Then, he helped me downstairs, hailed a cab and told the driver to take me to the hospital, that I'd had a bad fall down the stairs. I never saw him again. My parents came and brought me back home, and I withdrew from McInnes the next week."

Part of me is stunned by her revelation. Part of me is not. "Laurie, I'm so sorry. I had no idea."

"Julia, your friend Tony told me a little bit about what happened between you and Jeremy. That's the only reason that I agreed to see you. You need to know that you're in danger as long as you are a threat to him in any way. I've been following the Kreisler Competition. You and I both know that there was nothing accidental about Cal Burridge's death. If Jeremy thinks, for even a second, that you could somehow implicate him... well, I can only imagine how far he'd go to protect himself, his reputation."

"So... you think he killed Cal, too?" I ask.

"I don't doubt it for a second," she replies, almost before I can get the question out. I'm about to ask her something else, but she's suddenly looking at me so strangely, so intently. She finally takes her sunglasses off and I feel as if this woman can see right through me. And, as it turns out, she can.

"You're pregnant, aren't you?" It's more of a statement than a question. I find I can only nod, dumbly. "Does he know?" I shake my head. "Good, try and keep it that way."

"You can't think he'd...that he'd hurt me...not like that, do you? Not if he knew..."

Now Laurie is looking directly at me. She puts the glasses in her lap and reaches into her mouth, pulling out what looks like a denture. She smiles at me, and I see the gaps where there should be teeth. She pops the appliance back in.

"He knocked out six of my teeth that night. Between that and the damage from my broken jaw, I'll never play the flute again. I *know* he'd hurt you. Julia, he'd kill you in a heartbeat if you were so much as an inconvenience to him. And believe me, he's going to see your pregnancy as an inconvenience. If they can't get him on Cal's murder, then I strongly suggest you do what I did. Get out of town. Get as far away from the Corrigan brothers as you can and don't ever look back."

Before I can say another word, Laurie Daughtry stands up and starts to walk away from me. She never once looks back.

For the first time in weeks, I consider myself lucky.

Matthew is holding my hand as the plane banks south toward home. I told him about my conversation with Laurie, including her guess that I'm pregnant. It's been hanging over us like a brewing storm cloud for hours now.

"I know…" I start, and then stop.

"You know what?" Matthew coaxes gently.

I take a deep breath and try it again.

"I know you probably think I should have an abortion…"

"What?"

This one word, spoken with such shock, stops me mid-sentence. "I mean, don't you?"

He turns to face me, as much as he can within the constraints of the airplane seat, and looks directly into my eyes. "Julia, I may hate Jeremy, but that baby is a part of you. I would never want you to destroy a part of yourself," he says, his voice low and intense. "I'm not saying it's not right for other women, but I know you almost as well as you know yourself. There's no way you could live with yourself if you went through with it."

In one, overwhelming wave of understanding, I realize that this, right here, this is what true love looks and sounds like. It's not the sexy guy with the crinkly eyes, who is great in bed. At least, it wasn't in my case. No, it's the one man who has been, just as he is now, by my side, holding my hand. I have disappointed him and angered him. I have sent him away. But he never stops coming back. He never stops loving me.

I open my mouth to speak and quickly close it again. There are tears sliding down my cheeks now. I lean over and rest my head on his shoulder. He rests his chin on my head.

"There's so much, Matthew," I whisper through the tears. "I don't know what to feel first. I'm so, so sad. I didn't know it was possible to be this sad. I should be furious with him, but I'm just not there yet. Oh, God...and the baby..."

His voice above me is quiet, but firm. "You need to think of this as grief, Julia, because that's what it is. You're mourning the loss of someone you...someone you loved. Someone you trusted. There are stages to mourning, you know, like denial, anger, and acceptance. Well, I'm thinking the anger piece isn't too far off. And then, one day, you'll wake-up and it won't hurt quite so much. But that could be tomorrow, or a year from now."

I'm nodding, too choked up to speak. Small gulps and hiccups and gasps are slipping out of me as I fight the urge to weep openly in front of this plane full of strangers.

"And as for the baby, well, that's just fucking terrifying."

And just like that, the tears turn to laughter. "It is, isn't it? It's fucking terrifying!" I whisper back to him.

"You're going to be a mother, Julia," he says with a smile in his voice.

"I'm going to be a mother," I repeat, my hand instinctively finding its way to my belly.

"It's going to be okay. I promise you, Julia. I will be by your side no matter what, for as long as you want me there. You're not going to have to do this alone."

I look up at him with my tear-stained face and he smiles down on me. "I love you so much, Matthew. And I've treated you so badly…"

He shakes his head sharply. "No. No, we're not doing that. *Ever*. You are *not* to feel guilty about any of this, Julia. There were so many things that were out of your control."

"But you knew, and I wouldn't listen. And now…"

"And now, your heart is broken. I understand. And I'll do whatever I can to make it a little easier for you, but like I said, it's grief. It takes as long as it takes."

I don't know how long it's going to take me to fully get over Jeremy Corrigan, but the words of Laurie Daughtry have definitely put me on a faster track.

53

Roberto Vasquez is peering at us from across the narrow table in this tiny, beige, cinderblock room. A one-way mirror hangs on one wall and there are cameras mounted in the corners. On the cop shows they call it *'The Interrogation Room'* or simply, *'The Box.'* Vasquez claims this is the most private place for the three of us to talk, but I have the distinct feeling that someone is watching us from behind that mirror, mirror on the wall.

He clears his throat and opens up a small notepad in front of him. "So, tell me exactly what you saw, Miss James."

I sit up tall in the metal chair and meet his eyes squarely. "I followed Jeremy Corrigan up onto the stage while he and the conductor were trying to help Cal. While the Maestro was talking to Cal, trying to get him to stay responsive, Jeremy moved Cal's horn out of the way. That's when I saw him take the mouthpiece out of Cal's horn, put it in one pocket and pull another one out of his other pocket. That was the one he put back into Cal's horn. I think Jeremy may have put something on the first mouthpiece that caused Cal to have an allergic reaction, and switched it out so there wouldn't be any trace of it."

Vasquez is nodding as he jots down a few notes in his pad. "Why didn't you say something sooner?" he asks, looking up again.

"I was so upset at the time. I think I must have been in shock. Cal was a friend."

"So when did you realize what you'd seen?"

"I don't know. A few days ago, I guess. I didn't really want to believe it." I look down at my hands and up again. "I was seeing Jeremy at the time."

"But you're not now?"

"No."

"And who, exactly, broke off the relationship?"

"Wait," Matthew interjects. "What does that have to do with anything?"

Vasquez surveys him with raised eyebrows. "Mr. Ayers, if you can't stay quiet I'll have to ask you to step out."

"Excuse me? *We* came to *you!*"

"Exactly. And I have to wonder why. I mean, if you were all such good friends, why did it take you over a week to come forward with this information?"

"I just told you…" I start to protest but he cuts me off.

"Miss James, isn't it true that Mr. Corrigan broke off your relationship two days after Cal Burridge's death?"

"Well, yes but…"

"Is it possible, Miss James, that you're just hurt and angry and looking to get back at him for dumping you like that right before your recital?"

I'm staring at him in disbelief. Something isn't right here.

"Detective Vasquez," Matthew starts, "neither of us said anything about the circumstances of their break-up. How would you know the details?"

He ignores the question and comes back with one of his own. "Mr. Ayers, do you know a Tony Ruggiero?"

Uh-oh. I'm not sure I like where this is headed.

"Yes…" he answers cautiously. "Why?"

"Well, I know him, too. At least by reputation, and I know exactly what kind of work he does. I understand that Mr.

Ruggiero has been snooping around, prying into Jeremy Corrigan's background. Accessing files that he has no authority to access. Did you hire him to do that, Mr. Ayers?"

How would this man know about that? Unless…

"Have you spoken with Jeremy?" I ask suddenly.

He smiles at me. A placating smile that says *'I don't have to tell you anything.'* "I have, actually. He was in here yesterday discussing the possibility of filing a harassment complaint against the two of you and Mr. Ruggiero. I suspect you'll be hearing from his attorney."

I can't be hearing this correctly. Jeremy kills Cal and we're the ones who are in trouble?

"Making a false accusation is a very serious crime, Miss James. Especially when you're accusing the person of murder. You might just find yourself on the ugly end of a slander suit if you're not careful," he says.

I can tell Matthew has just about had it. He stands up and gestures for me to do the same.

"We're not done here," Vasquez says as he gets to his feet, too.

"Oh, yes we are," Matthew informs him. "You're a fool, detective. Jeremy Corrigan is playing you and you can't even see it."

The officer puts his palms down on the tabletop and leans forward so that he's only inches from us.

"What I see, Matthew, is a woman scorned. I see the silver medalist of the Kreisler Competition trying to cast dispersions on the gold medalist, knowing full well that if he's disqualified, she'll be next in line to the gold."

I can only stare at him, my mouth hanging open. This is exactly what Tony warned us would happen. The whole 'woman scorned' thing. Oh my God. This can't be happening.

"I—I can't believe you think that I'd do that," I stammer in an astonished whisper.

Vasquez smiles at me. "Oh, Miss James, I learned a long time ago that even the sweetest, sunniest little girl like you can wield the biggest, sharpest axe in town."

I hold up my wrist, still in its cast. "He did this to me, detective. He fractured my wrist. After that, he punched me in the face. This is not a good man. I mean, I thought he was. I thought I loved him…" I'm starting to get choked up.

I feel Matthew's hand on the small of my back as he gently pushes me toward the door.

"I didn't tell you that you could leave," Vasquez says in a flat, cold voice. He positions himself between us and the door.

"No," Matthew retorts, "you didn't. But if you try and stop us, then you'd better be prepared to charge us with something, Detective. And if you charge us with something, Detective, you'd better be prepared for the shit storm that is going to rain down on you when my five-hundred-dollar an hour attorney gets here."

Vasquez takes a second to size him up, his eyes never wavering from Matthew's. I know what he sees. And so does he, apparently, because he steps to the side as we walk out of The Box.

We take our hot chocolate and choose a bench in the tiny park outside City Hall.

"What can we do, Matthew?" I ask, warming my hands on the cup. "No one believes us. And I'm afraid of what Jeremy will do if we push this thing too hard."

"It's just too fucking much," Matthew says, shaking his head in disgust.

"Which part?" I ask.

"All of it, Julia. Everything he did to put you at a disadvantage. We're not talking about the usual petty head games. This guy had it in for you. He did his research, he stalked you, and he made a plan. Christ, he even beat us to the punch with the police!"

I stare at him. I hadn't really thought about it that way before now. I suppose I haven't wanted to.

"Julia, do you know how long Jeremy must have been working on this? He didn't know anything about your past. He had to dig, and dig deep, to get what he needed. And then, that sick fuck found your mother. All of it, just to give himself an advantage in a stupid competition. I mean, who does that?"

If what Matthew's saying is true, then Jeremy would have to be a monster, devoid of any feelings, totally indifferent to anyone but himself. There's no way I could have fallen in love with someone like that. Is there?

"Matthew, I don't know what to do. What am I supposed to do? You can't just un-love someone. It may not have been real for him, but it was, it is, real for me. And now, this baby…" He starts to say something but I cut him off. "No, please, let me finish. You're telling me that I've slept with a cold, calculating killer. That the father of my child is a…psychopath, or sociopath, or whatever. You're going to have to give me a little time to process this."

"Julia, time is one thing we don't have. Jeremy is off the rails, and no one seems to notice or care. He's got everyone fooled. We have to find a way to expose him for who—for what he really is before someone else gets hurt. Or worse."

We sit quietly side by side for a few minutes, sipping our drinks and watching the downtown traffic whiz by.

"I think that there is something we can do, Julia," he says, breaking our silence. "Something that might put the spotlight back on Jeremy, and maybe even force the police to take us seriously."

I turn on the bench and face him.

"I'm listening."

54

I'm not the only one who is skeptical about Matthew's plan. When we find Tony Ruggiero, he's sitting in Central Park, pretending to take pictures of the pigeons. In truth, he's taking pictures of the two men sitting on a bench just in front of the pigeons.

"We can come back later," Matthew offers, but Tony just takes a few more shots and waves him off.

"Nah, I've got all I need. I just had to prove those two are spending time together."

"Since when is that illegal?" I ask out of curiosity.

He puts the camera down and smiles at me. "Since the Securities Act of 1933. You're looking at insider trading right there," he explains with a nod to the harmless looking businessmen. "Anyway, come over here to this bench. No pigeons over here. I hate those fucking rats with wings."

When we settle on a bench, far away from the cooing 'rats,' Tony looks at us quizzically. "Okay, so what's this grand plan of yours?"

Matthew looks to me, as if for confirmation, and I nod. He turns back to Tony. "So, I'm thinking that maybe we can't go after Jeremy legally, but we can go after him professionally."

"What the hell is that supposed to mean?"

"Think about it, Tony. If we can get the word out there…the rumor…that Jeremy killed Cal to get his spot at the Kreisler's, I'd bet a whole lot of doors would start to close in his face."

"Get the word out to who? Your little field trip to the police station should have set you straight on that once and for all. As long Cal's death is on the books as an accident, no one is going to waste another second on an investigation. Based on what you've told me, it would seem that as far as the NYPD is concerned, this case is closed. Period. End of discussion."

"Come on, work with me here!" Matthew coaxes. "What orchestra wants that kind of a liability? The scandal, the cloud of suspicion? Jesus Christ, musicians are all so damned neurotic anyway. The bastard can take auditions all he wants, but no hiring committee is going to consider someone who has even the whiff of suspicion associated with them. I think we need to go public. We tell every orchestra, every conservatory, recording studio and musician's union within the sound of our voices that Jeremy did this, and that hiring him could put their organizations in jeopardy."

"Whoa!" Tony says, holding up his hands. "Proof, Matthew, *proof*! How many times do I have to say it? We don't have enough proof. They call it slander when you do shit like that and you don't have evidence to back it up. And you *know* Corrigan is just looking for something to throw at his lawyers."

"No! Don't you see? That's the beauty of it, Tony! We don't need proof to plant that seed of doubt. And tell me you can't find a way to get the word out without linking it back to us. If anyone can do it, it's you."

Tony is quiet for a long moment, looking down at the hands he has folded in his lap. When he looks up, it is with a face full of concern. Oh, I don't like this face on him. If Tony is worried, we all need to be worried.

"Matt, this is what I warned you about. It has 'back fire' written all over it. You may very well accomplish what you're talking about, but it's going to have a price tag attached to it."

"I'm not afraid of him."

Tony lowers his voice considerably and the effect is chilling. "You should be, Matthew. You should be afraid, if not for you, then for her." He swings his gaze around to me.

"If we do it right, he'll never know it was us," Matthew argues, leaning forward in excitement. It doesn't matter what Tony says at this point, he is committed to his plan.

Tony sighs in frustration and tries one more time. "You're not hearing me," he says more firmly. "He's not stupid—he'll figure it out. If you go through with this, if you succeed in blowing up this guy's career I don't know if I can protect you. I don't know if anybody can. Neither of you will be safe here. You'll have to give up your lives, your jobs, school, whatever. You'll have to get the fuck out of town and lie low—maybe even for the rest of your lives."

Matthew sniffs in disbelief. "Now you're just being dramatic."

"Julia, please, you've got to talk some sense into him," Tony implores, hiking a thumb toward Matthew. "Guys like Jeremy Corrigan don't forget who screwed them over. What you're proposing here can easily be done, but I'm begging you to take a little time to consider the fallout."

"Just do it," Matthew says in a tone that leaves no room for debate.

I know in this instant that, with those three words, he has sealed our fate. Whatever it may be.

55

DING!

I pick up the phone from where it sits on the side of the tub. Matthew's text is bright green on the screen.

Leaving rehearsal in five. General Tsao's?

I smile. I've done nothing but sleep, soak in the tub and eat Chinese food for the last week. I type back with pruned fingers, trying not to drop the phone into the bubble bath.

Yes! Please!

I lay my head back and close my eyes, taking a deep breath and exhaling slowly. I've had to do a lot of that lately, as the numbness has begun to wear off and the reality of my situation has started to settle in. Maybe it's the hormones, or maybe it's everything that's happened, but each day I wake to find myself in a new and different state of emotional distress. I feel lost and heartbroken because I gave my love to a man who intentionally hurt me. I'm terrified, because I'm going to be a mother—the mother of that man's child, no less. I'm furious because *my* mother opted to start a brand new family, with a brand new, shiny little girl, not an hour's drive from the orphanage where I spent nearly a decade.

And then, there's the tiniest part of me that's excited. Excited for the new life inside of me and for the new phase of my career as the recipient of the Kreisler Silver Medal. That excitement is swiftly followed by the guilt and regret. When I look at that silver disc hanging on the blue ribbon, it is a reminder. Not of my success, but of my failings. Of my foolishness in believing that a man as handsome, sexy and charismatic as Jeremy could ever love a Plain Jane like me. Why couldn't I see that? If only I had opened my eyes and seen it.

I haul myself out of the tub, towel off and wrap myself in a soft, pink robe. I'm rubbing a smaller towel over my wet hair when I step into my bedroom and find him there, sitting in the chair by my bed.

Holy. Shit.

I let the towel fall to the floor. "What are you doing here?"

"What, aren't you happy to see me, Jules? You used to like it when I was in your bedroom, remember? Remember how I fucked you in here? How I tied you to the bed and you told me about all your pathetic little scars that daddy left behind?"

Dammit! I left the phone on the edge of the tub. I look at the clock. Matthew was leaving rehearsal in five minutes. That was fifteen minutes ago. It'll take him nearly half hour on the subway, then another fifteen minutes for the takeout… Oh, hell. I'm on my own. I swallow hard and will my voice to sound normal rather than frightened. He can smell weakness.

"Can I get you a glass of wine?" I offer as casually as possible.

He squints a little, as if looking at me from a different perspective will make me easier to understand. "No. You and I need to have a little chat." He gets to his feet so that we're facing each other from opposite sides of the bed.

"What about?" I ask innocently.

"Oh, I think you know what," he says with a twisted little smile.

Is it possible that he knows I'm pregnant? No. No way. Or is it? I look back at him blankly and then shake my head. "No, Jeremy, I'm afraid I don't," I assure him. "Would you mind excusing me for just a second? I'm going to pop into the bathroom and put on some clothes. Then we can talk about whatever you like…"

I start to make a move toward my closet and the bathroom that is on the other side of it. "Stay right there," he barks, and I stop, startled.

"Jeremy, what is it? For God's sake, I just want to get dressed. And considering the way you dumped me, I'd rather not do it in front of you."

"Haven't you learned by now, Jules? I'm smarter than you, faster than you and stronger than you. If you take one step toward your cell phone—which I assume is in the bathroom—I'll have you flat on your face before you can clear the bedroom."

I can only stare at him, eyes wide.

Think, Julia, think!

I have to stall. It's the only option I have.

"Okay," I begin again slowly. "I won't get dressed then, but you don't have to be threatening about it, Jeremy. Please, just tell me what it is you want to talk about."

"I want to talk about what you've been up to since I beat your ass in the competition. Or didn't you think I'd find out?"

"I don't know what you're talking about. I've been here, home. Crying my eyes out because I love you and you—"

"Oh, please," he cuts me off. "You must think I'm as stupid as you are, Jules."

"What? Stupid?" I shake my head and furrow my brows, feigning confusion. "Jeremy, that's the last thing I'd call you. You're one of the shrewdest people I've ever met. When I've finally gotten over you, I'll probably even respect the way you…maneuvered all of this into place. There's no denying it was brilliant." I can't tell if the ego stroking is working or not, so I continue cautiously, not wanting to lay it on too thick. "But I'm sure you didn't come here to talk about that. What is it that you think I've been doing that has you so upset? Whatever it is, I'll stop it," I offer up. I'm going to say anything I have to in order to get him out of my bedroom.

"You've been a very busy little girl, haven't you, Jules?"

I'm not quite sure how to respond, so I don't.

"You went to the police, didn't you?" he accuses.

Oh, so that's what this is about.

"Yes, Jeremy, I did. And I was informed that you would press charges if I didn't leave you alone. So I have."

He's smiling again, wagging his index finger at me. He has also taken a single step to his left, toward the end of the bed. I pretend not to notice. "Now, Jules, if that were true, I wouldn't be here right now. You have had every opportunity to just take your lumps and get on with it. But now I understand you've been contacting orchestras, and newspapers, and schools."

I watch helplessly as he takes another step. "What on earth are you talking about?" I purposely try to sound confused.

"What did you tell them, Julia?" he asks, completing his route to the foot of the bed.

"Nothing…I didn't say anything to anyone, Jeremy. You beat me fair and square. I don't want to look like a sore loser," I say with as much sincerity as I can muster.

He's moving forward along the foot of the bed now, getting closer to my side with every tiny inch. "Don't you lie to me, Jules."

I shake my head and cling to the lie, hoping to eventually convince him it is true. "I swear, I didn't say anything to anyone…"

Two steps this time. He's about to make it to my side of the bed and that puts him within three feet of me. I take a step back toward the closet. If I could just get to the bathroom and lock the door… But there's no way. He's fast, and no telling what he'll do to me if I run. I keep seeing Laurie Daughtry's face, hearing her soft, flat voice.

"Don't you fucking lie to me!" It's clear he isn't playing with me. He aims to get an answer. "You've started a smear campaign against me, haven't you? You've been doing your damnedest to make sure no one will hire me."

"I didn't. I swear, Jeremy, it wasn't me," I insist, retreating further.

"I'm not going to ask you again," he threatens.

"That's right," Matthew says from the doorway. "You're not going to ask her again."

My heart practically leaps from my throat.

Oh, thank God!

Jeremy whips around toward him. "Well, look who's home."

"Why don't you pick on someone your own size for a change, Jeremy?" Matthew suggests, stepping further into the room.

Jeremy covers the final few feet between us, and stands next to me.

“What’s the matter, Matthew? Afraid I’m gonna hurt your fragile little flower?”

“Get. Away. From. Her.”

Matthew sounds more threatening than I’ve ever heard him in my life.

Unfazed, Jeremy doesn’t budge. “Now what would the fun in that be?” he smiles.

“She didn’t get in touch with all those orchestras,” Matthew says. “*I* did.”

Now Jeremy looks over at me at me, his expression softening. “No, you didn’t, did you?” he says, running the back of his hand along the curve of my face. It is an intimacy I used to relish. Now, it only sickens me.

I look him in the eye and shake my head. “No, Jeremy, I didn’t,” I whisper.

He drops his hand from me and turns around so that he’s standing squarely between Matthew and me. He’s so much taller than I am, that I can’t actually see past him unless I lean to the side.

“You know what, Matthew? I believe Jules. I think she’s too afraid and too pathetically in love with me to ever say a word against me.”

“Good,” Matthew spits. “Then leave her alone and get the fuck out.”

Jeremy throws another glance back at me and I see the smile is back. Not the scary one, but the faux-friendly one that’s all white teeth and crinkly eyes.

“Oh, I will in just a second. There’s just something I want to make…painfully…clear. Someone’s been snooping around, asking questions, making accusations. Someone’s been doing their level best to sabotage my career. It’s going to stop. Right. Now.”

“Get out, Jeremy,” Matthew repeats louder this time.

Jeremy continues as if he hasn't heard him. "And I mean right now, Matty Boy. Or sweet, innocent little Julia might find herself in an awkward position. You wouldn't want anything to happen to Julia, would you?"

And, in less time than it takes to blink, Matthew is in his face. "You want to think real hard about what you say next, Jeremy," he says softly. "I'm not afraid of you."

"You should be." He says these three words in an over-enunciated whisper. The effect is chilling. "If not for yourself, then for her," he continues with a nod in my direction. "Because I know, Matthew. I know that the surest way to hurt you is to hurt her. And you cannot possibly be there to protect her every minute of every day."

He's right, and all three of us in this room know it.

"Let's be clear here, Jeremy. I'm a man of more resources than you can possibly imagine—more connections, more power and more money. There is *nothing* that I cannot or will not buy to protect the people I care about. So if you think for a second that you're the only person in this room without something to worry about, you are very much mistaken. I might not be willing to kill you with my own bare hands, but I'm *not* above hiring someone else to do it for me. So again I say, get the fuck out of my home."

I can't see Jeremy's expression now, only that he's shaking his head very slowly.

"You have made a very, very big mistake, Matthew, and a stupid one at that. I mean really, if you think I killed Cal, then what makes you think I wouldn't hesitate to kill you? Or her? You know, I came here to offer you one last chance, but I've changed my mind. You can take your 'resources' and shove them up your ass, Matthew, because—I repeat—I can get to anyone, anywhere, anytime."

And with that he walks around Matthew, stopping briefly in the doorway to turn around and address me one last time. "Can you see the fall from here, Jules?" he asks with a twisted smile before heading down the hall and out the front door.

"Did that really just happen?" I ask incredulously. "Did I really just hear him threaten to…" I can't finish the sentence. I just slide down the wall until I'm sitting on the carpet.

Matthew joins me just the way he did that morning of the Kreisler auditions. God, it seems like a lifetime ago now. He takes my hand in his.

"What was that thing about the fall?"

"That day in Montauk. He took me to the lighthouse and I was afraid of coming back down the spiral stairs. He asked me why I wasn't scared going up too. I told him it was because on the way down, I could see the fall coming."

Just like now.

56

It is the last thing I can think of to do. It's a long shot, I know, but I have to try anyway. So when Brett Corrigan steps out of the backstage entrance of the theatre on Broadway, I'm waiting for him.

"Julia?" He's clearly surprised to see me there.

"Hey, Brett. I was hoping you might have the time to talk for a few minutes. Maybe I can buy you a nightcap somewhere? I won't take much of your time."

I can see that his curiosity is going to get the best of him on this one. "Uh, sure, I guess. There's a bar just over there," he says, gesturing to a small Irish pub.

I follow him across the street.

"How was the show tonight?" I ask, trying to make a little conversation as we walk down the block.

"The same," he groans. "It's always the same. You've played in Broadway pit orchestras before, you know how it goes."

"I do," I admit. "At least it pays well."

"That it does."

He holds the door open and I step into the dark bar ahead of him. The bartender nods to us, and we take a couple of empty stools at the far end of the big oak bar.

"Michelob," Brett says when he puts a coaster in front of him.

"I'll just have seltzer and cranberry, please," I say.

We wait quietly until the drinks are sitting in front of us.

"So…what's up?" Brett asks.

"I don't really know how to say this. Uh, it's your brother. It's Jeremy. He's making some pretty serious threats lately, threats against Matthew and me. And I was hoping you might..."

Brett's eyebrows go up expectantly, as if he's waiting for me to finish the sentence. "You were hoping...what? That I could intervene somehow?"

I shrug and take a sip from of my drink. "I guess. I hoped you could at least give me some guidance here. All I want is to get on with my life, Brett. He's got what he wants. He won the gold. He's going to have an amazing career. I'm going to steer clear. It's just that..."

He just stares at me, expressionless. This isn't going the way I'd hoped. Finally, he speaks, and he when he does, he doesn't hold anything back.

"What, Julia? What do you want? What is it that you think I'm going to tell you? Yes, my brother was a dick to you. I'm not surprised. In fact, I think you're the only one who didn't see that one coming."

Oh, this was *so* not a good idea.

"Brett," I say softly, locking my eyes on his. "He says he's going to hurt me."

"Wouldn't be the first time, now, would it, Julia? And I didn't see you running to the police, or packing a bag. If memory serves, you were sleeping in his bed both of those nights."

You know, I wasn't going to go there but he just opened the door. So, now I'm going to walk through it.

"Why didn't you do something? Why did you just let him hit me?" I ask quietly.

He looks away from me and swigs his bottle. "My brother and I have an agreement," he replies dispassionately. "I stay out of his affairs and he stays out of mine."

"Brett, I don't believe for a second that you would ever hit a woman," I say firmly. "So how could you stand by and let him do it?"

"You don't understand. My relationship with Jeremy is... complicated."

I'm never going to get through to him this way, so I might as well just throw it all out there. "You know he had something to do with Cal's death."

"I don't know that."

"You're not stupid Brett. He took peanut oil and put it on Cal's mouthpiece."

"Oh yeah? If that's so clear cut, then why haven't the police charged him with anything?"

"He switched the mouthpieces out when he was 'helping' Cal. I saw him do it, Brett."

"Again, why haven't the police charged him with anything?"

I sigh and drop my head in frustration and he continues, leaning down closer to me so that no one will overhear what he's about to say.

"You have fucked yourself here. Big time. If you had just let it go, everything would've been fine. Sure, your ego would have been bruised for a while, your heart would have been broken, but you'd have been okay eventually. I can't tell you that now. Did you know they're actually considering revoking his medal because of all this shit you and Matthew have stirred up?"

What? That could push Jeremy right over the edge!

"I know my brother better than anyone on this earth," Brett is saying, "and you better believe me when I tell you he holds a grudge. I'm going to give you a piece of advice, Julia, and I hope you take it."

He sits up again and takes a swig of beer. I stare at him, miserably, waiting for whatever it is he's going to say next.

"You, Julia, should get the fuck out of town, and take your boyfriend with you. If you stay here, there is nothing—and I mean *nothing*—that Jeremy won't do to punish you for this little stunt. He doesn't know it yet, but he'll be lucky to get a teaching job at a community college after your little publicity campaign. You took something huge from him, and I guarantee you that he will not rest until the score is settled."

I think I'm scared, that I'm going to grow pale and mutter and apologize for bothering him. But when I open my mouth, something miraculous happens. I fight back.

"Don't you think for a single second that I don't see your agenda here Brett Corrigan," I spit out at him. "You'd just love for us to leave town so you can just slip right into Matthew's seat at the Walton Quartet. That's what you're really thinking, isn't it Brett? Come on. Tell me the thought hasn't occurred to you before."

He smiles, and I have to make a concerted effort not to slap it off his face.

"Don't you feel even the least bit guilty?" I demand.

"Why should I? I haven't done a damn thing."

"Exactly."

"What?"

"You're worse than Jeremy. You just stand by and let him hurt people…kill people, Brett. You enable him to rape and beat women. You're worse because you *can* do something about it, but you make an active, conscious decision not to."

Now he's looking at me as if I've lost my mind.

"You know what, Brett? Forget it. Clearly coming here was a mistake. You're just as incapable of empathy as he is. Maybe all this time you thought you were teaching your brother how to be human. I think it's the other way around. He's been teaching you how to be a monster."

I've struck a nerve here. His jaw is slack, his brows are knit and it looks as if he's suspended in time. For an instant, I think I've won him over. But even I cannot undo a lifetime of conditioning from a master manipulator.

Brett regains his composure after a few seconds. He stands up, drops a ten-dollar bill on the bar and slings his viola case over his shoulder. "I've got this round," he says as he tucks his wallet back into his pocket. "You're going to need every cent you have to get as far away from here as possible."

And with that, he raises a hand goodbye and walks out the door without so much as a glance back over his shoulder.

57

The apartment is silent when I get back from my ill-fated peacekeeping mission. I put on my nightgown and try to sleep this horrible day away, but I can't. I make my way to the bedroom, Matthew's bedroom. The door is already open a crack, and I can see his figure, lying still underneath the covers on his bed.

I don't want to startle him so I ease the door open slowly and slip in, my feet padding noiselessly on the carpet. I lift up the covers and slide in next to where he's sleeping on his side, breathing in a soft, steady rhythm. I snuggle up against him, putting my head on his pillow and draping my arm over his waist.

"Matthew," I whisper into the darkness close to his ear.

"Hmmm…."

"Matthew, I have to talk to you."

The regularity of his breathing stops with a gulp of air, and his body stirs. "Julia?" he mumbles. "What's wrong?"

"We have to talk."

"What time is it?"

"About one a.m."

"Jesus, Julia, what are you doing up so late? You need your sleep," he mumbles and gravitates back toward slumber.

"Matthew, please. This is important," I say, still softly but more firmly this time. "I've just been to see Brett Corrigan."

That's all I need to say. Matthew is wide-awake and sitting up, staring at me in a matter of seconds. I pull myself up to join him in sitting against the headboard.

"What is it?"

"I think we're in some trouble."

"Jeremy?"

I nod solemnly. "I just heard that the Kreisler Committee is considering stripping him of the gold medal because of all the controversy around him. All the controversy that we helped to create."

He puts the heel of his hand to his forehead, closing his eyes as he speaks. "Oh, God. He's going to lose his fucking mind over this," he groans, echoing my thoughts. After a second he opens his eyes and looks at me. "Wait, why were you talking to Brett?"

"I was hoping he could do something—say something that would keep Jeremy from—I don't know. Doing whatever it is he's thinking of doing."

He shakes his head at me. "Julia, you can't reach a guy like Brett, anymore than you can reach Jeremy. They destroy lives. They don't care about anything or anyone other than themselves. You were never going to convince him to help," he says.

Well, I know that now. I sigh and put my hands over my face for a moment. "I can't lie to you Matthew, it's going to take some time for me to totally get over him, but now I have this—this other person to think about. If he finds out I'm pregnant, he'll hurt me. I know it in my heart. He'll do something to make me lose this baby."

"I know," he says simply.

"Do you think we're in danger? I mean, it kind of feels like that, but I don't know if I'm overreacting…"

"I'm not sure," he admits. "What did Brett say to you?"

I clear my throat.

"He recommends we leave before Jeremy has a chance to react." I purposely tone down Brett's comments so Matthew won't get even more upset."

I wait for a long moment before I ask him again. "What do you think?"

"I think I'm not afraid to stand my ground here," he begins. "And I know you're strong enough to weather whatever comes next. I think that if we commit to staying here, we can ride it out and hopefully Jeremy will move on, one way or another."

"But..." I say, certain there's another shoe he wants to drop.

"You know me too well, Julia. Of course there's a 'but.' But I can tell you right now it won't be easy. I'll be worried about you every second of every day. You'll be looking over your shoulder constantly, wondering what fucked up thing he's going to do next. Maybe..."

"Maybe we should go somewhere else and start over," I finish the thought for him.

He nods. "Although, I'd hate to let the son of a bitch think he's won."

"Oh, Matthew, it's not a win or lose situation. It's whatever will keep us safe and make us happy."

"But will you be, Julia? Can you be happy if you leave here with me? If you give up your life here, your degree, your career?"

"I can finish my degree and have a career somewhere else, Matthew. But you'd be giving up the Walton. You've worked your whole life for that."

He grabs my hand and holds it as if he's afraid I'm going to slip off the face of the earth if he lets go. "Nothing. That's nothing compared to you and the safety of your child, Julia. I'll give it up in a heartbeat and I won't look back if that's what we decide to do."

I don't know what to say, so I don't say anything. Finally, Matthew is the one to break the silence between us.

"Julia, I'm so sorry," he says in a strangled voice. My God, is he crying? "Tony warned me about pushing Jeremy and I didn't listen. Now—now I've ruined everything for us."

I can see the tears glistening down his cheeks in the darkness. And I thought I'd be the one crying over all of this.

"Oh, Matthew…" I take him into my arms, rubbing his back and soothing him as he sobs quietly into my shoulder.

"It's okay, we're okay," I murmur. This is my mantra. The words I use to get myself through scary times. Now I have broadened it to include him and the baby—all three of us.

He pulls his head back to look at me and I wipe the tears from his face. I can't help myself. When he leans in to kiss me, I don't pull away.

"Marry me," he breathes to me in between kisses.

"What?"

"Let me be your baby's father, Julia. Marry me."

And just like that, I'm overwhelmed by my love for this man. I have fought our attraction for more years than I can remember, but I can't do it for one single second more. I take his face in my hands and pull him into me. It happens so quickly, but it feels so right. I help him get the sweatshirt over his head and his pants are in a pile on the floor a moment later. I feel his strong, rough hands under my nightgown, his palms against the smoothness of my back.

"Take it off," I whisper breathlessly.

He helps me out of it and presses against me. The feel of his bare chest against mine is incredible. I can't take my mouth from his as his hands explore my body, cupping my breasts, outlining my hips, running up and down the outside of my thighs.

"I want to learn every curve by heart," he whispers. When he moves his mouth to my neck, I have to gasp. "Julia, are you sure? Are you really sure?" he asks, pulling away so I can see his face clearly.

I smile. "So sure," I say, putting a hand to his face.

I don't need to say another word. My legs wrap around his waist and he eases into me. I sigh, arching my head back. We fit together so perfectly. It's as if we were made for one another. Slowly, he starts to move, and I am with him. My eyes lock onto his and I meet every breath, every thrust until neither of us can stand it another second. And then we are moving faster and faster, building to a crescendo. I kiss him and pray silently that he will always be this close to me.

I feel as if, in this moment, I have finally found my home. My family.

Epilogue: Brett

As I take the stage at Carnegie Hall, I can see both Matthew and Jeremy, but they can't see one another. This is my first official concert with the Walton Quartet since I've taken over the seat that Matthew vacated. What a fool. He had the opportunity of a lifetime and he pissed it away. And for what? To defend a naïve little girl who was stupid enough to fall for my brother.

No one's seen Julia in weeks. Rumor is that she's withdrawn from McInnes. Jeremy tells me her phone is out of service and her emails bounce back. And this is the first time I've seen Matthew since Joe Dancy called to offer me his job.

Right now, my brother is seated in the audience, maybe six rows back from the stage. He's got a smug smile on his face because he's pleased that I've gotten this gig. Oh, not because he's happy for my success, but because it makes him look good to have a brother playing in the top chamber ensemble in the world right now.

Definitely not smiling is Matthew. He's standing back in a shadowy corner where he doesn't think anyone will notice him. But I do. Mainly because I've stood in those shadows myself a time or two, watching him take this very spot on stage and wishing it was me. And now it is.

I could probably find a way to tip Jeremy off to the fact that Matthew is there. But that's not what this is about. Matthew has come to say goodbye to his dream. I get it. By seeing me sitting in his chair, he can finally let it go and move on.

We tune carefully and open the music on our stands to the Schubert. When I look up again, Matthew is gone. Sorry, buddy, I have your life now. I'm the one with the great job and the career that's going to explode. If you're smart, you'll take Julia and you'll go away. Far, far away. Of course, that'll just buy you a little time. If there's one thing I know about my brother, it's that he always gets what he wants. And what he wants is to destroy you. It's just a matter of time.

When Joe Dancy nods for us to start, I put my viola under my chin and raise my bow to its strings. In an instant, the soft strains of Schubert fill the hall. It's the quartet he titled *Death and the Maiden.*

How very appropriate.

Acknowledgements

Thank you to the amazing people who made *Reverie* possible...

My sweet husband Tom who stood by me through all the angst, insecurities and tears. You're the love of my life.

My sister and my hero, Vanessa, and her beautiful family, Frankie Sr., Frankie Jr. and Ursula. You make me (and Mom) so proud every day.

Janet and Kwaku, more than my family, you are my closest friends. I love you more than I can say in words.

My family, including my grandparents, Mike and Crucita, aunts & uncles, Karen and Michael, Bonnie and David, Kim and David and cousins Laura, Michelle, Jessica, Cheryl, Jeremiah, Nathan, Joshua, Hannah, Angel and Noah. I love you all!

My mother, Marie. I know it's you, Mom. I know you're the one who whispers the words in my ear. I miss you.

My father, Gregory and grandparents Carol and Mario. You gave me a wonderful start in this world, but you left me way too soon.

My earliest readers and supporters, including Karen, Cathy, Myelita, Rita, Kate, Joan and Julie. You are extraordinary women with beauty, brains and heart.

My editor Jennifer Mishler, who made me a better writer.

Thanks to Ernie, who helped me to find my joy again, and for his lovely wife Stacey, my unexpected muse, untiring cheerleader and unrelenting quality controller.

Thanks to Jessica and her badass book club—Natalie, Jasmine, Mari, and Rachel.

About the Author

Award-Winning radio host Lauren Rico is one of the top classical music broadcasters in the country. Her voice is heard nationally on SiriusXM's Symphony Hall channel, as well as on radio stations in New York City, Charlotte and Tampa. Her love and passion for classical music have allowed her to breathe new life into the stories of the great composers.

And now Lauren is telling some stories of her own... Beginning with her erotic thriller, *Reverie* (Harmony House Productions, 2016) she set out to "put the sexy back in Bach" —creating a riveting tale of passion, deception and redemption set against the backdrop of an international music competition. She rounded out the trilogy with *Rhapsody* and *Requiem*.

From there, Lauren partnered with Entangled Publishing, LLC to create the first in her *Symphony Hall* series of romances, *Solo* (Entangled Publishing 2017). Her most recent release, *Blame it on the Bet*, is the first in the five-book *Whiskey Sisters* series (Entangled 2017). Upcoming projects include four more Whiskey Sisters romances and a follow-up to *Solo*.

Lauren hopes to bring classical music to a new audience by showcasing it in twisty, steamy stories that grab the reader and keep them turning pages—and YouTubing the music—into the wee hours.

When she's not on talking on the radio or typing on her laptop, Lauren enjoys time with her husband and spectacularly spoiled mini-schnauzer.

She is represented by Moe Ferrara of Bookends Literary Agency.

Made in the USA
Columbia, SC
25 February 2018